MURDER
at the
BEAUTY
PAGEANT

BOOKS BY HELENA DIXON

HELENA DIXON

MURDER
at the
BEAUTY
PAGEANT

bookouture

Published by Bookouture in 2023

An imprint of Storyfire Ltd.
Carmelite House
50 Victoria Embankment
London EC4Y 0DZ

www.bookouture.com

ISBN: 978-1-83790-068-8
eBook ISBN: 978-1-83790-067-1

Murder at the Beauty Pageant is dedicated with much love and thanks to Emily Gowers

PROLOGUE

Torbay Herald
April 1935

Silver Jubilee Celebrations

Celebrations have already commenced locally for the upcoming silver jubilee of His Majesty King George V. Events have taken place in Dartmouth, beginning with a Bonny Baby contest for infants under the age of one year. Competition was stiff and following a small altercation the eventual winner was announced as Norah Cope aged nine months. Contest organiser, Mrs Millicent Craven, former Mayoress of Dartmouth said, 'The contest was very successful, and the judges found it hard to choose the winner.'

This coming weekend sees the town hosting a beauty pageant, with the winner receiving the title of Miss Dartmouth Jubilee and a prize of ten guineas and a meat hamper. The contest is being generously sponsored by Venables butchers, purveyors of quality meats, poultry and game. Tickets for the pageant are available from the Dolphin Hotel where the event will be held. All proceeds from the events will fund a celebratory street party for the children in Dartmouth on Saturday 12th May.

EGYPTOLOGIST MUSEUM LECTURES

Sir Vivian Hardcastle, the celebrated Egyptologist who returned to Torquay a few months ago from Egypt is to give a further series of lectures at Torquay Museum. This follows on from the success of his previous lectures. The new subject matter will include the latest findings from the famous Valley of the Kings. Tickets are available from the museum.

CHAPTER ONE

Kitty Bryant stole a glance out of the large, leaded pane windows of her grandmother's salon in the Dolphin Hotel, Dartmouth. The sky matched Kitty's mood, grey and gloomy and she played absently with the still unaccustomed weight of the gold wedding band on her finger. Her mind drifted unhappily until a sharp reprimand recalled her back to the present.

'Kitty, you did make a note of that last instruction?'

'Yes, Mrs Craven.' Kitty suppressed a sigh of frustration and wondered how her life seemed to have brought her to a point where she had suddenly become Mrs Craven's secretary.

After her marriage at Christmas, with Mr Lutterworth now efficiently running the Dolphin and Matt's housekeeper, Mrs Smith, managing their home, Kitty had found herself at something of a loose end. She was accustomed to being busy and useful. This new life as a married woman had proved to be something of a change of pace.

Matt had presented her with her own printed business cards making her a full partner in Torbay Investigative Services. However, her role so far had consisted of comforting crying and distressed women and children, finding a lost kitten and filing notes. This was not how she had envisaged married life. Or, for that matter, her new career as a private investigator.

The ennui which had started to consume her had led her to accept Mrs Craven's request, or rather command, that she assist with the committee work for the forthcoming celebrations of King George V and Queen Mary's silver jubilee. The proceeds raised from the events were to be used to provide a street party and a commemorative gift for the town's children.

Her grandmother caught her eye and gave her a sympathetic smile. Mrs Craven was one of her beloved Grams' particular friends, but she had always had an unfortunate effect on Kitty's health, or rather her temper.

'Kitty, do you have the list of entrants for the beauty pageant?' Joan Ponsonby-Bell another of the committee ladies, asked as she set her delicate, floral-painted china teacup back on its saucer.

Kitty dutifully picked up the pile of forms she had collected from the hotel foyer before the meeting. There seemed to be a suitable number of entrants although she had not yet gone through them. She passed them across to Mrs Ponsonby-Bell.

'Now then, let's see.' The older lady donned a small, gold, wire-framed pair of reading spectacles and peered at the topmost sheet of paper.

'A Miss Betty Duke, ladies' maid.' She paused for Kitty to make a note.

'Oh, I rather think that may be Alice's cousin,' Kitty said. Alice was one of the chambermaids at the hotel and Kitty's particular friend.

'Hmm.' Mrs Craven appeared to catch Kitty's grandmother's eye and refrained from saying anything further. Kitty suspected that something derogatory had been hovering on the tip of the woman's sharp tongue.

'Naomi Coulter...' Mrs Ponsonby-Bell trailed off. 'She's my

goddaughter. I am most surprised that Naomi has entered.' Joan Ponsonby-Bell appeared quite taken aback.

'Felicia Felling, cinema usherette and actress,' Joan announced with a sniff after a moment to gather herself.

'That's the pretty blonde-haired girl who works at the picture house in Paignton. She lives in Kingswear, I believe,' Kitty's grandmother said.

'Dorothy Martin, Councillor Martin's daughter,' Joan continued. 'That means we cannot in good conscience allow someone from the council to be one of the judges.'

'Indeed no, not after the furore that went on with the Bonny Baby contest. I thought at one point Constable Oakes would have to arrest Mrs Worthing when she tried to slap Mrs Cope. Thank goodness the vicar intervened.' Mrs Craven gave a delicate shudder of distaste.

'Councillor Martin is such an objectionable man. I must admit I feel rather sorry for that girl living with him and her grandmother. I've known his mother for years; she was a sourpuss even when she was a young girl. Now this next one, Araminta Hardcastle. Sir Vivian Hardcastle's daughter. You know, the Egyptologist. His lecture series have been most popular by all accounts.' Joan had moved on to the next form.

'Which one is Araminta?' Mrs Craven asked. 'The man has been married several times and has about five daughters I believe.'

'I rather think she is the youngest. A bit of a wild child so I've heard or is that the other one, the stepdaughter?' Joan Ponsonby-Bell set the form aside and continued as Kitty made her notes. 'Peggy Blaine, the pharmacist's assistant.'

'Oh yes, quite a pretty girl, but something a little sly about her I've always thought,' Mrs Craven remarked. 'And the last entry form?'

Kitty knew Peggy from when she had collected prescriptions from the chemist's for her grandmother. The pharmacy was run by Peggy's much older brother, Alastair, a rather dour individual.

'Victoria Carstairs.' Joan placed the form on the top of the pile.

'That name seems familiar,' Kitty's grandmother said. 'What is her address?'

Joan picked the form back up, a crease formed on her forehead. 'She seems to have the same address as Araminta Hardcastle.'

'Of course, that's the girl you mentioned, Joan. Sir Vivian's stepdaughter from his last marriage. She must be a similar age to Araminta?' Mrs Craven asked.

'Yes, I rather think you are right, Millicent.' Kitty's grandmother gave a pleased nod of her head.

'Well, we seem to have a good selection of entrants. We do need to confirm the judges. Mr Venables from the butcher will obviously have to be asked since they are sponsoring the event.' Mrs Craven's expression soured slightly at this prognostication.

'Will you be a judge too?' Mrs Ponsonby-Bell asked. 'You are unconnected to any of the girls, and it is important that someone of taste and refinement is part of the process.'

Mrs Craven preened under Joan's praise and Kitty struggled to suppress a smile.

'Well, that is very kind of you to say so, Joan dear. I think the decision to keep the pageant tasteful and elegant by having an evening wear and a talent section rather than a bathing suit round was a good idea,' Mrs Craven said.

'Oh, most definitely, the weather is unseasonably chilly at the moment and since the Dolphin is to host the event it will be much nicer.' Kitty's grandmother agreed with her friends.

'So, there is the issue of the third judge.' Mrs Craven looked around. 'We need someone eminently respectable and above reproach unconnected with any of the girls.'

'I would have suggested the vicar but after the Bonny Baby

contest I rather fear he would not wish to take part.' Joan Ponsonby-Bell gave a regretful sigh.

'Why not ask Mr Lutterworth?' Kitty asked. 'He is most respectable and is here at the hotel and unconnected to any of the contestants.'

'Oh yes, capital idea, Kitty,' her grandmother agreed. 'I am happy to approach him if no one objects?'

Mrs Craven appeared to consider the suggestion. 'Yes, why not? Make a note of it, Kitty, and I shall work out everyone's tasks for the upcoming events. Kitty, you can contact the girls with the details for the rehearsal on Tuesday and the full run through on Friday. Instruct them to bring their evening attire for approval.'

Kitty dutifully added the decision to her notebook, relieved that the meeting was finally drawing to a close. She had promised to meet Alice later for a fish supper and a trip to the local picture house to see the latest film. Matt was attending a meeting of business owners at a club in Torquay and was not expecting to return until late in the evening.

'You seem very subdued of late, Kitty darling. Is everything all right?' her grandmother asked once Joan and Mrs Craven had taken their leave.

Kitty stopped tidying the tea things back on the trolley to discover her grandmother gazing keenly at her.

'I'm perfectly fine, Grams, I promise. I'm just adjusting to married life, I suppose.' Kitty gave her grandmother a reassuring smile.

'You would tell me if anything was wrong?' her grandmother persisted. 'You and Matthew are happy together?' Her grandmother appeared to be choosing her words carefully. 'You know that you always have a home here, Kitty, if you need it.'

Kitty hugged her grandmother, a tiny frisson of concern crossing her mind at her grandmother's increasing frailty. Her grandmother seemed to be so thin lately. 'Matt and I are very happy, I promise you. No, this is more to do with me finding my place in things.' She released her grandmother and met the elderly woman's gaze. 'Everything is perfectly all right.'

Her grandmother seemed somewhat mollified by Kitty's reassurance. 'Very well, my dear. Perhaps it's time you and Matthew planned that long-awaited honeymoon of yours?' she suggested. 'A change of air would restore the roses to your cheeks.'

Kitty smiled. 'You may be right. We have been looking at a few brochures.'

Her grandmother smiled back at her, apparently relieved. 'That's good. You had better run along then, my dear. Alice will be waiting for you in the lobby, and you know how much she loves attending the picture house.'

Kitty gave her grandmother a farewell kiss on her cheek and, taking her hat and coat, hurried away to meet her friend.

* * *

Matt ran a finger under the stiff, white collar of his evening shirt. The room was stuffy and filled with cigar smoke from the other gentlemen seated around the various mahogany tables. He never particularly enjoyed these kinds of events, but it was good business practice to attend. He would far rather have spent the evening at home with Kitty.

There had been much discussion about the Miss Europe beauty pageant to take place in Torquay in a few months' time. Matt suspected it would be a quite different event to the smaller, more decorous parade that Mrs Craven was planning for the celebration of the King's jubilee.

The meeting eventually closed and everyone began to move, ready to take their leave.

'Ah, Captain Bryant, allow me to introduce you to Sir Vivian Hardcastle. Sir Vivian, Captain Matthew Bryant.' Matt found himself being addressed by the mayor who was accompanied by a tall, distinguished-looking man with a deep tan and faint flecks of silver at the temples of his dark brown hair.

He had seen Sir Vivian's name in the newspaper the previous day in a report about a series of lectures the man was intending to give at the museum.

'I'm delighted to make your acquaintance, sir.' Matt shook hands with the Egyptologist as the mayor slipped away to greet another of his acquaintances.

Sir Vivian glanced about as if keen not to be overheard by any of the other men in the room. 'I say, Bryant, I hear that you're a private investigator?'

'Yes, sir, that's correct.' Matt's interest was immediately piqued.

'I wonder if I might have a word in private?' Sir Vivian gave another furtive glance around the rapidly emptying room.

'Of course.' Matt led the way discreetly to a darker corner of the room, out of earshot of any of the remaining attendees. 'How may I help you?'

Sir Vivian drew his silver cigarette case from his pocket and extracted a small, dark, exotic-looking cigarette before proffering the case to Matt.

'No, thank you, sir.' Matt waited while the man lit up and took his first inhalation of smoke.

'It's a rather delicate family matter. My stepdaughter, Victoria, I rather fear she may have become involved with bad company.' Sir Vivian paused and took another pull from his cigarette. 'You appreciate this is all confidential? The girl is quite touchy and does not get on with my other daughter, her stepsister, Araminta. I don't know how much of this is Araminta stirring up mischief or if Victoria is indeed in trouble.'

'I see, what kind of trouble, sir?' Matt asked.

'Drugs, cocaine to be precise. The curse of the modern age.' Sir Vivian grimaced. 'Victoria assures me that she takes nothing stronger than aspirin, but I have travelled extensively, and I know the signs.'

'I see. What is it that you wish me to do, sir?' Matt was curious about what the man wanted. He obviously had something in mind.

Sir Vivian finished his cigarette and extinguished it in a large crystal ashtray. 'I want you to find out who might be supplying her with the stuff.'

'Have you spoken to the police at all, sir?' Matt knew that his old acquaintance Inspector Greville, now newly promoted to chief inspector, had extensive knowledge in this department.

'No, not yet. If you can determine who it is, then I'll be happy to let the police take it further. My main concern is Victoria.'

'And do you have your own suspicions as to who may be supplying her, sir?' Matt asked.

Sir Vivian shook his head. 'Nothing definite. It could be any of that deuced crowd she runs around with. I want this to remain a private matter, for my daughter's sake and of course, my own. We have a reputation to maintain.'

Matt nodded. 'Very well, sir, I'll make some discreet inquiries.' He had the feeling that Sir Vivian had a very good idea who he suspected but wasn't prepared to share his suspicions at this point.

'I'll find a way to introduce you to the girls,' Sir Vivian said.

Matt agreed, and with a faint feeling of misgiving, watched his new client walk away. There was something that seemed just a little off with Sir Vivian's request.

'Bit of a rum cove that one. He intends to stand at the next election, or so I've heard,' a familiar male voice murmured next to Matt a few seconds later.

'Chief Inspector Greville, I thought I saw you arrive earlier.' Matt shook hands with the policeman. 'Congratulations on the promotion, sir. I expect Mrs Greville is very pleased?' He knew the chief inspector's wife had been very keen to see her husband advance his career.

Chief Inspector Greville's moustache drooped. 'She is delighted, Captain Bryant. In fact, she's been very busy of late looking at properties since she feels we should move to a larger home so we can have a guest bedroom.'

Matt could tell from the policeman's face that he didn't seem to share his spouse's enthusiasm. 'You don't wish to move?' he asked.

The chief inspector sighed. 'There are two problems with Mrs Greville's plan. One is that her mother would undoubtedly occupy the guest bedroom rather more than would be conducive for a peaceful home life, and secondly the houses she is considering are much closer to her mother.'

'Ah, I see.' Matt smiled sympathetically. He knew Kitty would be amused by this piece of news.

'Mrs Greville even considered Sir Vivian's house at one point. It's far above our means, however. He recently moved to a rented place in Paignton.'

'I'm sure you'll find a suitable property, soon,' Matt said.

'Let us hope so. Well, I expect Mrs Bryant will be waiting for you at home. Please give her my regards.' The chief inspector tipped his hat to Matt and took his leave.

CHAPTER TWO

Alice was in the hotel lobby waiting for Kitty.

'That blooming Mrs Craven gets more impossible every day,' Alice said with feeling as she waited for Kitty to button her coat and pull on her scarlet leather driving gloves.

'You don't need to tell me that, but what has she done to upset you?' Kitty adjusted her navy-blue hat with its cheerful cherry-red trim and prepared to walk out of the hotel with her friend. It was unlike Alice to get ruffled by Mrs Craven.

'She came down for her taxi with that friend of hers and told me as our Betty had entered the beauty pageant. And then her friend said, "Of course my goddaughter has entered too. Such a nice refined young lady."' Alice paused for breath for a moment, her cheeks flushed with indignation. 'Mrs Craven said as she hoped as Betty wouldn't let the side down as she intended it to be a respectable event. Like as if my family wasn't respectable.'

'Oh dear, she is quite impossible sometimes.' Kitty linked arms with her friend as they made their way out into the cool spring air. Her little red car was parked in the next street. 'Of course, everyone knows that your family is very respectable.

The only person letting the side down there was Mrs Craven. What a rude thing to say.'

'If my mother catches her saying anything like that, she'll give her what for and no mistake. I know as our Betty can have a bob on herself but really...' Alice marched along the pavement, forcing Kitty to scamper alongside her in order to keep up.

Alice halted on the pavement next to Kitty's car. 'Not as I think being in a beauty pageant is a good idea, but if our Betty wants to enter then she has as much right as anybody else.'

Kitty unlocked her car so Alice could take her place on the passenger seat. 'I agree. Betty is a pretty girl.'

Alice slid into the car looking slightly mollified. 'I take it that was what the meeting was about? This beauty pageant for the King's jubilee?'

Kitty took her seat behind the wheel and started the engine. 'Yes, and I'm just hoping it goes off better than the Bonny Baby contest.'

Alice giggled. 'The vicar still has a black eye from where that woman hit him when he tried to separate them from fighting.'

'That's probably why Mrs Ponsonby-Bell didn't think he would wish to be a judge for the pageant.' Kitty concentrated on steering her car through the narrow streets of the town towards the ferry ready to cross the river. They intended to see the film at the picture house in Paignton and then go for a fish supper near the seafront.

'Who is her goddaughter anyway?' Alice asked once they were safely aboard the ferry.

'Naomi Coulter, do you know her?' Kitty asked as she adjusted the collar on her coat. The cold seemed to be rising from the river and she guessed it would probably turn foggy on their journey back.

Alice appeared to be thinking, her snub nose wrinkled in concentration. 'I can't say as I do. Who else has entered then?'

Kitty gave her friend the names of the other contestants.

'I know that Felicia, she's another who likes to give herself airs. She's a friend of Betty's, thinks as she ought to be in the pictures not selling tickets to them,' Alice remarked as the ferry bumped to a gentle halt on the Kingswear side of the river.

Alice settled back in her seat as Kitty drove off the ferry and through the small village of Kingswear to take the lane leading past her house to Paignton.

'And as for being respectable, well if that Dorothy Martin is Councillor Martin's daughter...' Alice left the sentence hanging.

'Why? I don't think I know her either.' Kitty glanced at her friend.

'Let's put it like this, none of the tradespeople in Dartmouth lets her shop unattended. Got light fingers she has. Not as you'd think it to look at her. Snooty little madam. And, you know of her father...'

Kitty laughed. 'I wish you were on Mrs Craven's jubilee committee Alice. It would be a lot more fun.'

Alice grinned back at Kitty. 'No thank you. I'll leave the planning of them kind of things to my betters, ta ever so.' Alice gave a mock curtsey in her seat.

Kitty shook her head in mock despair. 'So, spill the beans on the other girls. Do you know them?'

'We both know Peggy. She works for that brother of hers at the chemist's. Nosy she is. Eavesdrops on people's conversations. Pretty though,' Alice said as Kitty overtook a man on a bicycle at Windy Corner.

'And Sir Vivian Hardcastle's daughters?' Kitty asked.

'I don't know them myself, but our Betty worked for Sir Vivian for a few weeks when he first come back to Torquay. She said as he were an old goat. A bit too handsy with the female staff.' Alice's smile widened. 'I reckon as Mrs Craven might have as much trouble with this pageant as she had with the baby contest.'

'Oh, Alice darling, please don't say that! Otherwise, you know that she'll find a way of placing the blame on me since it's being held at the Dolphin,' Kitty said, as she tried to stop laughing at Alice's tales about the contestants. Still, she hoped the pageant would go off peacefully. It would be too dreadful if there was a catfight at the contest.

'Have they decided who is to be the judges?' Alice asked as Kitty steered her car to a halt near the front of the picture house.

'Mr Venables from the butchers, Mrs Craven and Mr Lutterworth,' Kitty replied as she turned off the engine.

Alice's nose wrinkled as she gathered up her handbag. 'Well, Mr Lutterworth will be unbiased at least,' she said.

'I agree. Now, what is it we are to see this evening?' Kitty linked arms once again with her friend and they headed for the entrance of the large red-brick picture house which stood near the railway station.

'A comedy with Edward G Robinson. I've read in my magazine as it's very good,' Alice assured her as they purchased their tickets from the booth inside the entrance. Her friend touched the sleeve of Kitty's coat as they were about to make their way to the auditorium. 'Look! That's Felicia over there.'

Kitty watched as a statuesque blonde-haired woman in a smart navy uniform unceremoniously escorted a protesting young boy out of the cinema.

'No ticket. They tried to sneak in,' Felicia explained when she realised Kitty and Alice were watching her. 'Cheeky little blighters.'

'Oh dear,' Kitty sympathised.

Alice caught Kitty's attention once more as Felicia turned away to greet some other customers. 'And there's Alastair Blaine, Peggy's brother, with Celia Dobbs.'

Kitty looked in the direction that Alice was discreetly indicating. 'Mrs Dobbs? Is that the lady who was widowed around

October? I helped her with his wheelchair once. Matt knew her husband quite well. He'd been ill for some time, cancer I believe.'

'That's the one. Looks as if Mr Blaine is setting his cap at her,' Alice remarked as they made their way to their seats. 'That'll put his sister's nose out of joint, I bet. She runs rings around her brother does Peggy for all as he thinks as he's the boss of her.'

Kitty settled in her seat and offered Alice a boiled sweet from the bag in her handbag. It seemed the pageant would be a lot more interesting than she had first thought.

The lights were on at Kitty's house when she pulled onto the driveway after dropping Alice off in Kingswear. Her heart lifted as she realised this meant that Matt's meeting must have finished early and that he was already home.

A flurry of barks greeted her as she put her key in the front door and she braced herself for Bertie the cocker spaniel's enthusiastic welcome. The little roan dog's tail wagged ferociously as Kitty paused in the hall to remove her hat, coat and gloves.

'Matt?' She gave the dog the attention he was craving before going to look for her husband.

'In the sitting room,' Matt replied.

She pushed open the door to discover Matt, already in his burgundy fleece dressing gown and brown leather slippers, relaxing in front of the fire with a glass of port and a plate of cheese and biscuits.

Bertie promptly deserted her to station himself hopefully at Matt's elbow, looking for a tidbit from Matt's plate.

'You're home early, darling.' Kitty dropped a kiss on the top of Matt's head as she stole a biscuit and piece of cheese before dropping down into the seat opposite him.

Matt grinned at her as she nibbled on the edge of her purloined snack. 'Yes, not much business tonight, just more talk of beauty contests for the Miss Europe thing this summer. I did see Chief Inspector Greville though, he sends his regards. How was your day?'

'I was assisting Mrs Craven with this jubilee pageant planning. Honestly, I don't know what possessed me to agree to help out with it.' Kitty gave a tiny sliver of cheese to Bertie.

'It can be rather tricky to refuse to assist Mrs C,' Matt observed, still smiling. 'Anyway, I have a new client for us from this evening so at least my attendance at the meeting was not for nothing.'

'Oh?' Kitty immediately perked up. She hoped it would be something more exciting than a lost pet.

'I was approached by Sir Vivian Hardcastle, the Egyptologist,' Matt said.

'Good heavens, that family seems to be everywhere today.' Kitty rose from her seat and helped herself to a small glass of port from the decanter on the gilded bar trolley.

'The chief inspector says Sir Vivian is intending to stand for Parliament.' Matt looked at Kitty as she retook her seat.

'Well, public competition clearly runs in the family; his daughter and stepdaughter have both entered for the beauty pageant.' Kitty took an appreciative sip of her drink. It had been chilly driving back to Churston and the port warmed her throat nicely.

'Ah. Well, it's the stepdaughter Sir Vivian is concerned about, Victoria.' Matt gave the last piece of biscuit from his plate to Bertie.

'Yes, she's entered the contest along with Araminta.' Kitty frowned. 'What is the problem?'

'Sir Vivian thinks she has fallen in with the wrong crowd

and that one of them is supplying her with cocaine. Victoria has denied it, of course. He wants us to make enquiries and see if there is any truth in the matter and if so, who is responsible.'

'I have instructions from Mrs Craven to contact all the entrants to give them the details for the rehearsal on Tuesday evening at the Dolphin. She wishes to preapprove their evening attire and I need to run through the programme for the pageant,' Kitty remarked thoughtfully. 'That might be a good opportunity to assess the situation. The girls all have to practise their talent pieces so I can arrange music and any props they may require. Why has he not gone to the police, though?'

'That would work out quite nicely. I'm not certain quite what Sir Vivian hopes to achieve from our involvement. He did say that he would take whatever we discovered to the police, but he wished to be discreet.' Matt scratched the top of Bertie's head as the dog rested a hopeful nose on his knee.

'Do you think there is an ulterior motive beyond extricating his stepdaughter from her undesirable companions? It seems a bit odd to me,' Kitty asked.

Matt laughed. 'Obviously if the chief inspector is correct and Sir Vivian intends to put himself forward for Parliament, he will be keen to eliminate any hint of potential scandal. I think he is trying to live down his rather colourful marital past, so he needs to keep squeaky clean.'

'Naturally,' Kitty agreed. 'So, you think it's not so much Victoria herself that he is concerned about but rather his own reputation?'

Matt's smile widened. 'Indeed. He struck me as a rather self-centred sort.'

'It will be interesting to meet the daughters on Tuesday then. I wonder what they are like,' Kitty mused as she finished her drink.

* * *

Kitty was kept busy in the intervening days following Mrs Craven's numerous instructions. Matt contacted Sir Vivian and suggested that Kitty make the initial observations of the girls at the pageant rehearsal. Something Sir Vivian appeared happy to agree to.

By the time Tuesday evening rolled around, Kitty had set up a dressing area backstage in the ballroom for the girls and had organised a pianist should any of the girls wish to try the room for acoustics.

Mrs Craven arrived early to take tea with Kitty's grand-mother before the rehearsal started. Kitty decided that there was only so much of Mrs Craven's company she could take and decided to join Dolly and Mr Lutterworth for her own tea break.

'I really am very grateful to you, Cyril, for agreeing to assist in the judging,' Kitty perched herself on the edge of one of the desks in the tiny office at the back of the reception area.

'Not at all, Kitty.' Mr Lutterworth smiled at her. 'I am very used to such events from my time managing the Porteboy's club.' Before his arrival at the Dolphin, he had managed a pres-tigious gentleman's establishment in London.

Dolly handed her a cup of tea from the trolley. Alice's little sister had proved a very capable employee despite her young age, and Kitty was very fond of her.

'Our Betty is looking forward to taking part. My uncle wasn't none too happy until he found out as there wasn't to be any swimsuits and that it was being held here. I think until then as he thought it might not be very respectable.' Dolly passed another cup to Mr Lutterworth.

Kitty stirred her tea. 'How could the pageant not be respectable with Mrs Craven in charge?'

There was a ripple of laughter from her companions.

'Well, I can assure you I shall be scrupulously fair in my judging. I believe Mrs Craven has organised score sheets?'

Kitty nodded, rolling her eyes. 'Oh yes, marks for beauty, poise, elegance, deportment and talent. I think she wishes to avoid any controversy after what happened at the Bonny Baby contest.'

'I can understand that. What time are the girls all due? I might stay around to say hello to Betty before I go home,' Dolly said.

'Six o'clock onwards. I've divided up the dressing area backstage to ensure each girl has a hook, lamp and mirror. Hopefully they will all get along and there will be no arguments.' Kitty helped herself to a biscuit from the tea tray.

Mr Lutterworth raised his eyebrows slightly at her optimistic statement but refrained from speaking. Kitty had a feeling that she was probably going to be proved wrong in her wish, but she had done her best to ensure that all the contestants would be happy.

Kitty arranged with her receptionist that any of the contestants were to remain in the lobby until Mrs Craven came to greet them and take them to the ballroom. Each contestant had been allocated a space in the dressing room and Kitty had placed name cards on each spot. She was anxious that there should be no accusations of favouritism or cause for argument between the girls.

Betty was the first of the contestants to arrive, carrying her evening attire in a large box. Dolly had waited to see her cousin before leaving for the day and greeted her affectionately as she entered the lobby.

'Brr, it's cold out there tonight.' Betty adjusted the fake fur collar on her coat and shivered dramatically. 'Hello, Mrs Bryant, am I the first?'

'Yes, although I expect the others will be along shortly.' Kitty knew Betty from her involvement in some of the cases she and Matt had investigated previously. Betty was older than Alice and Dolly and an only child. This was something she liked to rub in her cousins' faces as their family was much larger and consequently, less well off.

Kitty had barely finished speaking when Felicia arrived, also carrying a large box. A small, perky dark-haired girl in an expensive-looking coat and hat was next. She introduced herself as Naomi Coulter.

Dorothy Martin followed her, entering the lobby in a gust of cold air and with a large number of boxes. She glanced around at the other girls with a disdainful stare.

'I don't suppose there is a porter to assist with our things?' Dorothy asked, looking at the receptionist.

Before the girl behind the desk could answer her, the sound of feminine bickering reached them from outside the hotel. A blonde-haired girl stormed into the lobby closely followed by a dark-haired young woman of a similar age.

Kitty guessed that these must be Sir Vivian's daughter and stepdaughter. From the glares they were bestowing on each other it seemed that there was little love lost between them.

The last of the girls to arrive was Peggy Blaine. Tall, and quietly dressed, she carried herself with an easy air of self-confidence.

Mrs Craven entered the lobby from the stairs. 'Ladies, welcome to the jubilee pageant, please follow Mrs Bryant to the ballroom and I shall be with you all shortly.'

Kitty bit her tongue as she considered who actually owned the Dolphin, but prepared to lead the contestants to the dressing room.

CHAPTER THREE

The girls trailed behind her, carrying their bags, Araminta and Victoria still bickering in hissed whispers, Dorothy bemoaning the lack of portage and Felicia making chatty conversation with Betty.

Dolly remained in the lobby to talk briefly to the receptionist before leaving for home. Mrs Craven had also remained in the lobby to await the arrival of the pianist. The lights in the ballroom had been left on as it was a dark and somewhat gloomy evening. If the weather didn't improve soon, Kitty could see that the hotel would end up hosting the children's jubilee celebration party too.

Kitty led the way to the white-painted door at the side of the stage and was somewhat surprised to discover it slightly ajar. Usually, she made a habit of locking the door behind her since the room was off limits to any of the hotel guests and she didn't wish anyone to go wandering in there accidentally.

The dressing room was in darkness as it had no window, so Kitty reached around the door frame for the light switch. The room filled with bright yellow light as she clicked the switch, and she stood aside to allow the pageant contestants to enter.

'There is an allocated space for each of you. You may leave any items here this evening and I will ensure the room is secured, if you do not wish to take your things back with you,' Kitty instructed as the girls began to look for their name cards.

She had deliberately chosen not to put Victoria and Araminta together, a decision she was congratulating herself on given the ill will they seemed to have for one another.

'Mrs Bryant, there seems to be a letter of some kind addressed to us all attached to my mirror.' Naomi Coulter pointed to a small nondescript white envelope tucked in the top corner behind her mirror. The words, *For the attention of the Pageant Contestants*, were typed in capital letters on the front.

'I expect it will be a good luck message,' Felicia said knowingly to Betty. 'Although flowers would have been nice.'

Kitty collected the envelope from the mirror with a sense of foreboding.

'Ladies, our pianist has arrived, so if you could all deposit your belongings and join me on the stage, please,' Mrs Craven announced, waltzing in, for once at a perfect moment. This caused an instant ripple of activity as the girls hastened to hang their gowns on the hooks Kitty had provided.

Kitty slipped the envelope into her pocket for now. She would open it once the girls were all busy on the stage. There was a great deal of hustle, bustle, grumbling and chatter as the contestants entered the ballroom.

Mrs Craven, resplendent in crushed garnet velvet, was armed with a clipboard. She checked off each girl's name and arranged them in the order in which they were to make their entrance for the pageant, giving them each a wristband with a number.

'You will ensure that these are worn during the event and will enter from the door at the wings when Mrs Bryant gives you your signal.' Mrs Craven looked at Kitty.

'I shall be present during your preparations in case any of you need any assistance,' Kitty said.

'I was expecting my maid to be able to accompany me to dress my hair,' Dorothy pouted.

'I'm afraid that will not be permitted as you've already seen we are limited for space in the dressing room.' Kitty could tell that Dorothy was going to be rather trying.

'What about pressing our gowns?' Naomi asked.

'There is a housekeeping facility here at the Dolphin. A member of staff will be more than happy to take your evening wear to press it for you should the need arise,' Kitty replied firmly.

'Now then, shall we begin?' Mrs Craven started to give out her instructions and the girls returned, still grumbling in Dorothy's case, to the dressing room.

They practised the entrance onto the stage, the walk along the room and return to the stage where they would introduce themselves before leaving to change into their evening wear. After the interval they would return duly attired in their gowns to demonstrate their chosen talent.

'Now, ladies, if you would arrange with Mr Jakes, our pianist, those of you requiring musical accompaniment,' Mrs Craven said and disappeared into the dressing room. Kitty presumed to inspect the girls' evening gowns for modesty.

Mrs Craven had already stated her concerns that any dresses deemed to be too revealing would not be permitted.

While the girls were otherwise occupied around the baby grand piano and poor Mr Jakes, Kitty took the envelope from her pocket. She discovered that it was not sealed and contained a single sheet of commonplace white writing paper, obviously torn from a pad.

She unfolded it and read the typewritten words.

To all contestants of this misbegotten pageant. Repent. Return to your parents' loving arms and seek forgiveness for your sin of vanity. Fear the Lord in all your actions that he may save you from sinfully displaying your flesh to strangers for profit. Failure to heed my warning may have dire consequences.

A well-wisher

Romans 6:23 For the wages of sin is death

'Oh dear.' Kitty spoke aloud without thinking, her words unluckily falling into a pause in the hubbub around the piano.

'Mrs Bryant, is something wrong?' Peggy Blaine hurried towards her. 'You have gone quite pale. Is it that envelope?' the girl asked, looking at the sheet of paper in Kitty's hand.

'What is it?' The other girls left the piano too before Kitty could stop them and gathered around her trying to see what she was holding.

Araminta wormed her way to the front and snatched the paper from Kitty's hand before she could stop her.

'Well, some crackpot has clearly taken offence at the idea of the pageant!' Araminta said.

There was an outbreak of shocked and excited chatter as the others read the contents of the note.

'Girls, whatever is going on in here?' Mrs Craven marched back into the ballroom.

'I'm afraid someone has left a rather objectionable note in the dressing room.' Kitty took the note back from Araminta and passed it across to Mrs Craven. It was useless to think about possible fingerprints now as all the girls had handled it.

Mrs Craven's immaculately painted arched eyebrows rose towards her hairline as she read the note.

'Well, really, some people have far too much time on their hands. I presume you will wish to report this matter to Chief

Inspector Greville, Kitty?' Mrs Craven handed the note back to Kitty, her lips pursed in distaste at the contents of the note.

'Yes, indeed. I shall alert Mickey, our security man, as well, to keep a close eye on things here at the hotel.' Kitty returned the note to its envelope and tucked it back inside her pocket.

'I'm sure this is the work of some harmless crank. Please do not be alarmed, ladies. Let us return to our business.' Mrs Craven fixed the girls with a steely gaze which quelled any discontented murmurs.

The rehearsal continued but a slightly subdued air now seemed to have fallen across the contestants. Once everyone had finished organising the things they required for their talent spots, and Mrs Craven was satisfied that everyone understood the order of proceedings, the practice ended. Mr Jakes collected up his music and departed.

'Thank you, girls. Remember, we shall meet here again on Friday evening for the talent run-through. Kitty will need to time everyone. Felicia, may I strongly suggest a corsage for the front of your gown. The neckline is showing too much décolletage. Victoria, please ensure you have appropriate foundation garments, or I may need to pin some parts of your dress on the day.' Mrs Craven looked around at the contestants. 'Any questions?'

Kitty half expected them to argue or protest but it seemed that none of them were in the mood. Even the loquacious Dorothy was silent.

'Jolly good. I shall see you all on Friday evening.' With that Mrs Craven bustled away.

Once she had gone the girls drifted off to the dressing room to gather up any items they wished to take home with them. Araminta and Victoria once more began their squabbles.

'Do you think it's worrying at all, Mrs Bryant, about that note?' Betty remained at Kitty's side accompanied by Felicia.

'I'm sure this kind of thing happens a lot. People do get very odd ideas. I expect it is someone who has issues with this kind of event. However, you know that Mrs Craven is the very model of decorum. There can be no reasonable objection to this pageant, which is after all being held to raise funds for the children's jubilee party. I shall alert the police and my staff though just to be on the safe side,' Kitty reassured the two women.

Peggy and Naomi came to join them dressed in their coats and hats. 'It's all rubbish if you ask me,' Peggy declared with a toss of her head. 'I mean, it's ridiculous. It's not as if we are even in our bathing suits.'

'Exactly.' Naomi nodded her neatly bobbed head in enthusiastic agreement.

'It's still not very nice.' Felicia looked doubtful. 'I mean it makes a threat after all and whoever left this is obviously unwell.'

'I can promise you that the Dolphin will take full measures for the protection of all of you,' Kitty said firmly. 'And as I said, I shall also alert the police.'

'Will our things be safe here?' Dorothy had also come to join the group with Victoria and Araminta following behind her.

'I shall lock the room and make certain the staff are aware that no one is to be given access without my permission.' Kitty walked away and locked the doors to the dressing area while the girls could see her.

They all appeared satisfied with her actions and wandered off to make their way out of the building. Kitty followed behind them.

'You may get your own taxi back to the house,' Araminta told Victoria. Kitty couldn't help but hear the girls' conversation as they were at the rear of the group.

'I wouldn't wish to be seen with you any way. Besides, Dominic is meeting me.' Victoria swished the tail of her fox fur stole more firmly onto her shoulder.

'You are more than welcome to both Dominic and his car,' Araminta informed her stepsister snippily.

The conversation halted as they reached the lobby. Peggy and Naomi walked off together as did Felicia and Betty. Araminta asked Bill, the hotel night porter, to arrange a taxi. On the far side of the lobby a tall, slim young man in an expensive dark grey suit and tweed overcoat rose from one of the armchairs to greet Victoria with a kiss on her cheek.

Victoria and her companion departed the hotel without a backwards glance at Araminta who stood a little forlornly beside the reception desk.

'I have a car and can drive you home, Miss Hardcastle,' Kitty offered as Bill went to pick up the black Bakelite telephone receiver to request a taxi for Araminta. 'It won't take me much out of my way as I have to cross the river to get to my own home in Churston any way.'

Araminta looked slightly doubtful for a moment. 'If you are quite certain, Mrs Bryant. I would be most grateful. Father is using the car tonight as he has a meeting about his talks at the museum in Torquay, so I had intended to call for a taxi. Victoria, it seems, has made her own arrangements.' She pulled a face in the direction of her departed sister.

'It's no trouble at all. If you will wait here for a moment, I just need to collect my things and say goodnight to my grandmother.' Kitty gave her a bright smile.

By offering the girl a lift home she should be able to find out a little more about Victoria and Araminta's rivalry. She might even get a hint about whether Sir Vivian's concerns for Victoria had any kind of foundation. And she wanted to know who the man was who had come to meet Victoria.

Kitty left Araminta in the lobby and hurried upstairs to bid her grandmother goodnight. Mrs Craven was already seated beside the fire enjoying a glass of sherry.

'Kitty, my dear, are you off home now? Millicent told me

about the note you found. Most distressing. I shall ask Mr Lutterworth and Mickey to tighten security around the ballroom area.' Her grandmother lifted her face to accept Kitty's kiss on her cheek as Kitty gathered her things ready to leave.

'Thank you, Grams. I've locked the room for tonight. I'm giving Araminta Hardcastle a lift home so I really must fly.' Kitty straightened up and buttoned her coat before pulling on her leather driving gloves.

'Very well, drive carefully darling,' her grandmother instructed as Kitty picked up her handbag and hurried out of the salon and back down the main stairs to the lobby.

Araminta was seated on the edge of one of the leather club chairs in the reception area but rose as soon as she saw Kitty approaching.

'I'm parked just along the street,' Kitty explained as she waved goodbye to Bill and set off along the pavement with Araminta at her side.

'It's very good of you to take me. I'm most grateful, Mrs Bryant,' the girl said as Kitty unlocked the door of her car.

'It's no trouble. You may have to give me some directions however when we get to Paignton.' Kitty smiled as she slipped into the driver's seat.

'Of course. We haven't been there very long. Just a few months. We had to sell our old house so this one is rented.' Kitty glanced across and saw Araminta's nose wrinkle as if in distaste as she spoke. It seemed this move was unpopular with the girl.

'Oh?' Kitty asked mildly as she started her engine and set off to wait for the ferry.

'A combination of Daddy's divorce from Victoria's mother and his need to fund his last expedition to Egypt,' Araminta explained as she gazed out of the passenger window at the ink dark waters of the Dart.

'Is there just yourself, your father and Victoria at home?' Kitty asked as she pulled forward onto the ferry.

'Yes, my older sisters Diana and Artemis and my half-sister Collette are all married. The only reason we are saddled with Victoria is that her mother has recently married some French Comte and is on her honeymoon, would you believe?' Araminta shook her head in disbelief, her blonde curls escaping from under her fashionable pale green felt hat.

'You and Victoria do not get along?' Kitty waited for the ferry to bump to a halt and the signal to be given for them to disembark into Kingswear.

'Gracious no, not all. We have absolutely nothing in common,' Araminta declared.

Kitty set off through the village and up the hill, her head-lamps illuminating the hedges on either side of the road. Over-head an owl hooted loudly somewhere, and the cold evening air chilled her face as they drove towards Paignton.

'I'm surprised that you both entered the contest then,' Kitty remarked.

'I had no idea that Victoria would have any interest in the pageant. I entered as I thought the money would be jolly useful. Plus, it's so frightfully dull being here. Not like when we were in Cairo where there were balls and parties.' Araminta sighed.

'So why has Victoria entered? Did she say?' Kitty asked as she obeyed Araminta's instruction to take a left turn inland.

'I swear she has done it to spite me. She is so frightfully jealous all the time. She says she wants the prize money. I can guess what for.' The girl must have thought she had spoken unwisely and stopped abruptly before giving Kitty another direction towards her house.

Kitty took the turn, thankful to see that at least there were a few streetlights. 'I suppose if she has a boyfriend though she may leave home in time,' Kitty said.

Araminta sniffed. 'I introduced her to Dominic at a party a few months ago. He was supposed to be my particular friend.'

Kitty spotted the name of the Hardcastle residence carved

into the stone pillar guarding the entrance of the driveway and turned in. 'I'm sorry. That must be awkward. What is his surname? I thought I recognised him from somewhere.' She pulled to a halt in front of the gothic-style rambling Victorian villa. Ivy covered the red-brick walls and rustled alarmingly in the wind.

'Really? I suppose he is quite well known. It's Dominic Peplow and she is quite welcome to him, I assure you,' Araminta declared as she prepared to exit the car. 'Thank you so much for bringing me home, Mrs Bryant. It was very kind.'

'Not at all,' Kitty said. She waited for the girl to climb out of the car and open the front door with her key before driving away.

The conversation with Araminta had certainly given her plenty to think about as she made her way back to Churston.

* * *

Matt examined the note and the envelope in the light of his desk lamp as Kitty reported everything she had discovered.

'You say the dressing room door was open?' he asked as Bertie came and dropped his ball in her lap, clearly delighted she had returned home.

'Yes, and you know that I always keep it locked. I didn't like to examine the door too closely with the girls all standing there, but it seemed to me that there were some scratches around the lock and I wondered if it had been picked.' Kitty petted the top of Bertie's head.

'We must ask Mary the receptionist tomorrow if she noticed any strangers in the lobby yesterday.' Matt replaced the note in the envelope.

Kitty could see he was unhappy with the letter.

'Yes, although the hotel is busy at the moment, so she may not have noticed anything in particular. Grams is going to talk to Mickey to increase security,' Kitty said. She really hoped the pageant was not going to be as problematic as the Bonny Baby contest.

Matt frowned. 'We'll take a trip into Torquay tomorrow and see what the chief inspector makes of it.'

CHAPTER FOUR

A fine shower of sleet peppered the windscreen of Kitty's car the following morning as they drove to the police station in Torquay. The weather so far had been unseasonably cold for spring in Devon.

Matt held a large black umbrella over Kitty as she locked her car and quickly walked the few steps inside the station.

'Morning, Captain Bryant, Mrs Bryant. 'Tis nasty out there today,' their old friend, the desk sergeant, greeted them as Matt carefully refurled the umbrella over the doormat to avoid soaking the lobby floor.

'It is indeed, Sergeant. Is Chief Inspector Greville available this morning?' Matt asked as he turned back to face the desk.

'I'm sorry, sir, he's gone to Exeter. A meeting with our new gaffer,' the sergeant apologised. 'Is it something as I can help you with?' The older man looked from Matt to Kitty.

'It's a rather unpleasant anonymous letter, making threats against the young ladies participating in the jubilee beauty pageant at Dartmouth,' Kitty explained.

'Oh dear, that does sound nasty. I can ask our new inspector if he's free to see you?' the sergeant offered.

'Oh, I didn't know you had a new inspector.' Kitty looked surprised.

The chief inspector hadn't said anything about a new appointment when Matt had seen him at the meeting a few days earlier, which made Matt wonder if this was someone the new chief constable had appointed very recently. The previous chief constable had retired a few months earlier.

'Oh yes, Mrs Bryant. Our new gaffer felt we needed a bit of a shake-up, and you knows what they say about new brooms. Well, now as Inspector Greville has gone up in the world, it left a vacancy.' The sergeant explained.

'You did not wish to apply for the post yourself?' Kitty asked.

The sergeant laughed. 'I'm a bit long in the tooth for that, Mrs Bryant. The chief constable is after recruiting bright, young thrusting officers. Our new inspector has come from a force in the north of England. Transferred, he has. Comes highly recommended apparently.'

'Well, if he is free to spare us a few minutes of his time we would be most obliged,' Matt said.

The sergeant picked up the receiver of the large black Bakelite telephone and dialled an internal number.

'Excuse me, sir, a lady and gentleman are here needing some advice about an anonymous letter. Can you spare them a moment?'

Matt couldn't hear the response to the sergeant's request.

'Yes, sir, I'm sure they appreciate that you are a busy man, but they are particular friends of the chief inspector so I'm sure he would be most obliged if you could see them in his absence.' Matt saw Kitty's delicate eyebrows rise slightly at the direction of the conversation.

The sergeant listened for a second then placed the handset back in its cradle. 'If you would like to follow me, the inspector can spare you a few minutes.'

He raised the hinged portion of the counter to allow them through to the other side of the desk before taking them into the cream-washed walls of the corridor which led to the offices and further on to the cells situated on the floor below.

The sergeant paused outside the green-painted door to what Matt knew had previously been Chief Inspector Greville's office and rapped loudly. On hearing the command to enter, the sergeant opened the door and stood aside to allow them access.

'Inspector Lewis, Captain and Mrs Bryant.'

The lean man in his early forties froze in the action of rising from behind his desk. Matt thought the look of dismay on the inspector's face was probably mirrored in the expressions on his own and Kitty's faces.

'Thank you, Sergeant. Inspector Lewis is an old acquaintance of ours.' Kitty was the first to recover her composure, extending a gloved hand for the inspector to shake.

'Yes, quite. Thank you, Sergeant.' Inspector Lewis recovered himself to dismiss the sergeant back to his post and to offer his hand to Matt.

Formalities completed, Matt took a seat on one of the wooden bent wood chairs in front of the desk next to Kitty. When the office had belonged to Inspector Greville, a pall of cigarette smoke had hung in the air and every surface including the chairs had been stacked high with untidy piles of brown manilla folders. Now the office was spotlessly clean with not a piece of paper in sight.

'This is quite a surprise, Inspector Lewis,' Matt remarked.

They had last seen the inspector in Yorkshire when he and Kitty had attended the wedding of Kitty's cousin Lucy to Rupert, Lord Thurscombe. The meeting had not been auspicious, and the inspector had not been at all happy to work with them.

The inspector straightened in his seat and adjusted the lapels of his smart brown tweed jacket. 'The chief constable was keen to recruit experienced men. He's a great believer in using modern methodology in policing. Chief Inspector Greville's promotion created an opportunity for me to progress my career more rapidly.'

'I see, congratulations then, Inspector. I hope you are settling in well?' Kitty said.

'Early days yet, um, Mrs Bryant. Now, how can I assist you? The sergeant mentioned an anonymous letter?' Inspector Lewis narrowed his foxy eyes.

Kitty opened her brown leather handbag and took out the note. 'I'm afraid it has been handled by all the pageant contestants. I wasn't swift enough to prevent them from touching it. This was left tucked behind a mirror in the dressing room at the Dolphin Hotel in Dartmouth. We are hosting the jubilee beauty pageant to raise funds for the children's party.'

The inspector's lips pursed in disapproval at this piece of information as he opened the envelope to extract its contents. 'Hmm, seems like your run-of-the-mill nut job. Vague threats, religious obsession. Anyone see anything that might indicate who could have left this? Is this dressing room easily accessible?'

Kitty explained the circumstances and her suspicion that the lock had been picked.

Inspector Lewis leaned back in his seat and steepled his hands together when she had finished her explanation. 'I see. And are any of the young ladies worried by this note?'

Matt considered that a slightly peculiar question.

'A little concerned obviously. It's not a nice thing to have happened.' Kitty looked puzzled.

'As you say, Mrs Bryant, it's not much use sending it for fingerprinting as it's been mauled by every Tom, Dick and Harriet. Nothing that stands out from the stationery which is very commonplace, and it's been typewritten. Best thing I can suggest is to keep a sharp eye out. Probably a disgruntled ex-boyfriend of one of the young ladies or an older busybody. Any worries, let the police in Dartmouth know about it and step up your security at your boarding house.'

Matt saw Kitty's lips compress into a thin line when the inspector referred to the Dolphin as a boarding house.

'Well, thank you, Inspector, for seeing us, and good luck in your new job.' Matt reached over to touch Kitty's arm signalling that they should leave. He could tell a sharp retort was hovering on the tip of her tongue.

'No trouble at all, Captain Bryant.' The inspector rose to see them out.

Kitty gathered her bag and stood ready to follow Matt.

'Perhaps though in the future if anything trivial like this occurs, your local constable could be your first port of call. This is a very busy department as I'm sure you'll appreciate. I know it's difficult sometimes for you amateurs to understand.' Inspector Lewis opened his office door.

'Of course, Inspector.' Matt kept his tone amiable despite his urge to punch the man on his nose.

Matt hustled Kitty along the corridor and away from Inspector Lewis as quickly as possible. He knew from the stiff set of her slim shoulders that she was just as angry with the man as he was. But it wouldn't help to antagonise the man.

'All done, Captain, Mrs Bryant?' the desk sergeant asked as he let them back out into the lobby.

'Oh, very much so,' Kitty said with some asperity.

'Ah, Inspector Lewis takes a bit of getting used to,' the sergeant said. 'Very keen on his new-fangled ideas and such, he is.' The older man gave them a sympathetic smile. 'You've met him before, you said?'

'Yes, we had the pleasure when we were in Yorkshire,' Matt explained.

The sergeant lowered his voice. ''Tis a pity he didn't stay there if you ask me, but then what do I know?'

Kitty smiled and patted the sergeant's arm. 'Thank you for your help and good luck.'

'I might need it and all,' the man replied as the telephone on his desk began to ring.

The sleet had stopped when they got outside the building, but it remained cold and damp. Kitty huddled down into the fur collar of her coat as they made their way to her small, red car.

'That smug, insufferable, beastly man. I cannot believe that he has now arrived in Torquay.' The words burst from Kitty's lips as soon as she was seated behind the steering wheel.

'I don't know who was the more surprised when the sergeant announced us.' Matt's lips quirked in amusement as he recalled Inspector Lewis's horrified expression at their arrival in his office.

'It is going to make our work rather more difficult,' Kitty observed. 'We cannot be bothering Chief Inspector Greville very often now he has moved up the chain so we will be stuck with that bone-headed man.'

Matt knew what she meant. When their paths had crossed in Yorkshire, the inspector had made it clear that he disliked private investigators and he especially disliked female investigators. His opinion seemed unaltered even after Kitty had effectively solved the inspector's case for him.

'We shall have to see how things go when he has settled into his position. Chief Inspector Greville is his superior officer so he may have to temper his distaste for working alongside us,' Matt remarked.

'Yes, I suppose that's true. He has already said he hopes this move will bring about a more rapid route to promotion so he will be keen to impress both the chief inspector and the chief constable,' Kitty said thoughtfully.

'I suggest we head back to Dartmouth and ask Mary if she noticed anything or anyone out of the ordinary yesterday. I know it's a slim chance but it has to be worth a try. Then I think perhaps some lunch?' Matt suggested. He knew the offer of food usually appeased his wife. She always claimed she did her best work on a full stomach.

'Very well, and after that we must take Bertie for his walk, or he will have eaten another hole in the rug behind the sofa. You know he hates being left at home.' Kitty started her car, and they pulled away in the direction of Kingswear.

* * *

Despite the bad weather the ferry was unusually busy and they had to wait quite some time before they could drive on board for the short crossing over the river to Dartmouth. The embankment was quiet with few pedestrians but unsurprisingly parking was at something of a premium. The bad weather meant that there were more cars, and carts in the narrow streets of the town.

Kitty had to park further from the Dolphin and nearer to the boat float, the small marina area where boats were stored or taken for repairs. The sleet started again as they left the car and the wind coming off the river buffeted the umbrella as Matt tried to hold it over Kitty's head.

'I shall be glad when this weather moves off. If it continues, the street party we are planning for the children on Jubilee day will have to be moved indoors,' Kitty said as they hurried inside the Dolphin's lobby out of the stinging icy needles of the sleet.

The lobby of the hotel was busy with guests. A family group were seated near the rack of leaflets arguing about what they should do for the day. An elderly couple were booking in at the desk and the young kitchen boy come porter was gathering up a large quantity of luggage to take it to the elevator.

Kitty waited with Matt while the receptionist dealt with the new arrivals. It felt odd to be at the Dolphin as a bystander instead of jumping in and working. Once the lobby had quietened down, she stepped up to the counter.

'Morning, Miss Kitty, Captain Bryant, sir.' Mary gave them her usual warm, welcoming smile.

'Good morning, Mary, this may sound a strange question, but did you notice any unusual strangers entering the hotel yesterday? Anyone who ventured in towards the lounges and the ballroom?' Kitty asked.

A frown creased Mary's forehead. 'It was very busy yesterday, miss. Any particular time of day?'

'We aren't certain. Someone managed to gain entry to the dressing room in the ballroom yesterday before the pageant contestants arrived,' Matt explained.

'Oh my word, was anything damaged? Or stolen?' Mary asked in alarm.

'No, just an unpleasant note left for the pageant entrants,' Kitty reassured her.

Mary still looked troubled as she tried to recall the events of the previous day. 'I'm thinking it must have been left on the afternoon, miss, as the maids was in the ballroom most of the morning cleaning. Mrs Homer the housekeeper wanted it looking nice all ready for the pageant contestants and there had been that big party in there the night before.'

'Well, that narrows it down a little,' Kitty said.

'The afternoon was busy as the weather were bad and several guests come back wanting to take tea in the lounges. Then there was the one man...' Mary stopped, a stricken expression on her face.

'What man?' Kitty asked. 'Do go on.'

'Well, he said as he was from the electrical company. There was a fault with the microphone in the ballroom. I didn't have time to check with Dolly or Mr Lutterworth and he were carrying his bag of tools. Oh dear, miss, do you think it was him?' The receptionist looked mortified as realisation dawned that she may have inadvertently allowed the letter writer to enter the hotel.

'Do you recall which company he said he represented?' Matt asked.

'No, it were one at Babbacombe, but I don't know the name, sir. I'm so sorry.'

'Don't worry, Mary. You were not to know that someone would do such a thing. Do you recall what he looked like or anything about him?' Kitty replied in a soothing tone, anxious to reassure her receptionist's concerns.

Mary's frown returned as she tried to think. 'He was an older man, about fifty, grey hair. Dressed in dark blue coveralls. He did look like an electrician.'

'Please don't worry about it. If you see him again let Mr Lutterworth or Mickey know straight away and don't let him in. We will check with Dolly and look in the trade directory to see if there is a firm in Babbacombe that may have sent someone out,' Kitty said.

Mary nodded, still looking worried. 'Very good, miss.'

Kitty knocked on the office door behind the reception before popping her head inside. Dolly was seated behind the large black typewriter, tapping away on the keys. The girl stopped the instant she saw Kitty and smiled a greeting.

'I'm so sorry to disturb you, Dolly, but did anyone request an engineer yesterday to see to a fault in the microphone in the ballroom?' Kitty asked.

'No, Miss Kitty. Is there a problem with it?' Dolly went to pick up the notepad and pencil which lay beside the typewriter.

'No, not as far as I'm aware. Please carry on.' Kitty withdrew and returned to where Matt was waiting at the desk studying the trade directories that Mary had provided.

'Dolly is unaware of any fault, and she doesn't know of any engineer being requested,' Kitty said.

'And there are no electrical companies listed at Babbacombe. Only one in Paignton and one in Torquay.' Matt closed the book and passed them back to Mary to stow away under the desk.

'Then it seems we have found our culprit.' Kitty grimaced. 'Now we need to look out for him should he try to return.'

CHAPTER FIVE

It seemed there was little more that they could do about the note or its mysterious sender for the time being.

'I seem to recall that you promised me a lunch,' Kitty reminded her husband as they said goodbye to Mary and prepared to leave the hotel.

'So I did, where would you like to go?' The dimple flashed in Matt's cheek as he smiled at her.

'The sleet seems to have stopped for now and the tearoom at Bayard's Cove has an excellent fire.' Kitty slipped her gloved hand into the crook of Matt's elbow.

'Then your wish is my command.' Matt chuckled as they headed back outside for the short walk to the tearoom.

The wind had died down a little and a weak and watery sun was making a brave attempt to break through the clouds over the river. The tearoom was busy, and all the tables seemed to be occupied.

Kitty was about to suggest they go and try somewhere else when she saw a hand waving imperiously at her from the far side of the room.

'I think Mrs Ponsonby-Bell has space at her table.' Kitty looked at Matt.

'Perhaps she is about to leave,' Matt said in a hopeful tone as he followed Kitty over to where Joan was seated at a large table apparently taking lunch with her goddaughter.

'Kitty dear, won't you and your husband join us? There is plenty of room and it's so very hectic in here today.' Mrs Ponsonby-Bell smiled up at them.

'Thank you, that's very kind. We were just about to go and try somewhere else.' Kitty shrugged off her coat as Matt pulled one of the dark oak chairs out for her.

Matt removed his overcoat and took their things over to the coat stand before rejoining her back at the table.

Naomi seemed quite taken with Matt, fluttering her blackened eyelashes at him. 'Will you be coming to watch the pageant, Captain Bryant?'

Kitty watched with a mixture of mild irritation and amusement as Matt ignored the flirtatious attempt to gain his attention as he studied the menu. 'I expect so. I like to support Kitty and she's putting a lot of work into raising money for the children's jubilee party.'

'Naomi was just telling me about that disgraceful letter that was left in the dressing room.' Joan Ponsonby-Bell pressed a bony and heavily bejewelled hand to her scrawny bosom. 'Have the police been informed?'

'We have been to the police station in Torquay this morning. Inspector Lewis will be giving the matter his personal attention. If you have concerns, I'm sure he will be most interested in assisting you.' Kitty smiled sweetly as Matt turned a laugh into a cough.

'Well, that's reassuring, isn't it, Naomi?' The older woman turned to her goddaughter.

'Oh yes, I must admit I was quite frightened when I read it.'

Naomi tried once again to engage Matt's attention by placing her hand on his arm.

'Inspector Lewis is a most thorough police officer. Kitty and I met him when he was based with the force in Yorkshire. I'm sure he will be keen to get to the bottom of the matter.' Matt discreetly withdrew his arm and summoned a passing uniformed waitress to take their order for lunch.

'Are you looking forward to taking part in the pageant, Naomi? What is your talent? I'm afraid I haven't had the opportunity yet to go through the final rehearsal list for Friday,' Kitty said as the harassed-looking waitress returned with a pot of tea and all the crockery.

'Naomi is very gifted. She had several options to choose from, didn't you, dear?' Mrs Ponsonby-Bell beamed proudly at the girl. 'She sings like a nightingale and can play the piano to concert standard.'

Naomi blushed delicately under her godmother's praise. 'I decided to sing. An aria from *Madame Butterfly*.'

'Naomi has had singing lessons from an early age.' Joan looked fondly at the girl.

Matt's brow lifted as he took a sip of tea, his gaze meeting Kitty's over the brim of his cup.

'That sounds delightful, and quite ambitious. I'm sure we shall all enjoy hearing you,' Kitty replied diplomatically as the waitress returned and placed plates of steak and kidney pudding with boiled potatoes and winter vegetables in front of her and Matt.

Naomi settled back in her seat and smiled complacently. 'Well, I do like to stretch myself. Some of the other girls seem to have put hardly any thought into their talent pieces. I mean Betty is doing a music hall turn.' The girl's pert nose wrinkled in distaste.

'Now then, my dear, not everyone has had your advantages

and the benefit of being exposed to culture,' Joan Ponsonby-Bell replied.

'I'm sure Betty's piece will be well received.' Matt applied himself to his steak and kidney pudding while Kitty tried to stifle a giggle at the expressions on Naomi and Joan's faces.

'I just hope the pianist is capable,' Joan said before draining her cup ready to leave the tearoom.

'Mr Jakes has played for all of the professional singers we've had at the hotel so I'm sure he will do well with Naomi's score,' Kitty assured her.

'Let us hope so. Naomi said he was quite elderly,' Joan replied as she gathered her things and called the waitress to pay for their bill.

'But as I said, very experienced. I shall look forward to hearing you sing at the rehearsal on Friday. I'm sure it will be a delightful treat.' Kitty forced herself to smile at Naomi.

'Thank you, Mrs Bryant, I shall see you, then.' Naomi pulled on her fine pale blue leather gloves and collected her coat while her godmother paid the waitress.

* * *

Matt relaxed back in his seat and dabbed the corners of his mouth with the white linen napkin after the two women had gone. 'Phew, that was um, interesting. Are you certain you're looking forward to Naomi's aria?' he asked. His blue eyes twinkled with amusement as he spoke.

'I rather think I need to double-check what all the girls are intending to perform. I was a little distracted yesterday by the note.' Kitty had a horrid feeling that the pageant might go the way of the baby contest if they were not careful.

Matt's smile widened. 'I'm sure Friday's rehearsal will be delightful. Perhaps you should invest in some cotton wool for your ears.'

Kitty laughed and shook her head in mock despair. She hoped that none of the other contestants were intending to attempt Puccini. She much preferred the thought of Betty's music hall turn.

They finished their meal and headed back across the river to Churston. While they had been eating, the sleet had at last ceased and a cool wind was helping to dry the road and the pavements.

Kitty parked her car on the drive and opened the door to climb out.

'Oh dear,' she said. Before they had even approached the front door, she could hear Bertie howling mournfully inside the house.

'I wonder what he has destroyed this time.' Matt led the way into the hall with Kitty following behind.

The housekeeper appeared from the kitchen, drying her hands on a towel as an unrepentant-looking Bertie pushed past her, wagging his tail in delight at their return.

'That blessed animal hasn't stopped howling for the best part of half an hour. I let him out in the garden, and he knocked over them pots as you were keeping for the summer plants, then he tracked mud all over my fresh mopped floors.' The older woman glared at Bertie who gazed up at her with large, soulful, brown eyes.

'I'm sorry, Mrs Smith. I'd better take him for a walk and use up some of his energy,' Kitty offered and picked up the leather dog's lead from the hall table.

Bertie bounded forward in delight and began weaving around their legs in anticipation at the mention of a walk.

'I'd be most grateful, Mrs Bryant,' the housekeeper said as Kitty caught hold of her dog and attached his lead.

'I think I might take the Sunbeam into Torquay and see what I can discover about that friend of Victoria Hardcastle,' Matt said as their housekeeper vanished back into the kitchen.

'Will you be all right taking Bertie by yourself?' He looked at the dog who already had his nose pressed to the front door.

'Of course, I think he intends to walk me!' Kitty agreed and stepped outside with the eager spaniel.

Matt changed his overcoat for the leather greatcoat he wore when riding his motorcycle and swapped his hat for a cap which fitted firmly to his head. He waved to Kitty as he set off along the road towards Torquay.

There was a certain billiards club at the back of the town which he had discovered. The clientele was somewhat varied, but it seemed that everyone there had information which could usually be acquired for the price of a pint of beer or over a game.

The road was still flooded in places, and he had to take care when passing close to the seafront. Angry waves were crashing over the sea wall and onto the road with the high tide depositing clumps of dark green seaweed in its wake.

The club was situated towards St Marychurch on the far side of the town centre. Matt parked his motorcycle and stowed his leather riding gauntlets away before making his way inside the club.

The billiards hall was situated in what he assumed had once been a small, whitewashed hotel. There were several ground-floor rooms containing tables with a central bar area. The dark-red carpet was slightly sticky underfoot from various spillages and a haze of blue cigarette smoke hung in the air.

The rooms themselves were dimly lit with shutters excluding all-natural daylight. The only bright lights were the green shaded ones above the tables, and the brighter ones in the bar area.

Matt stowed his outdoor wear in the cloakroom and went on into the bar to order a beer. He nodded a greeting to the barman who recognised him from previous visits.

'Afternoon, sir, is it still bad out there?' the barman asked as he started to pull the pint.

'It's cold but improving, the sleet has stopped now. The sea is still a little rough today however,' Matt affirmed as he handed over the money for his drink. 'I was hoping for a game, is anyone playing?'

'Try the room over yonder, sir. There are some fellows in there might give you a go.' The barman nodded his head in the direction of the furthest room.

Matt suspected that there might be wagering going on but if he could find out any information on Mr Peplow, Victoria's boyfriend, then it would be worth the payment. He stepped quietly into the room and stood sipping his pint while watching the match in progress.

There were two men engaged in a game. An older man dressed in the clothes of a working man, a hand-rolled cigarette clamped firmly between his lips, and his opponent, a much younger lad in clean but shabby attire. From his appearance Matt guessed the boy was not well off and he hoped the lad hadn't wagered too much on the game.

The game progressed quickly, and the older man was soon the victor; the points on the board which were being marked by a third man told their own story. The lad replaced his cue in the stand, his shoulders drooping dispiritedly as his opponent scooped up the meagre pile of coins from a nearby table.

'Better luck next time, eh, lad,' the man said as the boy left the room.

He picked up his pint glass and took a long pull at the contents before turning to Matt. 'You up for a game?' Matt could see the man's dark eyes assessing the cut of Matt's clothes as if judging how much to ask for the wager on the game.

'Why not?' Matt set down his own glass and selected a billiard cue from the polished wooden rack on the wall before applying chalk to the tip of the cue.

'A little something on the side to make it interesting?' the man suggested.

'Very well, although I am in the market for some information too.' Matt drew out his wallet and tipped out some coins. He affected not to notice the slightly wary glance the men had exchanged when he mentioned the need for information. 'I am not the police, so you need have no worries on that score.'

He piled the coins up on the table. He had judged the amount to be enough to tempt his opponent but to be an amount the man could match. The two men exchanged looks once more before the scorekeeper gave the other man a faint nod. The billiard player added his own coins to the pile.

'What kind of information you after then?' the player asked as he indicated that Matt should start the game.

Matt refrained from replying until after he had bent and taken his shot. 'I work as a private investigator. This is not a criminal matter or any case of wrongdoing. I am acting on behalf of a concerned father.'

His opponent stepped up to the table to take his turn. He glanced at Matt before bending to make his shot sending a ball into the pocket. 'Lass in trouble?' he asked.

'I don't believe so. More that the parent thinks this gentleman to be an unsuitable companion.' Matt watched as the man potted two more balls before standing aside.

'Got a name, this bloke?' the player asked as Matt took his turn, potting a ball himself before replying.

'Dominic Peplow.' Kitty had done well to discover the man's name from Araminta.

His opponent shrugged his shoulders. 'Not someone I know of.'

The other man who had been keeping the score spoke. 'I thinks I know of him. Young fellow, flash motor car.'

'That sounds like it could be the one,' Matt agreed as his opponent cleared half the table.

'I don't know him personal like except from where I do a spot of casual work from time to time.' The man moved slightly into the light and Matt saw that the man's face had a livid scar running from his hairline to his jaw and he held himself somewhat awkwardly.

It was clear that he had either been involved in some terrible accident or more likely, judging by his age, he was like Matt, a war veteran.

'I see.' Matt took another drink of his beer and waited for the man to speak.

'Runs with quite a fast crowd of young people. All loud music and drinking and such,' the man continued.

Matt sensed a little more financial encouragement might be needed if the man was to be more forthcoming. 'And what do you know of his reputation?' He drew a note from his wallet and placed it separately to the coins set out for the billiards.

Both of the men's eyes widened and the scorekeeper licked his lips.

'He seems to organise a lot of parties around the bay. Big houses, rich people, all the bright young things. A bit too bright if'n you ask me.' He gave Matt a meaningful look.

'Drugs?' Matt asked casually as he stepped up to the table to take a shot.

His informant exchanged another slightly wary look at Matt's opponent before a glance back at the money on the table seemed to loosen his tongue.

'Aye, sir, I reckon so. I don't know for sure as this Peplow is behind it all, but he certainly seems to be the man in the middle.' The scorekeeper marked up Matt's point on the polished wooden scoreboard.

'Does he live locally?' Matt asked, missing his next shot and allowing his opponent to step forward.

'He has a villa overlooking the bay near Ilsham on the coast road. I only know because I heard him inviting a couple of

young ladies back there the other night,' the scorekeeper
replied.

Matt's opponent made short work of clearing the remaining
balls from the table, winning the game.

'Well done.' Matt shook hands with the man.

'Pleasure, sir, you fancy another game?' His opponent pock-
eted the coins from the wager.

Matt shook his head. 'Another time, perhaps. Thank you
both for your assistance, gentlemen.' He swallowed the last of
his pint and went to collect his things ready to return to
Churston. He knew that Kitty would be very interested to hear
what he had learned about Peplow's character and his
reputation.

CHAPTER SIX

Matt told Kitty the results of his trip to the billiard club as soon as he returned home. Kitty agreed with him that they should continue to see what else they could learn about Dominic Peplow and Victoria Carstairs over the course of the pageant weekend. In the meantime, Matt decided to take a tour around the Ilsham area the following day to see what else he could discover.

Kitty's plans to join him for some sleuthing were halted by a telephone call from Mrs Craven during breakfast. The discovery of the anonymous letter seemed to have upset the pageant committee and she insisted that Kitty should go to the Dolphin to check the security of the dressing room personally.

So, later that morning after seeing Matt off on his motorcycle, she bundled Bertie into her car and left for Dartmouth. The weather had improved and although it was still cold for late April, at least the rain and sleet had stopped. Even the spring flowers along the embankment seemed to have perked up with the sight of the sun.

She managed to park near the hotel and collected Bertie from the back seat. He trotted ahead of her on his leash as she entered the wood-panelled lobby of the Dolphin. The reception area was considerably quieter than it had been the previous day and Bertie bounded up to the desk to be fussed over by Mary.

'Good morning, Miss Kitty.' Mary found a biscuit from the drawer of her desk and slipped it to Bertie.

'Morning, Mary, Mrs Craven and the pageant committee have asked me to check that all is secure with the dressing room for tomorrow evening,' Kitty said.

'Of course, miss. Mickey has been keeping an eye out like you and Mrs Treadwell asked,' the girl assured her.

'Thank you. I'll just pop along and double-check. Then I can report back to her with a clear conscience.' Kitty smiled and gave the dog's lead a gentle tug to signal she was about to move.

She left the lobby and made her way along the corridor towards the ballroom. She passed the guest lounges which were virtually empty and pushed open one of the oak double doors to the ballroom. The space had been prepared ready for the pageant with a short catwalk having been built out from the stage extending into the dance floor. The seating had been altered so that everyone would have a view of the contestants as they walked along and as they performed their talent. A table and chairs had been set up on the side of the stage for the three judges.

Everything was clean, polished and prepared with red, white and blue decorations on the tables. Kitty and Bertie headed for the door at the side of the stage. She breathed a sigh of relief at finding it securely locked. In the clearer light of day, she could see the recent scratches around the lock barrel confirming her suspicion that it had been picked.

Kitty took out her master key and unlocked the door, switching on the dressing room light. The room smelled slightly musty, a sign that it had been closed up. Kitty released her hold on Bertie's leash, knowing that he would stay by her side as she checked that everything was in order.

A quick look at the mirrors showed no signs of any more objectionable notes. Most of the girls had left their gowns carefully covered on padded hangers and their evening shoes in bags beneath the dressing areas she had prepared for each contestant.

Dorothy Martin's area was full of bags, cosmetics, two pairs of shoes and a large pink feathered fan. Kitty decided that she really did need to check what talent each girl intended to perform. Satisfied that nothing had been disturbed, she called Bertie and came out of the room taking care to lock it back up again.

Before leaving, she walked up the couple of steps at the side of the stage and checked that the other door from the dressing room into the wings was also still locked. Bertie followed at her heels his leather lead rustling along the wooden boards as he sniffed hopefully at the painted flats at the back of the stage.

The black baby grand piano was opposite the judges' table and Kitty could see that Mr Jakes had left a copy of the running order of the girls' performances on the leather topped piano stool.

Mrs Craven had placed the contestants to appear in alphabetical order so there would be no accusations of favouritism. Peggy Blaine would be first with a poem and Dorothy Martin would finish the turns with a song. Kitty could only assume Dorothy's song made some kind of use of the pink feathery fan she had seen in the dressing room.

Kitty picked up Bertie's leash and walked back towards the reception area. She would say hello to Dolly and Cyril before calling on her grandmother. Then she would telephone Mrs Craven to assure her that all was well.

As she entered the lobby, she saw Mary was not behind the desk but at the far end of the room peering out of the leaded window. Mostly hidden behind the curtain, it was clear that she didn't wish to be noticed by someone outside the hotel.

'Mary?' Kitty asked, careful not to raise her voice too loudly.

'I thought I saw that man again, miss. The one who came the other day pretending to be from the electrical company.' Mary dropped the dark green velvet curtain back into place and walked back towards the desk.

Kitty hurried down the room to take Mary's spot at the window. Much to her disappointment there was no one in sight. 'There's no one out there now.'

'I saw someone walk past the door and took no particular notice because people are always passing by,' Mary explained. 'But then the sun come out and I got this funny feeling like as if I were being watched. I looked up and saw a man stood on the pavement. I couldn't see his face properly as the sun were behind him. He catched me looking and moved off sharpish so I run down to the window to have a look and I swear it was the same man. It was his eyes, burning into me, like,' Mary said, a distressed look on her pretty face.

'Hmm, perhaps he was looking to see how busy the lobby was. I suppose he might have been thinking he would try again to leave another note. What was he wearing?' Kitty asked.

'Normal clothes this time, a dark overcoat and a grey hat, but I'm certain it was him,' Mary said.

'Go and let Mickey know. I'll watch reception until you return,' Kitty instructed.

The girl darted off to locate the hotel maintenance and security man in his small office near the kitchens. Kitty drummed her fingers on the highly polished surface of the reception desk. Bertie sat obediently at her side and sniffed the air hoping for another biscuit from the desk drawer.

Mary returned a few minutes later. 'Mickey says he will ask the kitchen staff to watch out the back in case he tries to sneak in at the trade entrance when we has a delivery. He'll keep watch over the front, and he'll let Bill, the night porter, know to watch out tonight.'

'Thank you, Mary. I think that's all that we can do for now. Well done for spotting him. Hopefully if he thinks he has been noticed it may prevent him from returning.' She gave the girl a reassuring smile.

Kitty rapped on the door of the office behind the reception area and peeped inside. She let Dolly and Cyril know that the suspicious man had been sighted again and the precautions that were being taken.

Dolly looked anxiously at Mr Lutterworth.

'I'll check on the dressing room and stage myself a little later for you, Kitty. Please don't be alarmed, I'm sure this man will turn out to be a harmless crank,' Mr Lutterworth said.

Kitty suspected his words were intended to soothe Dolly as much as herself.

'I think you are probably right, I shall let Mrs Craven know in a moment. She is most anxious about the whole pageant especially after what happened at the baby contest.' Kitty took Bertie upstairs and knocked on the door of her grandmother's salon.

Her grandmother was seated at her writing bureau dealing with her correspondence when Kitty entered.

'Darling, Millicent said she had asked you to check all the arrangements for tomorrow's rehearsal.' Her grandmother looked up and smiled as Kitty and Bertie entered.

'Yes, everything is secure, and nothing has been tampered with.' Kitty went on to tell her grandmother about the man Mary had seen while she took off her coat and hat. Bertie took himself off to stretch out on the hearthrug in front of the fire.

'How very vexing. I'm sure that Mickey will keep a good look out. Is it worth telling the constable that this man has been seen again?' her grandmother asked as she packed away her correspondence.

'Unfortunately, we don't have a good description of him,

and we can't go around accosting perfectly innocent men just in case they are the anonymous letter writer,' Kitty said.

Her grandmother chuckled. 'You have a point, my dear. Millicent is calling in shortly so you can reassure her in person. I think the baby show business did rather upset her. She sounded quite flustered on the telephone. I know she will be glad when the jubilee is over, it is such a lot of work.'

Kitty had never known much to perturb Mrs Craven. Even when she had once been witness to a murder on board her carriage on a train. Her grandmother ordered a tray of tea and Kitty had just settled herself comfortably in front of the fire when Mrs Craven arrived.

It was clear from the older woman's demeanour that she was perturbed. Her cheeks were rosy and flushed, a spark of indignation was in her eyes and her jowls wobbled slightly. She swiftly divested herself of her outdoor coat and fur stole while greeting them.

'I have come here straight from the police station in Torquay. I really must have words with the new chief constable. I mean, things were disgracefully slow before but now, my dears, they do not seem to be taking anything seriously.' Mrs Craven glared at Kitty as she spoke as if her complaint were somehow all Kitty's fault.

'Millicent, do sit down and have a cup of tea. Whatever has happened?' Kitty's grandmother picked up the silver teapot and poured tea into the extra china cup that was ready on the tray.

'Another one of those ghastly letters, that is what is wrong. A dreadful thing, making all kinds of scurrilous accusations against me. Me, of all people.' Mrs Craven's eyes flashed.

'A letter? Like the one that was left here for the contestants?' Kitty asked.

'Yes. Typewritten and anonymous just as before. Obviously, I was furious. Joan Ponsonby-Bell has received one too. She told me that you had said an Inspector Lewis was dealing with the matter, Kitty.'

Kitty had a horrid feeling that her flippant comment to Joan was about to come back and bite her. She had left the house before their post had arrived and she wondered if she too might have a letter waiting for her when she returned home.

Mrs Craven took a sip of her tea before continuing. 'I telephoned the inspector, as I believe Joan has too. He was most unhelpful. I have been to the station and left a complaint with Chief Inspector Greville. Not that I suppose it will do much good. How that man Greville got promoted is beyond my comprehension.' Mrs Craven spluttered to a halt and looked at Kitty for a response.

'My post had not arrived when I left. I wonder if I have had a letter too?' Kitty mused.

'The other two ladies who are assisting with the fundraising for the party have received one also.' She looked at Kitty's grandmother. 'Have you had a letter?'

'I must confess I haven't yet collected today's post. Indeed, I had just finished replying to yesterday's correspondence when Kitty arrived.' Her grandmother looked at Kitty. 'Perhaps you could run down, dear, and see if there is anything downstairs for me?'

Kitty set down her cup, and after cautioning Bertie to wait for her she hurried down to the lobby.

After Kitty requested her grandmother's mail, Mary passed her a slim pile of post from the pigeonholes behind the desk. Kitty thanked her and started back up the stairs, sorting through the post as she went along.

Sure enough, there was a flimsy typewritten envelope addressed to her grandmother that seemed to her to be the same sort as the one they had found on Tuesday. The two women broke off their conversation as she re-entered the salon and looked at her expectantly.

'Well?' Mrs Craven demanded.

'I think it's this one.' Kitty held up the suspicious envelope.

Before passing it to her grandmother she slit it open carefully with the small brass paperknife from her grandmother's writing bureau and eased the contents out with a pair of tweezers, taking care not to handle it.

'Better not to touch it in case our writer has been careless and left fingerprints,' Kitty explained.

'Of course.' Her grandmother rose from her seat on the sofa and crossed to the bureau where Kitty had opened up the letter. Mrs Craven came to join her and all three of them studied the contents.

Dear Madam,

I am shocked that you are continuing to be involved in condoning and encouraging such wickedness under the roof of your establishment. The flaunting of the flesh of young ladies before the leering eyes of respectable men is to be deplored. Repent and withdraw your support for such a misguided scheme or pay the price for your sins.

A well-wisher

Romans 13:14 Instead, put on the Lord Jesus Christ, and make no provision for the flesh to arouse its desires.

'He does seem rather fond of quoting Romans,' Kitty remarked, trying to make light of the matter in an attempt to reassure Mrs Craven.

'I gave my letter to the constable here in Dartmouth and Joan was taking hers to Torquay police station. I believe she intended to try and see the chief inspector too,' Mrs Craven said.

'Matt has gone to Torquay on another case. I think he was calling in at the office.' Kitty picked up the telephone receiver.

They had a small office on the main street in Torquay just above a gentlemen's outfitters. The office shared a landing with a company that made dentures. It gave them a postal address for the business and space to arrange appointments to meet clients about cases. Kitty had spent more time there recently dealing with files and sorting out paperwork for Matt.

The line was connected, and Kitty waited, hoping that Matt was in the office.

'Matt, I'm so glad I've caught you.' Kitty spoke before her husband could get much further than hello.

'Steady on, old girl, is something wrong?' Matt's voice was calm and reassuring even though she detected a note of concern.

'It seems that Mrs Craven, Grams and the other ladies on the committee have all received anonymous letters in the post this morning. Our post had not come when I left so I don't know if I have received one too,' Kitty explained as Mrs Craven nodded her head vigorously in agreement.

'Tell Matthew that I have complained to Inspector Lewis,' Mrs Craven interrupted.

Matt's low chuckle sounded in her ear. 'Hmm, I don't suppose that was terribly effective.'

'No, she has taken it up with Chief Inspector Greville and I believe Mrs Ponsonby-Bell has also complained,' Kitty said.

'Keep the letter your grandmother has received, and I'll meet you back at home. We can see if there is anything there for you,' Matt advised.

'I presume we can then make another journey to Torquay to see Inspector Lewis?' Kitty asked.

'Who else?' Matt laughed. 'I'll see you at home shortly, give my regards to the ladies.'

'Well?' demanded Mrs Craven. 'What does he advise?'

'I shall take this letter with me, Grams, if that's all right and I'm meeting Matt at home so we can check our post before going to see Inspector Lewis again.' Kitty replaced the handset on its cradle as she spoke before easing the note carefully back inside its envelope.

'I hope you have better luck than myself or Joan,' Mrs Craven said somewhat huffily as she retired back to her seat on the sofa to finish her tea. 'Please keep me informed, Kitty, and I shall expect you here early tomorrow afternoon for the pageant run-through.'

Kitty's grandmother exchanged a speaking glance with Kitty while her friend's attention was on her teacup.

'Do be careful, my dear. I shall see you tomorrow.' Grams kissed her cheek as Kitty put on her coat and gloves before calling Bertie from his inspection of Mrs Craven's handbag that she had carelessly placed on the floor.

Matt rode back from the office to discover Kitty's little red car was already parked on the drive next to the house. He pulled up at the side of her vehicle and stopped his engine. He suspected that Kitty had probably opened whatever post had come that morning.

He entered the house and was greeted enthusiastically by Bertie. Kitty was in the dining room, the day's post on the dining table in front of her.

'Have you received a letter too?' Matt asked as he smoothed back his hair that had been somewhat disarranged after he'd removed his cap.

'Yes.' She indicated a sheet of cheap writing paper on the table.

Madam,

I urge you most strongly to reconsider your actions in supporting this ungodly event. Withdraw at once or risk the consequences.

A well-wisher

Colossians 3:25 For he who does wrong will receive the consequences of the wrong which he has done, and that without partiality.

'Well, that makes a nice change,' Kitty remarked drily.

'How do you mean?' asked Matt as he came over to the table.

'At least it's not Romans this time. Whoever it is knows his Bible,' Kitty replied.

'I take it you have opened it with care?' Matt asked. He saw the letter opener from the sitting room beside the envelope and Kitty was still wearing her red kid driving gloves.

'Naturally.' She returned the note to the envelope and slid it into her handbag next to an identical one which he assumed must be the note her grandmother had received.

'Let's go back to the police station then, and our friend Inspector Lewis.' Matt guessed the inspector would be harbouring very unfriendly feelings towards himself and Kitty if he had already fended off Mrs Craven and Mrs Ponsonby-Bell.

* * *

The desk sergeant greeted them with a wide smile as they entered the lobby of the police station.

'Good afternoon, Captain Bryant, Mrs Bryant, would you be wanting a word with Inspector Lewis?' he asked.

'Only if he is not too busy with his other important tasks,' Kitty responded.

'Oh, I'm sure he'll find the time to see you, Mrs Bryant. Come on through.' The sergeant lifted the hinged portion of the desk, and they entered the corridor leading to the offices.

Matt could hear the sound of male voices engaged in what sounded like a somewhat heated discussion. As they drew closer to Inspector Lewis's door, he realised the argument was being conducted inside the office.

The sergeant knocked loudly on the door and the voices stopped.

The sergeant opened the door and peered inside. 'Sorry to disturb you, sirs, but I have Captain and Mrs Bryant here to see you.'

He stood aside to allow them to enter. Inspector Lewis was seated behind his desk looking rather red in the face while Chief Inspector Greville was standing to one side.

'Captain Bryant, Kitty, do come in and have a seat. I expect you are here about the letters?' Chief Inspector Greville greeted them warmly and offered a chair to Kitty.

'Thank you, sir, I'm afraid we are. My grandmother has also received a letter and when I returned home, I discovered that I too had been sent one.' Kitty took the envelopes from her handbag and put them on the empty desk in front of Inspector Lewis.

She went on to tell the policemen that Mary thought she had seen the man responsible lurking outside the Dolphin again earlier in the day.

'I see, do we know if any of the young ladies have also received letters today?' Chief Inspector Greville asked.

'Not as far as I'm aware but apart from Sir Vivian Hardcastle's daughters, the other girls are at work and may not get their post until they return home. I'm not sure about Naomi Coulter, Mrs Ponsonby-Bell's goddaughter or Dorothy Martin, councillor Martin's daughter, but I'm sure they would have come forward if they had received anything like this today,' Kitty said as Inspector Lewis carefully extracted the contents of the envelopes and opened the notes so he and the chief inspector could read them.

'The pageant is on Saturday afternoon?' the chief inspector asked.

'Yes, sir, and the girls have a dress rehearsal tomorrow evening,' Matt said.

'I take it you will be attending both events?' Chief Inspector Greville's level gaze locked with Matt.

'Yes, sir,' Matt confirmed.

'We shall ask the Dartmouth constabulary to be present for the pageant and the aftermath. Mrs Bryant, I take it that the Dolphin will also have security?' Chief Inspector Greville asked.

'Of course, sir. My staff have already been alerted,' Kitty affirmed.

'This may all be the work of some harmless delusionist but better to be safe than sorry. I'm sure Inspector Lewis here will be delighted to offer his support.' Chief Inspector Greville gave his junior officer a pat on his shoulder and made his farewells.

Inspector Lewis was left facing them with a distinctly sour expression on his foxy face.

CHAPTER SEVEN

Friday teatime saw the beauty pageant contestants clattering back into the Dolphin ready for the run-through. Mickey, Kitty's maintenance man and head of security matters at the Dolphin, was discreetly stationed in a corner of the lobby.

Inspector Lewis had requested the local constable to patrol the embankment more frequently as a visible deterrent should the letter writer reappear. Naomi was busy telling the other girls about the anonymous letters that the event organisers had received. To Kitty's relief, none of the contestants appeared to have received a letter.

'That does sound quite frightening,' Victoria said when Naomi had finished her tale.

'Well, I'm not scared of such nonsense.' Peggy Blaine tossed her pretty head and sniffed scornfully.

Kitty unlocked the dressing room doors so the girls could enter and was relieved to see that everything was as she had left it the day before. Mr Jakes was seated at the piano and was busy checking the music which some of the girls had provided for their talent pieces.

Mrs Craven bustled to and fro, checking hemlines and

décolletage for modesty. Dorothy was complaining and Victoria was bickering once more with Araminta. Naomi effectively drowned them all out by practising her scales to warm up her voice. This drew a united chorus of disapproval from the other girls.

After reminding the girls of how the pageant would run, Mrs Craven issued Kitty with a clipboard and requested she time each girl's talent piece before they did a full dress rehearsal. Matt stationed himself at the back of the ballroom near the bar and prepared to watch the rehearsal.

Peggy was first with a soulful recitation of the 'Lady of Shalott'. Kitty noted the time and waited for Naomi with 'Un bel di vedremo'. After ignoring Naomi's fussing about Mr Jakes' playing and Betty's not so quiet mutter of 'Lawks what a racket,' she noted Naomi's time on the sheet.

Betty performed 'You Made Me Love You', Victoria gave a demonstration of movement to music and Felicia performed a tap dance. Araminta then recited Shakespeare's sonnet 'Shall I compare thee to a summer's day'. Dorothy then appeared with her fan to perform 'Five Foot Two, Eyes of Blue'.

Mrs Craven approved the timing for all the pieces and had strong words with Dorothy about making less suggestive movements with her fan.

'You are not Miss Josephine Baker, Dorothy.'

With all the performances approved, Kitty organised refreshments for the girls before they started the dress rehearsal in full. Trolleys of tea, and sandwiches with cake were brought into the ballroom and the girls were given the opportunity to have a short break.

Matt went to check on Mickey to see if there had been any issues downstairs.

'Well, that seemed to go well, I thought. A nice mix of items both cultured and popular,' Mrs Craven murmured to Kitty as they stood aside looking over Kitty's notes.

'Yes, let's hope the full run-through goes as smoothly,' Kitty agreed before she was called away by Felicia requesting advice on where she should stand to best advantage on the stage.

A few minutes later the rehearsal commenced with the parade of daywear and introductions followed by a break to change clothes and the talent spot before the end parade and mock announcement of the winner.

By the time the rehearsal had finished, and the girls had gone, Kitty was exhausted.

'Tomorrow is the big day. Ticket sales have been brisk, and we have some lovely prizes for the raffle. Thank heavens there has been no sign of the letter writer,' Mrs Craven declared as she put on her coat and picked up her gloves. 'Kitty, I shall leave you to lock up and I shall see you tomorrow.'

Kitty blew out a sigh of relief and bade goodnight to Mr Jakes.

'Mickey says there were no problems downstairs so we may have frightened our villain away,' Matt said as he accompanied Kitty while she locked the doors once more.

'I feel quite frazzled so I shall be glad when tomorrow is over and there is just the children's party left to organise.' Kitty collected her own coat and gloves and they set off back to Churston.

Perhaps the increased police presence had deterred the letter writer after all. Still, she knew she would not fully relax until after the pageant was over. The threats contained in the letters had made her uneasy.

* * *

The day of the pageant dawned bright and breezy. Kitty and Matt had scarcely sat down to breakfast when they heard the telephone ring. A moment later, the door of the dining room opened.

'Begging your pardon, Mrs Bryant, a Mrs Craven wishes to speak to you urgent she says.' Kitty's housekeeper sounded apologetic.

Kitty thanked her and abandoned her soft-boiled egg.

'Kitty, Joan Ponsonby-Bell tells me that Naomi has received a letter this morning advising her not to participate in the pageant. If she has had a letter no doubt the other girls will also receive one.'

'Is Naomi all right? Does she still intend to take part?' Kitty asked. She had a feeling that Mrs Craven was right. If one girl had been sent a letter, then it was very likely to be the same for the other contestants.

'Well, she is shaken, of course. These things are most unpleasant. I have advised her to take it up with Inspector Lewis. I do hope the other girls will not be deterred.'

Kitty agreed with Mrs Craven. 'Yes, it would be terrible if it put them off. Why someone would get so het up about this I cannot imagine. The girls are not even going to be wearing bathing suits.'

'Quite so, and the money raised will provide a splendid celebratory treat for our young people to honour their majesties.' Mrs Craven sounded most indignant about the whole business.

Kitty spent a few more minutes soothing the older woman before returning to her rapidly cooling breakfast.

'I dare say you will have to wait until later to see if everyone turns up,' Matt said when Kitty told him about the call. 'We shall have to be on our guard in case this fellow attempts to disrupt the contest in some way.'

'The sooner it's over the happier I shall be. I wish we knew what he looked like.' Kitty poked her egg with the spoon.

'We can focus on Sir Vivian's case once the pageant is over. I drew a blank at Ilsham looking for that Peplow chap,' Matt said.

'He may be at the Dolphin this afternoon to support Victoria,' Kitty suggested, buttering the last triangle of toast from the rack.

'Yes, good thought. I wonder if Sir Vivian will attend too.' Matt passed her the small, pressed glass dish of marmalade.

'We shall soon see,' Kitty replied as she gave the end of her toast to the ever-waiting Bertie.

* * *

Joan Ponsonby-Bell, accompanied by Naomi, was already waiting for them when they arrived at the Dolphin.

'Captain Bryant, Mrs Bryant, have you heard? Naomi received one of those dreadful letters this morning.' Joan held on to the sleeve of Matt's coat with a bejewelled hand. 'I informed the police, but no one seems to be taking it seriously. What if the girls are in real danger? This letter writer sounds quite unhinged.'

Naomi rolled her eyes. 'Honestly, the pageant will be over in a few hours, Aunt Joan. I'm sure it will all be perfectly fine.'

Dorothy Martin hurried into the lobby clutching a small round leatherette vanity box. 'I say, I had one of those letters this morning. I took it to the constable. I daren't tell Daddy about it, he'll stop me from entering.' She looked excitedly around the group.

'I had one too. I expect everyone has received one,' Naomi said.

A few minutes later, Felicia and Betty arrived together. 'We've had letters.'

Kitty soothed the babble of excited chatter and led them down to the ballroom so they could begin to get ready. She had just unlocked the dressing area when Araminta and Victoria entered with the same tale. It seemed they had received a letter addressed to them jointly.

'Father was most annoyed when he read it. He telephoned Mrs Craven, and she told him to contact Inspector Lewis,' Araminta reported.

'Dominic was furious when I telephoned him, he has insisted that he will be here this afternoon to make sure I'm safe.' Victoria cut her eyes at her sister, apparently looking to gauge Araminta's reaction.

The reaction she got was a faint snort of derision.

'Whatever is all the fuss about?' Peggy Blaine was the last girl to arrive. She looked around at the others. 'Don't tell me that idiotic letter has you all riled up?' She carefully took off her hat so as not to disturb her smooth dark bob.

'Did you get a letter, Peggy?' Felicia asked.

'Oh yes, but I shan't let it bother me.' Peggy took her place in front of her mirror and took out her powder compact.

Kitty breathed a small sigh of relief and went to report to Mrs Craven that all the girls had arrived and intended to participate. Matt had gone to liaise with Mickey to make sure he was aware of the latest developments as the audience had started to arrive.

'Ah, Kitty, the very person. I was just assuring Sir Vivian that you and Captain Bryant have been working with the police to ensure the safety of the contestants,' Mrs Craven said as soon as Kitty approached. She assumed the tall, distinguished man next to Mrs Craven was Sir Vivian.

'Mrs Bryant, delighted to make your acquaintance. I know your husband.' Sir Vivian bowed over her hand in a slightly old-fashioned gesture.

'Likewise, Sir Vivian. Matt is with my head of security for the hotel now and the police have assured us that they are taking these letters seriously.' Kitty withdrew her hand.

'I'm pleased to hear it. These threats are quite concerning. Now, I think I should take my seat as it's getting quite busy in here.' Sir Vivian looked around the rapidly filling ballroom.

Kitty saw Alice, Dolly and the rest of the Miller family all in the front row next to Mrs Ponsonby-Bell. Sir Vivian took his place next to a man she recognised as Councillor Martin. The two men immediately started up in conversation and she assumed they knew each other well. Mr Lutterworth was already seated at the judging table on the stage talking to a florid-faced man who she assumed must be Mr Venables, the sponsor of the event.

Kitty stationed herself at the dressing room door that led to the stage and waited for her cue from Mrs Craven for the pageant to begin. As she did so she noticed Dominic Peplow slipping into the back of the room accompanied by a gaggle of attractive young girls and well-heeled men.

Mr Jakes struck up on the piano and the room fell silent as Mrs Craven took centre stage to make the opening announcements. The first half went smoothly. There were a few stumbled introductions and some silly answers here and there to the judge's questions. A steely glare from Mrs Craven calmed the catcalls and high spirits of a group of naval cadets present in the audience.

During the intermission Kitty went to check with Matt that all had gone smoothly while the girls changed for the evening wear and talent show part of the event. The other committee ladies were engaged in the sale of raffle tickets and the bar was busy.

'No problems reported from the lobby, Kitty. It seems to be going well, it's very busy out there with people stepping in and out,' Matt reported.

She made her way back towards the dressing room after stopping off for a quick chat with Alice. Several of the girls seemed to have slipped out for various reasons. Only Felicia and Betty were still applying their make-up in front of the mirrors.

'Five minutes to go. Where are the other girls?' Kitty asked.

'There's a big queue for the ladies'.' Dorothy slid back into the room.

Araminta came back in looking cross. 'Victoria is drinking with Dominic. Father will be furious if he sees her.'

Naomi returned a minute later. 'Victoria is coming. Has anyone seen Peggy?'

Kitty looked at her watch as Victoria entered, her cheeks flushed and her eyes a little glassy.

'Peggy went out ages ago,' Victoria said, having heard Naomi's question as she entered the room. 'She said she needed a breath of fresh air before she got changed.'

Peggy's evening gown was still on its hanger. There was less than two minutes before the second half was due to begin and Peggy was the first girl due to perform. Kitty hurried out onto the stage to scan the ballroom for any sign of the missing girl.

'Are we all ready?' Mrs Craven bustled forward to meet her.

'Peggy Blaine is late,' Kitty explained.

'Well really, these young women today. I expected better of Peggy, she always seems so reliable at her job.' Mrs Craven checked her own tiny gold wristwatch. 'I'll tell Mr Jakes that we are moving her to the end and Naomi can come on first.'

Kitty nodded and hurried back to the dressing room to warn Naomi to get ready. Once Naomi had gone out onto the stage Kitty left Betty to get ready to follow Naomi's turn and went out to look for Matt. Thanks to the timing sheet from the previous day, she knew she had a few minutes in hand.

Kitty found her husband at the rear of the ballroom, stationed where he could watch the pageant and keep a discreet eye on Dominic Peplow.

'Matt, thank goodness. Peggy Blaine hasn't returned to the dressing room. No one knows where she is. Can you alert Mickey and the constable and ask them to look out for her? She's still in her daywear.'

'Very well, do you think something may have happened to her? Or has she been struck by stage fright?' Matt asked.

'I don't know. Peggy doesn't seem the kind of young woman to be afraid of performing, or indeed of anything, but who knows. I must get back to the other girls.' She looked at her watch again. Naomi's aria was almost at its climax.

'Very well, go back. I'll alert everyone,' Matt said.

Kitty returned to the dressing room just as the audience started to applaud Naomi. She sent Betty out onto the stage as the other girl arrived back in the room, flushed and smiling from her performance.

'Is there still no sign of Peggy?' Kitty looked at the girls. She was sure something was very wrong.

They shook their heads, Araminta shrugged and Victoria continued to apply her lipstick.

'Did she say anything about where she was going?' Kitty went to Peggy's area of the dressing room and started to look amongst the girls' things. Perhaps if Peggy had developed stage fright, she might have left a note of some kind.

'Just that she needed a breath of fresh air. I assumed she was going onto the embankment for a quick smoke,' Dorothy said.

'Perhaps that brother of hers has made her go back to the shop,' Felicia suggested. 'Peggy said as he didn't approve of her taking part and that letter didn't help matters.'

'She'll have to come back for her things,' Dorothy said, casting a covetous look at Peggy's shagreen-covered vanity box.

The sound of applause reached them from the ballroom and Kitty hustled Victoria into place ready to go on as Betty came off. Kitty longed to abandon her post to go and see if Matt had found the missing girl. However, Felicia had managed to knot the laces in her tap shoes and there was insufficient time to nip out and get back before Victoria's act ended.

Dorothy was the final act and there was still no sign of Peggy. Kitty ran around to the front of the ballroom to the judges' table to discreetly let Mrs Craven know that Peggy had not returned.

The audience applauded her song and dance and Dorothy returned to the dressing room while they waited for the raffle to be drawn and the judges to total their scores to determine the winner.

'Here, you don't think as that letter writer has got her, do you?' Betty asked as the contestants titivated themselves, ready for their final stage appearance.

'Peggy? I pity the bloke if he tried anything with Peggy, she's as hard as nails that one,' Dorothy remarked.

'Even so, it's a bit queer, her just going off like that and leaving all her things here.' Felicia patted her blonde locks into place.

'It'll be her brother like you said. He's a bit of an odd one.' Dorothy added a dab of perfume, scenting the air with roses.

Kitty hoped Dorothy was right.

CHAPTER EIGHT

Once the girls had all left the dressing room to go back on stage for the final results, Kitty went out to look for Matt. She could see no sign of him in the ballroom and assumed he must have gone out to the lobby to see Mickey.

A round of applause broke out as she reached the door, and she glanced back to see Felicia graciously accepting the blue satin sash and sparkling tiara. The corridor was quiet as she walked swiftly to the reception area, checking the resident lounges as she passed just in case Peggy might have gone into one of those.

'Matt, is there any sign of her?' Kitty reached her husband's side where he was standing with Mickey.

'No trace of her, she could well have left the hotel at the interval. Mickey says quite a few people came out for a quick stroll and a cigarette.' Matt's face creased in concern.

'That's right, Miss Kitty, and of course I were watching for a suspicious bloke trying to get in, not a girl going out,' Mickey said.

'Of course,' Kitty agreed. 'It just seems so odd. She has left all her things, no note or message. She just told the other girls she was going out for a breath of fresh air and then vanished.'

'I've informed the constable and he's gone round to the chemist's to see if her brother has seen her. You know in case as she might have gone home like,' Mickey said.

Kitty knew that Peggy and her brother lived above the shop in the heart of the town. 'Thank you, one of the girls said they thought her brother disapproved of her entering the contest and might have come to persuade her to drop out.'

People started to file past them, chattering and talking as they left the hotel.

'Who won?' Matt asked as he drew Kitty aside to allow a large family group to go past.

'Felicia. I think it was ending her tap dance with the splits that did it,' Kitty said absently as she nodded farewell to various people that knew her.

'Not Dorothy's big pink fan?' The corners of Matt's lips turned up in a brief smile.

Kitty knew he was attempting to distract her. She appreciated the sentiment but couldn't shake the feeling of dread that had enveloped her.

The constable pushed his way through the exiting crowds, his navy uniform and helmet visible in the throng.

'Mr Blaine hasn't seen his sister since this morning, sir. He said as he last saw her at breakfast when they had argued about her taking part. She had received one of those nasty letters.' The constable was red-faced and slightly out of breath from where he had clearly hurried back to the Dolphin from the chemist's.

'We should go and speak to the other girls again before they leave.' Matt looked at Kitty.

They made their way against the flow of people back to the dressing room. The ballroom was half empty now of people. Mr Venables and Mr Lutterworth were engaged in what seemed to be amiable conversation at the judges table.

Mrs Craven was with Mrs Ponsonby-Bell and the other committee ladies at the raffle table where they appeared to be counting the proceeds. The various families of the pageant entrants were collected in small groups waiting for the girls to change clothes and bring their things out of the dressing room.

Matt waited at the dressing room door while Kitty went inside to check that all the girls were decent before Matt could join her.

'Did you find Peggy, Mrs Bryant?' Araminta asked.

'Not yet, no,' Kitty said and opened the door to permit Matt to enter.

'I'm afraid Peggy seems to have disappeared. She hasn't returned home, and her brother hasn't seen her. Did she say anything at all before she went outside that might indicate where she was going?' He looked around at the girls.

There was a mass shaking of heads. 'No, she just said she was stepping out for a breath of air,' Felicia said. The others all murmured agreement.

'I told her she would be cutting it fine to get ready, but she said it would only take her a minute,' Betty added.

'Did anything happen before she said she was going out? Did she leave the dressing room for any reason or say anything at all that might give us a clue to where she might be?' Kitty asked.

'She did go out into the ballroom for a few minutes and got a drink,' Felicia said slowly. 'She seemed all pleased, and I don't know, sort of flushed and giggly when she came back in. That was when she said she was stepping outside.'

'Yes, you're right. She took her handbag with her. That's why I assumed she must have intended going for a cigarette.' Naomi looked at Felicia.

'Hmm, do you think it possible that she saw someone or met someone in the ballroom and went off to meet them for some reason?' Kitty asked.

'Ooh yes, that would be why she looked so, well, pleased with herself. Like a man friend you mean?' Dorothy's eyes brightened.

'Has Peggy got a boyfriend?' Matt asked.

Felicia and Betty shrugged. 'Peggy always kept herself to herself where her own business was concerned,' Felicia said. 'I never saw her at the picture house with anybody in particular.'

'I think she did have a gentleman admirer...' Dorothy paused in her packing. 'I was in the chemist's a week or so ago and they had a new perfume in stock. Smelt lovely it did, very expensive. I remarked on it, and she got this kind of smile and made a comment about how much she liked it but would never pay that much herself. Well, blow me down if she weren't wearing it here, got a big bottle of it in her box.'

'But no one saw her speak to anyone?' Matt asked.

Again, there was a collective shaking of heads. Kitty noticed that Araminta and Victoria had remained quiet, but she supposed they probably didn't know Peggy as well as the other girls did.

'She didn't say if she expected anyone to come to see her take part in the pageant?' Matt asked. 'I know the rest of you all have friends or family here.'

'No, she said her brother had to work. Peggy wasn't the kind of girl to have friends,' Dorothy said.

Kitty could see they were getting nowhere, and the girls' families were all waiting for them, so she and Matt were compelled to stand aside to allow them to leave.

'I'll lock the room and leave Peggy's things here until she comes to collect them,' Kitty said, firmly placing the missing girl's vanity box further away from Dorothy's pile of bags and boxes.

The girls all trooped out to be greeted by their nearest and dearest while Kitty secured the room.

'Do you think she will be back?' Kitty asked Matt in a low voice once the girls were out of earshot.

'I'd like to say yes, but I fear that you and I are both thinking the worst,' Matt replied.

Everyone else had left the ballroom. Only Kitty's grandmother, Mrs Craven and Mrs Ponsonby-Bell remained.

'Have you discovered where Peggy Blaine has gone?' Mrs Craven asked as soon as they approached the now empty raffle table.

Matt shook his head. 'Not yet, Mrs Craven. Still, I take it the event was a success?' He looked at the grey metal money tin.

'Marvellous,' Joan replied with a beaming smile. 'Better than our expectations. The children of Dartmouth will have the most delightful celebration of our dear King's jubilee.'

'That's very good news, and Felicia won, I understand?' Matt said.

Mrs Craven nodded. 'I was overruled. I personally considered Naomi to have scored more highly. That finishing part of Felicia's dance, most unorthodox. She did not attempt the splits at the rehearsal.' The older woman appeared most put out.

'Of course, dear Naomi is much more cultured, but one must bow to populist opinion I suppose.' Joan's mouth took on a puckered appearance. 'Fortunately, she is not too disheartened. She has gone with Miss Hardcastle now, I believe for supper and drinks. Sir Vivian kindly offered to treat them.'

'Is Victoria not joining them?' Kitty asked.

Joan's nose wrinkled in disapproval. 'Oh no, she has gone off with that Peplow boy and his gaggle of chums. I don't think Sir Vivian is very impressed.'

'It's very strange, Peggy going off like that.' Kitty's grandmother looked worried.

Kitty agreed and glancing at Matt, she knew that he too was concerned.

'I think we should speak to Inspector Lewis and make

him aware of this development. If Peggy turns up unharmed having just got cold feet, then we can take a little ribbing from the police,' Matt said, confirming Kitty's thoughts.

'I think that would be sensible. One can't be too careful as the girls all received one of those nasty letters today,' Mrs Craven said, closing the money tin.

Kitty and Matt went back to the lobby where the constable was taking a drink of tea in Mr Lutterworth's office, accompanied by Mickey.

'The girls had nothing useful to add. I think we should inform Inspector Lewis of Miss Blaine's disappearance.' Kitty reached for the telephone receiver.

The constable drained his tea from the thick white china mug. 'Here, best not be too hasty, Mrs Bryant. It's not been long. Peggy could have just gone for a walk, to clear her head if she was suffering from stage fright.'

Kitty fixed the constable with a steely gaze. 'Constable, you know Peggy Blaine as well as I do. Has she ever struck you as the kind of young lady who might suffer stage fright or have a predilection to go walking without informing someone of her whereabouts?'

The constable's cheeks grew rosier, and he dropped his gaze. 'No, Mrs Bryant.'

'Perhaps you and Mickey could go out and start looking for her. Take Albert, the kitchen boy, if he can be spared,' Matt suggested.

'I would be happy to assist too.' Mr Lutterworth unfolded himself from his seat and reached for his overcoat.

'Thank you.' Kitty waited for the office to empty before lifting the receiver.

'Hello, Inspector Lewis? This is Kitty Bryant, we have a problem at the pageant.'

Matt had dropped into one of the freshly vacated seats and

looked quizzically at her while she listened to the rest of the inspector's remarks.

'All of the contestants received a letter this morning in the post. I believe the letters contain similar threats to the ones people have received previously. The constable here in Dartmouth has collected them. During the pageant interval, one of the girls, Peggy Blaine, went missing and has not returned either here or to her home.'

'I see. Have you any reason to suspect anything may have happened to her, Mrs Bryant? She may just have changed her mind about participating.' Inspector Lewis didn't sound concerned.

Kitty could feel her irritation with the man increasing. 'Peggy is not the kind of young woman to just walk out without saying something. All her belongings are here at the hotel, including some recently acquired and very expensive perfume.'

'What time was she last seen?' Inspector Lewis asked.

'At three o'clock during the interval.' Kitty released a breath. Perhaps he was taking her worries seriously after all.

'With all due respect, Mrs Bryant, it's not even six o'clock yet.' The inspector's tone implied that she was foolish for raising her concerns at this point.

'Inspector, I am worried. In the light of these letters, Peggy vanishing is immensely troubling. Time may be of the essence if she is any kind of danger.' If the inspector had been standing in front of her, Kitty thought she may have wanted to smack him.

'I appreciate your concern, have the constable keep a look out for her and if she is not home by say ten o'clock, let the station know.'

Before Kitty could protest, the inspector bade her a good evening and rang off.

'Well!' She banged the receiver back into its cradle. 'Inspector Lewis is clearly not taking this at all seriously.'

She had scarcely finished speaking when the office door

flew open and Albert, the young kitchen lad, stood there, crimson-cheeked and breathless.

'Captain Bryant, come quick, we've found her, Peggy – dead in the park!'

Matt uttered an oath under his breath and raced off after the lad. Kitty picked up her coat and hurried after them, wishing she was wearing a lower-heeled pair of shoes.

They caught up with the boy at the white-painted wrought-iron bandstand in the centre of the small park. Red, white and blue bunting hung limply from the roofline. The gardens were quiet as the light was already starting to fade. The constable and Mr Lutterworth were inside the bandstand while Albert and Mickey stood at the entrance, shielding the inside from any curious passers-by.

Kitty caught her breath as she followed Matt up the steps inside the bandstand. Peggy was slumped in the corner, sitting on a seat. To a casual observer it would have appeared as if she were sitting admiring the view. Her neat navy-blue felt hat with the bunch of primroses trim was pulled low over eyes that were open and unseeing. A slightly startled expression was on Peggy's pretty face and a dark red stain marked the front of her pale green cotton printed frock. Blood had oozed out below the hem of the dead girl's navy wool coat and dripped in a small, sticky puddle on the floor.

Kitty pressed the back of her hand to her mouth in shock.

'We need to alert Inspector Lewis.' Matt turned to her. 'Run back, Kitty old girl, and telephone.' He squeezed her hand tenderly, sensing her distress at the scene.

Kitty nodded wordlessly and sped off, her ears buzzing and bile bubbling dangerously close to the back of her throat.

* * *

Matt peered cautiously under Peggy's jacket to see what had killed the girl. A small brass knife with an ornate handle, set with blue stones, glittered in the dim light. It seemed clear to Matt that whoever had killed Peggy had taken her by surprise. Had she come here to meet someone? It was a popular lovers' trysting spot and would have been quiet with most of the town attending the pageant.

'Best not touch much, Captain Bryant. Inspector Lewis is very keen on these new-fangled methods of investigating,' the constable warned.

'Yes, and don't worry I haven't touched a thing.' Matt looked around the bandstand for anything else that might provide a clue to who Peggy may have come to meet. For it had been a rendezvous, he was sure of it. The floor of the bandstand was dry and dusty with small patches of damp mud in the corners covered with small pieces of detritus that had been blown inside. No helpful footprints or dropped buttons were in evidence.

'Ahoy, there, Captain Bryant! Or should it be a more musical reference?' Matt was greeted by the ever-cheerful voice of Dr Carter who was walking along the narrow pathway carrying his leather doctor's bag.

'You received Kitty's telephone call? I'm afraid we have another victim for you, doctor.' Matt stood aside to allow the doctor to enter.

'Stabbing?' the doctor said, eyeing the bloody puddle on the floor.

'One of the pageant contestants,' Matt said. 'The girls had all received threatening letters.'

The doctor frowned as he looked more closely. 'Good grief, it's young Peggy from the chemist's.' He was careful, like Matt, not to disturb the scene before Inspector Lewis could arrive to see it for himself.

Matt told the doctor about Peggy stepping out during the interval.

'Well, judging by the viscosity of the blood I would say that fits with the window for her murder. I was in Dartmouth at the hospital when Inspector Lewis telephoned to say there had been a death, hence my prompt arrival. I assume my wife must have told him where to find. He said Mrs Bryant had made the call.' The doctor gave Matt a shrewd glance. 'I daresay this will upset Kitty since the pageant was at the Dolphin?'

Matt nodded. 'Yes, she was worried from the moment Peggy didn't return. She said it was unlike the girl.'

The doctor agreed. 'Yes, Miss Blaine was always most conscientious. Someone will have to break the news to Alastair, her brother. He's virtually raised Peggy, him being so much older and their parents passing away when she was just a girl.'

'It's a bad business.' Matt looked across the park and saw Kitty coming back towards them, huddled up in her winter coat against the breeze that had sprung up once again from the river.

'The inspector is on his way,' Kitty confirmed when she reached them. 'I believe Inspector Greville may be coming too.' She said hello to the doctor who greeted her as affably as if he were simply out for an evening stroll.

True to her word, a black police car pulled to a halt on the road at the edge of the park just as the street lamps started to flicker into life.

'What's this Lewis chap like?' Dr Carter asked. 'I've heard mixed reviews.'

'We'll let you judge for yourself,' Kitty said with a hint of a smile.

'That bad, eh?' The doctor waited for the inspector and his accompanying constable to draw nearer.

'What are all you people doing inside there? There has been a serious crime committed here.' The inspector glared at them and Matt, Kitty, Mr Lutterworth, the constable and Dr Carter all obediently exited the bandstand.

'You, there, are you the doctor?' Inspector Lewis popped his head back out to look at Dr Carter.

'Yes, would you like me to come back inside, sir?' Dr Carter said innocently and winked at Kitty. He walked back up the steps.

'Mr Lutterworth, would you go back to the Dolphin please and let Grams know what has happened and perhaps have some refreshments prepared? If Chief Inspector Greville does come I'm sure he would welcome them,' Kitty suggested.

'Of course, Kitty. I daresay you and Captain Bryant are in need of something to eat too. It's been a very busy day.' Mr Lutterworth called Albert and Mickey and the trio set off back to the hotel.

The two constables took over their posts at the entrance of the bandstand.

'Are you all right, Kitty?' Matt asked as they listened to the rise and fall of male conversation from inside the bandstand.

'Yes, I think so. I was just shocked to see Peggy like that. Do you think the other girls are safe? What if the letter writer attacks them?' Kitty asked, looking up at Matt. 'Or the other committee ladies? Much as I have often wished to kill Mrs Craven, I truly don't wish anything to happen to her.'

Matt placed his arm around his wife's narrow waist and pulled her close. 'Let us see what Inspector Lewis has to say on the matter.'

Kitty's expression clearly demonstrated that she didn't think Inspector Lewis would have anything useful to say.

'Captain and Mrs Bryant, I heard that you found the missing pageant contestant?' Chief Inspector Greville had approached them unnoticed out of the gloom.

Matt quickly informed the chief inspector of the circum-

stances surrounding Peggy's disappearance and the discovery of
her body.

'I see.' The chief inspector's sad and untidy moustache
twitched. 'This will of course be Inspector Lewis's case.
However, since he is still unfamiliar with some of our procedures, I shall be supporting him.'

'Thank you, sir. He is in the bandstand now with Dr
Carter. Matt and I were heading back to the Dolphin. You and
the inspector are most welcome to join us when you are free. I
have asked Mr Lutterworth to provide refreshments. It's very
cold out here now the sun has gone,' Kitty said.

Matt knew that the chief inspector was seldom able to resist
the prospect of food despite Mrs Greville's desire for him to lose
weight. He also knew that Kitty hoped to find out more information about Peggy's death by offering the police tea and cakes.

'That's very kind of you, Mrs Bryant. I'm sure the inspector
will wish to speak to you about Miss Blaine and the circumstances surrounding her disappearance. He told me he was most
concerned when you reported her missing.'

It was hard to tell in the fading light, but Kitty could have
sworn the chief inspector gave her a quick wink.

CHAPTER NINE

Matt steered Kitty away from the murder scene and back to the Dolphin before she could tell the chief inspector what had really been said during the first telephone conversation.

'That wretched man!' Kitty exploded as soon as they were out of earshot. 'He lied to Chief Inspector Greville. Most concerned, my foot!'

Matt for once found himself having to speed up to keep up with Kitty. Her anger making her march along at a rapid pace.

'I know, but we are likely to be stuck with Inspector Lewis for quite some time and our paths will keep crossing.' Matt would have liked a few choice words with Inspector Lewis, but they needed to play a long game.

'You do realise, that when we solve this murder and catch Peggy's killer – *and we will!* – he will try and take all the credit?' Kitty halted so suddenly he almost bumped into her.

'I know, old thing, but if we antagonise him even more, he can make it very difficult for us to get the information we need for our cases.' Matt fell into step beside Kitty once more as her pace slowed.

'You mean we shall catch more flies with honey than with

vinegar.' Kitty glanced up at him and he could see that she understood what he meant.

'I agree, Inspector Lewis is exasperating but we have little choice. We cannot run to Chief Inspector Greville with every small complaint no matter how justified. I believe the chief inspector has the measure of him.' Matt followed Kitty into the busy lobby of the hotel.

Guests were entering and exiting ready for dinner and there was an air of bustling normality that completely belied the grisly scene just down the road at the bandstand.

'I have prepared some refreshments in the office, Kitty,' Mr Lutterworth said, greeting them discreetly.

'Thank you, Cyril. I think the chief inspector and Inspector Lewis will be over in a while.' Kitty gave her hotel manager a warm smile.

Matt followed Kitty into the office and saw that Mr Lutterworth had set up a small table with sandwiches, cakes, pork pie and sausage rolls along with all the accoutrements for tea.

'Oh this looks wonderful. I am so hungry.' Kitty slipped off her coat and hung it up before sinking into her old leather office chair with a sigh. 'Poor Peggy. I know the other girls didn't like her much but it's such a terrible thing to happen.'

Matt could see from the light of the green shaded desk lamp that his wife was still pale with shock from their discovery.

'Here, I'll pour us some tea and I think a splash of brandy is in order for medicinal purposes,' Matt said. He laced their teacups with a small amount of brandy from the decanter Kitty always kept to hand in the hotel office.

Kitty took a reviving sip and set her cup down so she could fill her plate with food. 'Do you think the letter writer is responsible for this murder, Matt? Are the other girls or the committee in danger? I know I asked this before but now Peggy is dead.'

Matt scratched his head as he took his seat opposite his wife. 'I don't know, Kitty. As you said, many people were not keen on Peggy. It could be a personal attack. A lover perhaps? Peggy went there to meet someone, I'm sure of it. Now, unless the letter writer is a person we know, then it has to be someone with a more personal connection to the girl.'

Kitty nodded. 'Yes, I see what you mean. The way the girls described her demeanour in the dressing room before she left, it sounded as if it were likely that Peggy knew her attacker. Of course, I suppose the letters could be a bluff to make it look as if Peggy were killed by a stranger.'

'Or the murderer took advantage of the girls having received letters to murder Peggy,' Matt said as he helped himself to a plate of food.

There was a tap on the office door and Chief Inspector Greville came to join them. His face was pale and his expression grim. Kitty poured him a cup of tea as he took off his hat and coat.

'Inspector Lewis has gone to see Mr Blaine, the dead girl's brother.' The policeman took one of the spare seats from behind Dolly's desk. His eyes lit up at the sight of the loaded table.

'Ah yes, they have a flat above the chemist's,' Kitty said after inviting the chief inspector to help himself to food.

'So I understand. Miss Blaine seems to have been pretty well known in the town. I take it a good many people would have had contact with her?' The chief inspector picked up a large slice of pork pie.

'Yes, I think so, through her work. She was employed by her brother in the chemist's shop. She wasn't particularly friendly though. Prickly and rather stand-offish. I think it was Mrs Craven who described her as "sly", which seemed a little too far but you get the picture.' Kitty poured a cup of tea and passed it to the chief inspector.

'Dr Carter said she always seemed to know everybody's business,' the policeman observed before tucking into a cheese and pickle sandwich.

'I think she used to eavesdrop on conversations, and I suppose she would find out a lot of things about people by assisting her brother,' Kitty said.

Matt gave the chief inspector the information they had learned from the other pageant contestants.

'Dorothy Martin seems to think that Peggy had a wealthy admirer,' Kitty passed on Dorothy's story of the perfume.

'We thought Peggy may have gone to the bandstand to meet someone,' Matt said.

The chief inspector finished his sandwich before responding. 'From the position and place in which Peggy was found, I think that is a reasonable supposition. It fits with the information the other girls gave you.'

'Do you think the other girls, or the committee might be in any danger, sir?' Kitty asked. 'If the murderer is connected in some way to those dreadful letters that everyone received?'

Matt knew that this was Kitty's main fear. As one of the organisers of the pageant, even though her role had been mainly secretarial, he knew she felt responsible as it had been hosted by the Dolphin.

'I think it unlikely. I will be surprised if Peggy's murderer turns out to be the writer of the letters. It seems to me that she went to the bandstand to meet someone she knew. It's possible I grant you, but those letters were intended to deter participation in the pageant. The event has finished now. I would very much like to discover the letter writer's identity, however, if only to rule them out.' The chief inspector helped himself to a slice of sponge cake.

Matt watched a cascade of crumbs drop onto the chief inspector's dark green tie. 'I presume the inspector will wish to interview the other contestants?'

The chief inspector nodded. 'He will no doubt cover the same ground you have covered with them, as well as talking to you and Mrs Bryant. Inspector Lewis said he was involved in that case in Yorkshire last year? Your cousin Lady Woodcombe's wedding?' He looked at Kitty.

'He was. He doesn't really approve of private investigators, especially female ones,' Kitty said, a touch glumly.

The chief inspector chuckled. 'Then he had better become more accustomed to it.'

Matt saw Kitty's face brighten at the chief inspector's remark. He had to admit feeling somewhat relieved himself. They had developed a good working relationship with the local police, and had both been concerned that Inspector Lewis's arrival might upset the apple cart in some way.

They had almost finished eating when there was another, louder more impatient knock on the door.

'Inspector Lewis, do please come and join us, I'll send for a fresh pot of tea,' Kitty said as she opened the door.

The inspector looked somewhat taken back to discover his senior officer ensconced in the room, with cake crumbs on his tie.

'I've just come from the Blaines' home, sir.' Inspector Lewis addressed himself to Chief Inspector Greville before somewhat reluctantly taking the last vacant seat in the small space.

'That must have been very distressing,' Kitty murmured as she offered the inspector a plate.

'Of course, he was extremely upset. He has been his sister's guardian for much of her life. He was twenty-seven when his parents died in the Spanish flu outbreak. His sister was considerably younger.' Inspector Lewis took the plate and picked up a ham sandwich from the depleted selection.

'Did he know if Peggy had any admirers?' Kitty asked.

Inspector Lewis gave her a dour look. 'He said he thought she had been walking out with someone but he had not been introduced to the gentleman. Miss Blaine was inclined to be secretive by all accounts.'

'Hmm, any arguments or disagreements with anyone? I assume that her brother has an alibi?' Chief Inspector Greville asked as Mr Lutterworth deposited a fresh pot of tea on the table and withdrew.

'Mr Blaine was working in the pharmacy all afternoon as he had not approved of Miss Blaine taking part in the pageant. There was an assistant with him who can vouch for him not having left the premises. The shop closed at five thirty.' Inspector Lewis accepted a cup of tea from Kitty.

'And any particular female friends or disagreements with anyone that he knew of?' the chief inspector asked, after Inspector Lewis had taken a drink of tea.

'There was an argument with a Miss Dorothy Martin a week or so ago. It was quite nasty apparently and Miss Blaine turned her out of the shop.'

Matt saw Kitty's eyebrows rise at this unexpected piece of information.

'It seems Miss Blaine kept herself to herself and didn't have any particularly close friends. She had developed an interest in Egyptology lately however and had attended lectures at Torquay Museum.' The inspector picked up the last piece of sponge cake, an action that caused the chief inspector to sigh heavily.

'What about the knife?' Matt asked. 'It seemed quite unusual. The handle looked ornate with those turquoise blue stones.'

Inspector Lewis looked as if he was about to protest at the question but a look from Chief Inspector Greville compelled him to respond. 'We shall know more when the doctor examines Miss Blaine at the mortuary. However, it did seem quite distinctive. With any luck someone might recognise it.'

'Well, I shall leave you to your investigation, Inspector. Thank you for your hospitality, Mrs Bryant, most kind of you.' The chief inspector rose, brushed the crumbs from his front and with a regretful glance at the now empty plates said a warm goodbye to Kitty and Matt.

'I expect you would like the names and addresses of the pageant contestants so that they can be interviewed?' Kitty asked the inspector.

'Yes, thank you.' Inspector Lewis set down his plate as Kitty handed over the entry forms the contestants had completed when they had entered the contest.

'Dorothy Martin? The same one that had the altercation with Miss Blaine?' The inspector looked at Kitty.

'Yes, Councillor Martin's daughter. She seemed to know more about Peggy than the other girls. Did she not report receiving a letter? How strange,' Kitty said, unable to resist a small, barbed comment. She knew that Dorothy's father had created quite a stink about her letter.

'Hmm.' The inspector folded up the forms and tucked them into the inside breast pocket of his jacket. 'Thank you for the refreshments, Mrs Bryant.' He rose from his chair ready to leave. 'I would however remind you that Miss Blaine's murder is a police matter, and all information must be given to myself or my officers. I am in charge of the investigation. You will also keep anything you know or discover confidential from members of the public.'

He replaced his hat and donned his coat.

'Of course, Inspector,' Kitty replied sweetly.

He gave her a suspicious look and departed, closing the office door behind him.

'I'll give you a hand,' Matt said as Kitty started to tidy away the dirty crockery onto a tray on the table.

'It seems we now have two cases to investigate,' she said.

'It does indeed. Miss Blaine's murder and Sir Vivian's request. I wonder if there is a degree of overlay if Peggy attended Sir Vivian's lectures.' Matt stacked the plates.

'It gives us a reason to contact several of the contestants to

double-check if there is any information we may have missed.'
Kitty looked at Matt and he saw there was a mischievous
twinkle in her blue-grey eyes.

'Absolutely. However, I think tomorrow our first port of call
may have to be Mrs Craven and Mrs Ponsonby-Bell,' Matt said.

Kitty's shoulders drooped. 'They will be very distressed by
Peggy's murder. I'm surprised Mrs C hasn't arrived back here
already. No doubt Grams will have telephoned her the moment
Mr Lutterworth returned to the Dolphin and told her what had
happened.'

'I'm certain you are right. Both those ladies, however, have
an uncanny knack for knowing everything that happens in
Dartmouth. If Peggy did have an admirer, then they are the
people most likely to know and to be able to discover his identity,' Matt said.

CHAPTER TEN

Kitty woke early the following morning to find that Matt had risen even earlier and had already taken Bertie for his morning perambulation across the common.

'Have you any thoughts on how we can discover who the letter writer might be?' Kitty asked as she attacked the top of her soft-boiled egg with a spoon.

'It's a difficult one. Mary saw the man who was purporting to be an electrician, so if he is the letter writer and she didn't recognise him as someone she knew, I'm inclined to think he is not from Dartmouth.' Matt poured himself a cup of coffee from the tall chrome-plated coffee pot.

Kitty considered this as she chewed her toast. 'He seemed familiar with the local area though as he mentioned Babba-combe to Mary. He must also have seen information about the pageant in the *Herald*.'

'The paper said where tickets could be obtained and where the pageant was being held. He must have seen posters in the town. How would he discover who was taking part?' Matt asked.

'The names of the committee members are a matter of

public information as there has been all sorts of notices in the parish magazine and in the newspaper in the run up to the baby contest, so that would be easy to discover.' Kitty dipped her toast soldier in her egg yolk. 'I think he may have obtained the contestants' names when he left the first letter. The one tucked in the mirror in the dressing room. I had put a name card on each girls' dressing station. He could have made a note of it from there.'

Matt looked thoughtful. 'Some of the girls would be easy to find an address for but he would need some local knowledge.'

A shiver ran down Kitty's spine. 'Then he must not be far away. I wonder if he has done this kind of thing before? Written letters or protested against something he disagrees with. He clearly found the idea of a beauty pageant distasteful.'

'I think you may have something there, perhaps he may have written to the local paper?' Matt's eyes lit up and he grinned at her.

'I know that even if they agree to print a letter anonymously, they insist upon having a name and address in their records for the contributor.' Kitty's admirer from when she and Matt had first met had worked for the local newspaper and she had learned a great deal about its operations.

'Perhaps after we have seen Mrs Craven and Mrs Ponsonby-Bell, we should go to the newspaper offices and see if they might have something in their archive. They may well be open, as they print every day,' Matt suggested. 'There was a beauty contest last year in Paignton. That might be a good starting point for our search.'

Kitty nodded. It seemed likely that the letter writer might have stepped up his activities from merely writing to the press if he thought such events were becoming more widespread. Without an initial starting point, she could see an archive search at the newspaper offices would be like looking for a needle in a haystack.

After finishing breakfast, she made a couple of telephone calls and was assured that Mrs Craven and Mrs Ponsonby-Bell would meet them at the Dolphin after church. The weather was still chilly, but the sun was making a valiant attempt to break through the clouds as they set off for Dartmouth once more.

A few daffodils were nodding yellow bonneted heads in the hedgerows and the fields were fresh and green as they drove into Kingswear to take the ferry.

'We shall need to be careful not to step on Inspector Lewis's toes,' Kitty said once they were safely across the river.

Matt smiled, the dimple flashing in his cheek. 'Yes, he was very clear that he did not wish us to be involved.'

'Indeed, as a mere *lady detective*, I may as well give up now, knowing things are in his oh-so capable hands,' Kitty commented tartly.

The ladies were already installed in Kitty's grandmother's salon when they arrived. Mrs Ponsonby-Bell pounced upon them as soon as they entered the door.

'Captain Bryant, Kitty, what is happening at the chemist's this morning? Have they arrested Peggy's brother?' she asked, an eager expression on her narrow, wrinkled face.

'I'm sorry? What do you mean?' Kitty asked. From what they had learned yesterday evening, Alastair Blaine had an alibi for the time of Peggy's death since he was working in the dispensary of his shop. As far as she knew he also had no motive to kill his sister.

A disappointed expression crossed Joan's face. 'I thought you might know. There was a constable outside the entrance to the Blaines' flat this morning when I passed by on my way here. The shop was closed of course, as one would expect in the circumstances and it being Sunday. I asked the constable at the door what had gone on, and he said he was not at liberty to say what had happened.'

'Alastair Blaine has always been a most respectable man. I

hardly think it likely that he would have killed his sister. No, perhaps there is some other reason. They may have found a clue to the murderer in Peggy's things.' Mrs Craven's face brightened.

Kitty's grandmother looked disapprovingly at her friends. 'I hardly think idle speculation will help in such tragic circumstances. Now, Kitty dear, I presume you and Matthew have a reason for asking us to gather here this morning?'

The three elderly ladies turned their gaze towards Kitty, and she swallowed nervously, keen to strike the right tone. 'Dorothy Martin seemed to believe that Peggy had an admirer, a wealthy man. No one seems to know who this might be. Felicia hadn't seen her with anyone at the picture house and her brother didn't know his identity. Matt thought that as you ladies are well connected you perhaps may have some ideas.' Kitty looked at them hopefully.

Mrs Craven visibly preened herself at Kitty's subtle flattery and Joan too looked flattered.

'I know one shouldn't speak ill of the dead, but you know I always considered there was something a little sly about Peggy. She struck me as a very secretive kind of girl and quite avaricious.' Mrs Craven screwed up her face in thought. 'Of course, she was very pretty, and she liked nice things. Last year I believe, there was an older man from Torquay that took her out to tea a few times, but I heard that his sister disapproved of the match and he has since married a girl from Totnes and moved away.'

Joan Ponsonby-Bell nodded her head in agreement. 'Yes, I remember that. Peggy was quite disappointed I think at the time. He was quite well to do.'

'But neither of you know about anyone else she may have been seeing?' Matt asked.

Both ladies shook their heads regretfully.

'If you do happen to discover anything in that way, could you let us know?' Kitty asked.

'We know we can trust your discretion on such a delicate matter,' Matt added with a smile that seemed to perk up the ladies' spirits at their failure to provide a name for Peggy's beau.

'We seem to have drawn a blank there,' Kitty observed as they stepped back out of the hotel. 'I wonder what has gone on at the Blaines' flat? If Mrs Ponsonby-Bell is correct it does sound a little odd.'

'Shall we take a short stroll?' Matt suggested.

Kitty rested her gloved hand lightly on the crook of her husband's arm and they set off for the chemist's near the Butterwalk.

'There is the constable, he is just leaving.' Kitty spotted the policeman from yesterday making his way along the street towards them.

'Constable, has something else happened at the Blaines' home?' Kitty asked as the man drew near.

The policeman immediately took on a slightly evasive expression. 'I don't know as I can rightly say, Mrs Bryant. Inspector Lewis...'

Matt interrupted, 'You know that we are to be trusted and are already involved in this matter. We will not tell anyone that you have given us any information.'

'Indeed no, you won't get into any trouble with the inspector,' Kitty said, seeing the man was undecided about what he should say.

'Well then, you haven't heard it from me, but Miss Blaine's room has been searched by someone. Mr Blaine discovered it this morning when he opened her door. Everything was all upside down. No one thought to look in there last night so we don't know exactly when it were done or what they were looking for.' The constable looked about nervously to ensure they could not be overheard.

'Was anything missing?' Kitty asked. She was surprised no one had thought to look in Peggy's room last night.

'No, Mrs Bryant, not to Mr Blaine's knowledge, all her jewellery was still there and some money as she kept in a shoebox in her wardrobe. A fair bit of cash there was in there too, and in her bank,' the constable said.

'I see, that does sound most peculiar.' Kitty thought it sounded as if whatever the burglar had been looking for, and had possibly found, might provide the motive for Peggy's death.

The constable wished them a good morning and continued on his way. Kitty and Matt turned around and started back towards the Dolphin.

'I wonder what the burglar was searching for?' Kitty asked.

'And if he found it.' Matt frowned.

They reached Kitty's car and got in. 'Torquay next?' she suggested.

'I think so. We need to visit the newspaper offices to see if we can find out anything from there that might give a clue to the identity of our letter writer,' Matt said as Kitty started her car.

'If the letter writer killed Peggy, why her? And why was her room searched?' This new development seemed to cast a doubt in her mind as to who the murderer might be. It seemed to her that Peggy's murder and now this search of the girl's room must be linked.

'Perhaps she recognised him? Knew him somehow. Then he would kill her to hide his identity and search her room to make sure she hadn't left anything there that might incriminate him,' Matt suggested.

Kitty tried the suggestion out in her mind. It was plausible but why would Peggy not just have told someone who the man was? Unless she hadn't been sure, perhaps. They could only hope that a trawl through the newspaper archives might provide a clue to the letter writer's identity.

The offices of the *Torbay Herald* were situated in a square white building at the top end of the town. Kitty suppressed a faint shudder at the memories the building evoked from when she had first met Matt. A dark-haired young woman was seated behind the polished mahogany and glass counter in the reception area.

Matt handed her his business card and asked if it were possible to speak to the proprietor or the chief editor.

'I can see if Mr Leeds is free?' the girl said in a doubtful tone looking at Matt's card.

'It's a simple enquiry and we very much hope he will be able to help us,' Kitty reassured her.

'Can I ask what it's about? Only he's a busy man and he shouts a lot.' The girl's hand hovered indecisively over the telephone receiver.

'It's connected with the recent murder in Dartmouth.' Matt's words seemed to spur the girl into action. She called through and explained their business to whoever was on the other end.

'Mr Leeds says he can spare you a few minutes if you would just wait here,' the girl said as she hung the receiver back on its cradle.

They stepped back from the counter and waited for Mr Leeds. In the distance Kitty could hear a faint hum of conversations and a clicking and crashing which she could only assume must be the presses. She knew the *Herald* published a Sunday version of its weekly paper and would print the early Monday edition ready for the stands on a Sunday.

Eventually a door marked private opened to the side of them and a short, stout man in his late fifties appeared. Black-framed spectacles were perched precariously on the top of his thinning hair and a half-smoked cigarette dangled from his lower lip.

'Captain Bryant? Come this way.' He ignored Kitty, and she gritted her teeth in irritation at his rudeness. She followed Matt and their host up two flights of concrete stairs, past a large no smoking sign and into an untidy, smoke-filled office.

'Now then, what can I do for you?' Mr Leeds asked as he studied Matt's business card which he'd taken from the girl at the front desk. 'Something to do with that murder in Dartmouth, the girl said? Main reason we're printing now, a special edition with a big spread for morning. Got to get ahead of the London papers. Took some nice pictures at the pageant of the girls.'

'It's really a little background research. The matter may be relevant to Miss Blaine's murder, or it may not,' Matt said. Kitty realised he was treading carefully in case the newspaper editor decided to use anything Matt said and print it in the *Herald*.

'This is of course, off the record, but the beauty pageant contestants all received anonymous letters before the event. It seemed likely to me that the writer may well have sent a similar letter into the newspaper either for this event or the one held last year in Paignton.' Matt looked at the editor.

'Yes, that new inspector, what's his name? Lewis? He said as there had been anonymous letters in the statement he gave us.' The editor frowned, and strode the couple of paces to his office door. He flung the door open and yelled out into the corridor.

'Miriam!'

A moment later Kitty heard another door further down the corridor bang and a small, thin elderly woman in a green floral print frock appeared in the office.

'What do you want? I'm busy.' She addressed the editor, taking absolutely no notice of Matt or Kitty's presence in the room.

'Miriam deals with all the post. She knows everything about everything,' the editor explained as Miriam continued to scowl furiously while tapping the toe of her black patent shoe at having been called from her work. 'Did we get any protest letters about the beauty pageant in Dartmouth?'

'A couple. One from Mr Jeavons, as usual and one from a Mr Smith.' Miriam looked bored and impatient.

'Mr Jeavons writes in regularly and complains about everything,' the editor explained. 'What about this Smith bloke? Has he written in before?' He addressed the question to Miriam.

'Let me check.' Miriam disappeared back into the corridor letting in a welcome blast of fresher air as well as noise from the distant presses.

'Do you think as this letter writer might be a suspect?' The editor looked at Matt.

'It's hard to say. I think it would be wise to exclude him. I presume Mr Smith wished to be published anonymously?' Matt asked as Miriam re-entered the room carrying two pieces of paper.

She handed the letters over to the editor who looked them over before passing them across to Matt. Kitty peered around Matt's arm so she could see them for herself. The one from Mr Jeavons appeared to be a straightforward complaint about commercialisation of the town by entertaining the lowest common denominator of holidaymaker.

The other letter however certainly had some strong similarities with the anonymous letters.

'Did you receive any letters last year about the Paignton beauty pageant?' Matt asked.

Miriam rolled her eyes and disappeared once more, presumably to search her files. She returned a minute later with another letter. 'Mr Smith again. We didn't publish either letter,' she said.

Matt looked at the second of Mr Smith's letters. 'I think I can see why.'

Kitty could see the letters were a tirade about the degeneration of the youth of today littered with Biblical references. Typewritten on cheap paper, they seemed to her to resemble the anonymous letters received by everyone connected with the pageant.

'Can I get back to work, now? I'd like to finish in time to cook my Sunday dinner.' Miriam looked at her employer, clearly feeling that she'd done her duty.

Mr Leeds gave a nod and the woman vanished.

'Miriam's worked here for years. She's a mine of information,' the editor explained. 'Those what you were looking for? Is he the bloke?'

'I think it is very likely. The letters certainly appear similar. May I take these? I shall of course pass them on to Inspector Lewis,' Matt said.

The editor shrugged. 'If you think it will help. Can't have innocent young women getting themselves killed in the bay. Bad for business. Of course, I'd appreciate any information on the progress of the case for our readers. An exclusive like.' He looked at Matt.

'I understand.' Matt folded the letters and slipped them into the pocket of his overcoat. 'Thank you very much for your assistance, Mr Leeds.'

'Got to do my civic duty.' The editor opened the door to his office and Kitty followed Matt back out of the building into the cool, crisp spring air.

CHAPTER ELEVEN

Kitty waited until they were seated inside her car before turning to Matt. 'May I see those two letters again please?'

He extracted the letters from his pocket and handed them to her. 'They seem to be very similar in content and on the same kind of paper as the others. The Bible quote at the bottom is our clearest indication that this may be the man responsible for the anonymous letters.'

'Romans again,' Kitty said as she read the notes once more. 'Mr Smith? His real name or a pseudonym do you think?'

Matt laughed. 'Your guess is as good as mine. The question is probably whether Mr Smith provided his actual address or gave a fake one.'

Kitty mentally kicked herself for not realising that both the name and the address on the letters could be false. She gave the letters back to Matt.

'I suppose there is only one way to find out.' She started the car. 'Do you know where the street is?'

Matt frowned as he studied the address. 'Paignton. Hmm, I think this is in the town not far from Winner Street. Head that way and we can always stop and ask for directions once we are closer.' He replaced the letters back inside his coat pocket as Kitty put the car in gear and pulled away.

They headed towards the area where Matt thought the address was situated. When they reached Paignton, they stopped to ask a passer-by in Winner Street for directions. It seemed that Matt had been correct about the location and soon Kitty found herself driving along a steep, narrow road lined with terraced cottages in various states of disrepair.

'I think most of these cottages at this end of the street are lodging houses.' Kitty slowed to a halt and peered through the windscreen at a couple of taller properties that had probably once belonged to more affluent people.

'I think you are correct,' Matt agreed as he checked the address on the letters once more.

A small group of street urchins aged about seven or eight appeared from a nearby alleyway to goggle curiously at Kitty's red car and its occupants.

'Wait here, I'll go and check out the address.' Matt tucked the letters back in his pocket and crossed the street to one of the lodging houses. Kitty watched from the car as he knocked at the door. It took several minutes before the door cracked open a few inches and Matt was able to speak to the occupant. It seemed clear to Kitty that her husband was not meeting with much success as she saw him gesturing towards some of the other houses on the street.

The children in the meantime had drawn closer to Kitty's car. She wound down the window to speak to them.

'Do any of you children know a Mr Smith that lives around here?' she asked.

There was a collective shaking of heads.

She glanced back to where Matt was still conversing with whoever was hiding behind the lodging house door.

'Do any of you know an older gentleman who perhaps behaves a bit oddly? Perhaps disapproves of young ladies like myself, who drive cars and things?' Kitty decided to try a different tack. Even if this so-called Mr Smith had given a fake name and address, he must be familiar with the area. Perhaps they could track him down using a slightly different method.

Two of the boys looked at one another before the one who appeared to be the older of the two spoke up. 'What's in it for us?'

Kitty fished inside her leather handbag and drew out her purse to check her change. 'Sixpence if the information is good,' she suggested.

The younger boy's eyes widened as she drew the small silver coin from her purse, and he clutched at the older lad's tattered shirt sleeve. 'Tell her about Preacher Bob,' he urged.

'Preacher Bob?' Kitty asked. 'Who is Preacher Bob?'

The younger boy tugged even harder at his companion's sleeve.

'I'll throw in some pear drops.' Kitty took out the small paper twist of boiled sweets she usually carried with her.

'Preacher Bob has rooms in the house down there, he lives with his mother. She's at least one hundred years old.' The older boy nodded his head towards a house further down the street on the opposite side of the road from where Matt was making his enquiries.

'She's a witch an all.' The younger boy's eyes were wide.

'Tell me some more about Preacher Bob.' Kitty looked at her little gang of informants.

'He's proper creepy. He talks in the street in Torquay near the market standing on a box telling you about going to Hell. He doesn't like anything or anybody.' A little girl with a mop of untidy dark blonde curls pushed her way in front of the boys.

'You keep quiet, our Daisy.' The younger lad gave her a push in the small of her back, causing tears to appear in the girl's big, blue eyes.

'Preacher Bob tells ladies off in the street if he thinks their dresses are too short and he goes down the beach in the summer to tell the bathers to cover up.' The older lad scowled at his companions, clearly eager to regain the upper hand.

'I see. Thank you. Do you know his last name?' Kitty asked as she saw Matt turning to return to the car.

'Mr Price, but everybody knows him as Preacher Bob. He quotes the Bible at you all the time,' the older boy said.

'You've all been very helpful.' Kitty handed the bag of sweets to the younger boy and gave the older lad the sixpence. She delved back in her purse and gave two pennies to the little girl.

The children melted away back in the direction of the alley as Matt approached the car to rejoin her.

'Any luck?' Kitty asked once he had retaken his place in the passenger seat.

'No Mr Smiths there or in the houses nearby. At least that was what the wretched woman who finally answered the door said. I could smell the drink from the step and her speech wasn't terribly clear so I'm not sure if she could be relied upon as a source of information.' He glanced at Kitty. 'You look very pleased with yourself. I saw the children gathering round the car.'

'I tried a different tack and some bribery. The children believe a man called Preacher Bob may be the man we want. He lodges further along the street and is fond of quoting the Bible and correcting young women on their attire. Apparently, he lives with his aged mother who may or may not be a witch.' Kitty couldn't resist a small smile of triumph as she relayed her information.

'I see. Any surname?' Matt asked, the corners of his mouth twitching upwards.

'Price.' Kitty started her car and turned it around in the street to head back towards the group of houses further down that the children had indicated.

Matt's grin grew wider. 'How much did your informants extract from you for this information?'

She stopped her car outside the house and pulled on the handbrake. 'One bag of pear drops, a silver sixpence and tuppence.'

Matt prepared to clamber out of the car once more. 'A bargain.'

Kitty went to open her car door to follow him.

'Darling, stay with the car for now. If this man is the letter writer, he may also be Peggy's murderer. We know he dislikes women, and I don't want you to get hurt.' Matt dropped a quick kiss on her cheek to soften his words.

Reluctantly, Kitty waited inside the car while Matt strode off the short distance along the street to try his luck at the house the children had indicated. The logical part of her brain could see Matt's point but at the same time it was most frustrating to feel sidelined from the action yet again.

As she gazed around the street her attention was caught by the entrance of another narrow alley. It seemed to run off the street where she had parked, to go behind the houses where Matt was now knocking at the door.

She slipped out of the car and walked across the road towards the alley curious to see where it led. If this Preacher Bob was the man they were after he might try to avoid Matt and slip out of the back of the house. If he did, then she would be waiting to see where he went.

Almost immediately as she entered the passage, she heard a faint mewing sound. The alley was narrow with brick walls on both sides and a gutter running down the middle. She looked around the weedy cobbles and at first saw nothing other than some stinking metal dustbins.

Taking her bearings, she judged she must be more or less behind the lodging house where Preacher Bob was reported to dwell. Each house seemed to have a tiny backyard with a wooden gate opening into the alley. The end of the passage was bricked off so if anyone did leave the houses via their back gate they would have to leave via the way Kitty had entered.

Satisfied that she would be able to see Preacher Bob if he did make a bolt for it, Kitty decided to return to her car to wait for Matt. She stepped over the gutter and started back when she heard the mewing sound again. Holding her breath against the stench, she investigated the metal bins. She was about to give up her search when she realised that a piece of sodden sacking next to one of the dustbins was moving.

Cautiously, she lifted the edge of the sack to discover a tiny brown and white tabby kitten, its fur wet and plastered to its body and green eyes crusty.

'Oh, you poor little thing.' Kitty bent down and scooped it up into her arms.

The little cat mewed piteously and snuggled against Kitty's coat. Kitty started to walk back towards her car, still holding the kitten. She couldn't leave it in the alleyway. Someone had clearly abandoned it amongst the rubbish. Though how anyone could do such a thing to a poor defenceless animal was beyond her comprehension.

The sound of raised voices met her as she reached the entrance to the alley. Male voices shouting mixed with that of an older female, high-pitched and shrieking. Kitty rounded the corner into the street and realised that Matt was engaged in a tussle with an older man. A bent, old lady was on the doorstep hurling abuse at both of them.

'Matt!' She hurried forward. If this was the letter writer and possibly Peggy's killer, her husband would need her help. This man could be a murderer. He appeared to be a burly individual in late middle age, fitting Mary's description of the letter writer. She assumed the old lady must be his mother.

At the sound of her voice the man broke free from Matt's

hold, but instead of running away as she had expected, he came charging towards her.

Kitty held on tightly to the kitten and skipped backwards as Preacher Bob charged at her, sticking her foot out as she did so. The man clattered into her outstretched foot, the momentum of his charge sending him sprawling face forward into the road.

Matt ran up and grabbed hold of the man's jacket collar at the back of his neck, hauling him to his feet.

'Here, leave go of me, you've no rights attacking a man in his own home.' The man attempted to wriggle free from Matt's grasp.

Kitty gasped in horror. 'What happened?' she asked.

'He attacked me, that's what happened.' The man made another attempt to free himself, wriggling like a fish on a hook.

'Perhaps we should see what the police have to say on that matter.' Matt gave his prisoner a shake.

The man glared at Matt and tried to lunge at him. Matt held on tight to his captive and dodged the intended blow.

'Mr Price, I assume? Or Mr Smith?' Kitty asked.

The man swung around to face her, his face red and contorted with anger. 'Who wants to know? What's this all about anyways?'

'From the way you were attempting to flee, I'd say you know full well why my husband wished to speak to you,' Kitty said.

'I don't know what you'm on about.' The man straightened up, glowering at her, his fists still clenched.

'A number of letters written by you and sent anonymously to the entrants of the Miss Dartmouth Jubilee beauty pageant,' Kitty said crisply. 'Threatening letters.'

The man's demeanour changed abruptly. His bluster seeming to dissipate as if by magic.

'I didn't write no letters.' He glanced around as if fearful that his neighbours might have overheard what she'd said.

Kitty was pretty certain that they were being watched

through the windows of several of the nearby houses. Preacher Bob's yelling would have attracted attention in the quiet street.

'Really, and yet we have evidence to prove that you did,' Kitty bluffed and watched as small beads of sweat started to form on the man's temples. 'I'm sure Inspector Lewis will be very interested to speak to you regarding Peggy Blaine's murder in Dartmouth yesterday.'

The man visibly started at the mention of murder and once more started to try to struggle free from Matt's grasp. 'Here, don't you go putting me in the frame for no murder.'

'But you know of her death?' Matt asked as he hung on tightly to the man's coat and shirt.

The man was now visibly sweating profusely. 'I heard as a woman had been killed when I got home this morning. I work shifts, see, on the railway, and one of the blokes there heard about it from his brother. They said as it was the girl from the chemist's.'

Kitty glanced at Matt. 'And you knew that Peggy was one of the pageant girls because you had sent her a letter warning her not to participate.'

The kitten clawed its way up her coat, and she was forced to extract its claws and settle it down. The unexpected movement drew a bemused look from Matt when he realised what she was holding.

'Now hold on a minute there, Mrs. It's one thing to send someone a friendly warning note. It's something else to be accusing an innocent man of murder.' Preacher Bob had the expression of a man who knew he had been bested.

'I don't think sending someone a death threat is a friendly warning,' Kitty said.

'Well, they'll all go to Hell, the hussies. Shameless they are, putting muck on their faces and raising their skirts to lead good, honest men astray.' Flecks of spittle appeared at the corners of Preacher Bob's mouth. 'I'm doing the Lord's work.'

Kitty was relieved to see the familiar blue uniform of a police constable approaching them rapidly from further down the street. She guessed that one of the neighbours must have sent a message to the police station in Paignton.

'I think you can explain everything to the police. Where were you on Saturday afternoon while the pageant was on?' Kitty asked.

'Minding my own business, that's where. I was in the marketplace in Dartmouth, preaching and spreading the word of the Lord. That's what I was doing. Trying to save souls from temptation to not attend that wicked event.' Preacher Bob's eyes took on a fanatical light as he spoke.

The constable caught up to them and Matt explained the situation interrupted by protests from Preacher Bob.

'Right, well I'd best get this settled at the police station. I reckon as Captain Bryant here is right. Inspector Lewis will want a word or two with you.' The constable placed handcuffs on Preacher Bob's wrists and Matt handed the policeman the letters from the newspaper files.

'Do you think he is our man?' Kitty asked Matt as the constable hustled Bob along the street back towards the town centre and the police station.

'For writing those letters, definitely. He admitted as much. For Peggy's murder and searching her room I think it unlikely. He has an alibi for the time of the murder, and I can't see a reason why he would have broken into the Blaines' home.' Matt frowned at the rapidly retreating figures.

Kitty agreed with him. Whoever had ransacked Peggy's room had been looking for something and it seemed to her that person must have been the same person who had killed the girl.

The kitten gave a piteous mew and tried to wriggle up Kitty's coat once more.

'Darling, why are you carrying a cat?' Matt asked, his attention drawn back to the bedraggled kitten.

'I found it dumped in the alley. We need to get it home so I can get it cleaned and fed.' Kitty stroked the top of the kitten's grubby head with a tender finger.

Matt sighed gently and took off his woollen muffler to wrap the kitten. 'I don't know what Bertie will think of it, but yes, let's go home and plan our next course of action.'

Kitty's stomach rumbled as she climbed back into the driver's seat as Matt stowed the kitten safely on his lap for the journey.

'Good idea, I'm starving.'

CHAPTER TWELVE

Their housekeeper had finished for the day by the time they arrived home as she only worked for a few hours on Sundays. A cottage pie for their supper was in the pantry and everywhere appeared neat and tidy. Bertie greeted them at the door with his usual enthusiasm, made even more excited by the mysterious woollen bundle that Matt was carrying.

'I do hope they'll get along,' Kitty said as she removed her hat and coat in the hall.

Matt crouched down and unwrapped the scarf a little so that the dog could meet the tiny kitten. Bertie stuck his nose in to sniff the new occupant and was rewarded by a swipe from a tiny paw. The dog jumped back and woofed indignantly causing the kitten to arch its back, hissing and spitting in response.

'Oh dear.' Kitty came to take the bundle from Matt so he could remove his own coat.

Bertie looked up at her with reproachful eyes as she carried the kitten into the kitchen to start cleaning the animal, ready to feed it.

'Never mind, Bertie old man, she still loves you.' Matt grinned and patted his dog before heading into the sitting room.

Kitty emerged a little later to join him. She deposited a tray with a pot of tea and a plate of sandwiches onto the table in front of the sofa. 'The kitten is asleep on the kitchen counter. I've cleaned her and fed her. She really is the prettiest little thing. How can people be so cruel? She would have died if I hadn't found her.'

Bertie lifted his head from where he had been snoozing at Matt's feet to look sorrowfully at her. It seemed the dog didn't share Kitty's sentiments regarding the kitten.

Matt helped himself to sandwiches and a chunk of pork pie as Bertie sat up to sniff hopefully in the direction of his plate. 'I take it you were thinking of keeping her?'

Kitty lifted the lid of the smart chrome teapot to stir the contents. 'I would like to, but I suppose we shall have to see how she and Bertie get along together.'

Matt could see his wife was taken with the little kitten so he hoped that somehow Bertie would be able to accept a new companion.

They ate their late lunch quickly in companionable silence with Bertie receiving his share of bits of ham and cheese.

'It would be good to speak to Sir Vivian to find out if he noticed Peggy in attendance at any of his lectures,' Kitty said after she had finished the last of her cup of tea.

'We still have to discover more about this Dominic Peplow fellow and if he is indeed involved with supplying Victoria with illicit drugs,' Matt agreed. Kitty had mentioned that Victoria's demeanour had seemed altered after the interval at the pageant, during which she had been out to see Dominic and his friends. It seemed to him that Sir Vivian had been remiss in not mentioning Mr Peplow as a suspect when he had commissioned them.

Peggy's murder had distracted them somewhat from their

client's investigation and they needed to get back on track. With luck they might be able to combine both cases with a visit to see Sir Vivian. Perhaps he might be more forthcoming on the subject of Victoria's young man this time.

'Why don't you telephone Sir Vivian and see if we can call while I clear these tea things away?' Kitty suggested as she jumped to her feet. 'We could go and see him and perhaps find out more from him and his daughters about Mr Peplow. They may even have remembered something more about Peggy that could be helpful too.'

Matt agreed as the afternoon was wearing on already and it would be nice to make a breakthrough. Sir Vivian was amenable to a visit when he telephoned so Matt took Bertie out for a quick stroll while Kitty ensured the kitten was in a safe spot before they set off in the motor car once more.

'I do hope they'll be all right together,' Kitty fretted as they sped towards Sir Vivian's house. 'I put Bertie in the kitchen and the kitten is inside the scullery in a basket with the door closed.'

'Judging by the way your new little chum swiped Bertie on the nose I think he will be more cautious anyway if he tries to approach again. The door is shut so they should both be safe enough for an hour or so,' Matt reassured her.

* * *

Before long they were turning into the driveway of Sir Vivian's house. Matt thought the house looked just as forbidding in daylight as Kitty had said it had by moonlight. Ivy covered most of the red-brick walls and the paint was peeling from the windowsills and on the front door. The whole building had a slightly decaying air of faded grandeur.

'Araminta said her father was renting this house as he'd sold their previous property to fund an expedition and to pay for his divorce from Victoria's mother.' Kitty peered around as she prepared to exit her car.

'Hmm, let's go and talk to Sir Vivian and see what we can discover about his lectures at the museum. We can also assure him of our work on his own case.' Matt closed the car door and joined Kitty at the front of the house. He pushed the unpolished brass bell, setting off an unmelodic clanging sound deep within the house.

A moment later an older woman in a slightly grubby maid's uniform opened the front door. Matt handed over his card. 'Sir Vivian is expecting us.'

'Then you'd best come in, sir, madam. He'll be in his study.' The woman led the way along a dingy hallway lined with dark and gloomy oil paintings of various local scenes. She paused in front of an oak door and knocked, opening it only when a bellow from inside the room commanded her to enter.

'Captain Bryant, and Mrs Bryant.' Sir Vivian rose from his seat behind a vast mahogany desk as they entered the room. The maid had vanished without waiting to see if refreshments were required.

Kitty shook hands with Sir Vivian and stared wide-eyed at the contents of the study. Interspersed with different somewhat moth-eaten examples of taxidermy confined within their glass cases were various antiquities that she had only ever seen before inside a museum.

Framed photographs showing the pyramids and close-up shots of statues were hung on the walls next to mounted scarabs and shelves holding various pieces of pottery and other interesting objects.

'I see you are admiring my collection, Mrs Bryant. This is quite modest. Most of the pieces are in storage. The larger and most valuable pieces are of course in various museums.' Sir Vivian noted her interest.

'It's quite fascinating,' Kitty said as she took a proffered seat next to Matt in front of Sir Vivian's desk.

'My life's work and indeed, my true passion,' Sir Vivian exclaimed genially as he opened a black lacquered cigarette box and offered it to both of them. When they both declined, he took a cigarette for himself, closed the box and resumed his place in the dark green leather upholstered chair on the other side of the desk.

'We thought we should update you, sir, on your case,' Matt said as Sir Vivian lit his cigarette.

Matt proceeded to explain what they had learned so far and that they had some leads which they were following.

'A Mr Peplow, a friend of Victoria's, seems to be of interest,' Matt said.

Sir Vivian looked at them shrewdly. 'The fella is as slippery as an eel. He's been avoiding me as he knows I don't think much of him. He was at the pageant though. Hanging about like a bad smell with those reprobate friends of his. He was taking rather too much interest in the other girls taking part in the contest if you ask me. He has a reputation as a ladies' man.'

'Indeed, sir. The girl who was murdered, Peggy Blaine, did you know her at all?' Kitty asked. From what Betty had told Alice about Sir Vivian's own reputation she wondered if the older man might be jealous of Mr Peplow's popularity with women.

Sir Vivian frowned. 'Not that I'm especially aware of. I saw her that afternoon, during the first half of the thing.'

'Peggy was known to have an interest in Egyptology and her brother said she had been attending your lectures at the museum in Torquay. Do you recall seeing her there at all?' Matt asked.

Sir Vivian blew out a thin pale blue stream of smoke. 'My lectures are very well attended. However, now you come to mention it, yes, I do recall her. She would stay behind sometimes and ask questions. People often do, you know, especially the ladies.'

'Did anyone accompany her?' Kitty asked. 'A friend, or companion?'

Sir Vivian appeared to consider the question. 'A lover, you mean? No, no, not that I can recall, she came by herself. Pretty little thing, nice ankles.'

This line of enquiry seemed to have drawn yet another blank. 'Are Araminta or Victoria at home? I was concerned that Peggy's death may have upset them,' Kitty said.

'Victoria is out with that wastrel Peplow somewhere. I agree with you that he is probably of interest. I didn't mention him before as I didn't want to prejudice your enquiries. Minty is probably in the library. She spends most of her time in there when she's not off riding that wretched horse of hers.' Sir Vivian stubbed his cigarette out in the large onyx and brass ashtray on his desk. 'Well, do keep me informed about Victoria and that Peplow character. If he is behind anything shady, I want him caught. The library is the last door on this side of the corridor if you want to see if Minty is in there.' Sir Vivian rose, and recognising that they were being dismissed, Kitty and Matt saw themselves out of the study and back into the hall.

'Let's try the library then, shall we?' Matt murmured.

Kitty followed him as they walked a little further along the hall and tried the door that Sir Vivian had suggested.

Araminta was curled up on an old brown leather chesterfield sofa in front of a meagre fire. A small dog was asleep on her lap and a battered-looking novel of the type sold at station stalls was in her hand.

'We're dreadfully sorry to interrupt you, but we called to see your father and it seemed rude to leave without saying hello,' Kitty explained as Araminta sat herself up on the sofa.

'Oh no, that's perfectly fine. It's quite nice to have some visitors. Victoria is out as usual and father spends all of his time in his study, looking at dead things,' Araminta said. 'Would you like some tea?' She looked around as if she were about to summon the maid.

'No, really, we're fine,' Kitty assured her as she and Matt took a seat on the overstuffed button back armchairs that faced the sofa. 'I was concerned that you may have been feeling distressed over Peggy's death. It's all so awful. Have you seen Inspector Lewis at all?'

Araminta gave a careless shrug. 'No, he sent some constable to the house this morning to interview both me and Victoria. Not that there was anything much we could tell him. Neither of us knew the girl. I mean, I had seen her before obviously when we called into the chemist's in Dartmouth, but we usually went to the one in Paignton so at best I'd only seen her a couple of times.'

'Dorothy Martin seemed to think Peggy had an admirer who had given her that expensive bottle of perfume. You didn't see her talking to anyone at all during the interval before she went outside or at the start when people began to arrive?' Kitty was aware she had covered this ground before, but she knew that sometimes people would remember something later that at first they had not thought important to mention.

Araminta frowned. 'I wasn't really taking much notice when I went out during the intermission. I saw her walk past Victoria and Dominic and then I think she collected a drink from the bar, she was carrying a cocktail when she came back into the dressing room. Felicia told her off as I think she was worried that something could get spilled on one of the gowns. Peggy just laughed and tossed it back. She was in a good mood. Then she said she was stepping out for a moment, and off she went. Felicia put the glass back in the ballroom.'

Kitty thought that would account for why she hadn't seen any empty glasses in the dressing room. The girls had been instructed by Mrs Craven not to take any drinks or food in there during the event, but still she'd been surprised not to find a few empty ones.

'Your father gives lectures at the museum in Torquay and Peggy's brother said that she often attended. Did you ever go to your father's lectures at all?' Kitty asked. It was a bit of a long shot but perhaps if Araminta had seen Peggy at the museum, then she might have observed something that Sir Vivian hadn't noticed.

Colour crept into Araminta's cheeks, and she made a fuss of moving her little dog, dropping her gaze from Kitty's. 'I've only been to a couple of father's lectures. When one lives in what feels like a museum, attending a lecture on the subject is hardly thrilling. I only go if father needs assistance in some way,' the girl explained.

'But you have attended some?' Matt asked. Kitty wondered if he too had noticed that Araminta appeared perturbed by their line of questioning.

'Father required some help with a couple of his talks, you know, slides, so I offered to help. Peggy was in the audience for both of those, I think,' Araminta admitted in a reluctant tone.

'Was she accompanied by anyone?' Kitty asked.

The girl shook her head. 'No, she was all dressed up though and sat in the third row right in Father's eyeline. She always stayed behind to ask questions.' Araminta seemed torn between telling them anything about Peggy's presence at the lectures and telling them too much.

It seemed odd to Kitty that Araminta should remember so much about Peggy's presence when she had claimed earlier that she barely knew the girl. 'Yes, your father said she would ask questions.'

A flicker of some indefinable emotion crossed Araminta's face. 'Well, there you are then.'

They were clearly being dismissed and the subject closed. Kitty tried to decide what she had just seen – fear, panic? There was something about Peggy's attendance at the museum lectures that both Araminta and her father were hiding. She was sure of it.

'Thank you for your help and I'm glad the news of Peggy's death has not upset you unduly.' Kitty rose from her seat and collected her bag.

'It has cast a dreadful shadow over what should have been a fun event. It must be frightfully hard on Felicia. I think she hoped it might raise her profile. She was saying she hoped to become an actress,' Araminta said as Matt joined Kitty.

'At least the money raised from the pageant will provide a nice jubilee party for the children in the town,' Kitty said.

'A small consolation, I suppose. Peggy must have been well known as most people used the chemist's,' Araminta mused.

'Which makes the burglary such a strange thing...' Matt started to button his coat.

'Burglary? What burglary?' Colour leached from Araminta's face.

'Peggy's room in her brother's flat was robbed yesterday. Probably just after she was killed. Her brother discovered it this morning when he opened her bedroom door,' Kitty said.

Araminta's eyes widened. 'Do the police know if anything was stolen?'

Kitty shrugged. 'Nothing of material value which is rather odd, don't you think?'

Araminta licked her lips as if they had suddenly dried on hearing about the robbery. 'Yes, I suppose it is. Perhaps this letter writer was responsible. He may be some kind of pervert looking for something personal of Peggy's.' Araminta shuddered at the idea.

'Perhaps,' Matt agreed. 'Well, we must be off. Thank you again for your help. We shall try and catch up with Victoria when she's free, just to make sure that she is all right.'

Araminta pulled a face. 'Good luck with that. Victoria is everywhere except here these days, usually with Dominic.'

They said their goodbyes and made their way back along the gloomy hallway leaving Araminta in the library. The door to Sir Vivian's study was closed and Kitty thought she could hear the faint strains of opera music coming from inside the room.

The fresh, cool air outside the house was a relief.

'Was it just me, or did you feel that Araminta and her father were both holding something back?' Kitty mused as she unlocked the door to her car and slid inside. Once she had opened the passenger door, Matt took his seat beside her.

'There was definitely something, wasn't there? And Araminta's reaction to the news of the burglary was odd too.'

Kitty placed her key in the ignition and started her car. 'I got the feeling that Araminta knew what a burglar might have been looking for and for some reason it troubled her.'

'I agree. I just wish I knew what it might have been so that we could determine if whoever broke in managed to find what they were looking for,' Matt said.

CHAPTER THIRTEEN

Matt was surprised when he unlocked the door to their house not to be greeted immediately by Bertie. Kitty followed him into the hall.

'Where is Bertie?' She looked around as she unfastened her coat.

Matt hurried into the kitchen where they had left the spaniel asleep in front of the range. The rag rug mat was now empty and the door to the scullery was slightly ajar.

'Oh, Matt, the kitten!' Kitty brushed past her husband to open the scullery door wider.

To their astonishment they discovered Bertie was curled up near the back door on the red quarry tiles. The wicker basket which Kitty had lined with an old towel lay on its side and the tiny occupant of the basket was missing.

'What has happened? Where is the kitten?' Kitty's questions stopped abruptly, and Matt realised that fast asleep between Bertie's front paws lay the missing cat. He nudged Kitty's arm and pointed.

'Oh, how sweet...' Kitty pressed her gloved fingertips to her lips in surprise.

'I don't think we need to worry about Bertie getting along with the kitten.' Matt grinned at her as she bent down to retrieve the sleeping feline from Bertie's protective custody.

As soon as Kitty had retrieved the kitten, Bertie stood and shook himself before somewhat sheepishly nudging Matt's leg in order to be petted. Kitty popped the kitten back in its basket.

'Darling, Bertie, you are so naughty opening the door. I'll put our supper in the oven to start warming,' Kitty said to Matt.

Matt left Kitty to her ministrations in the kitchen and returned with Bertie to the lounge where he stoked up the fire. The light was starting to fade now, and the room had grown cool while they had been out. He would be glad when the weather started to become more springlike. This cold, damp start to the season made the aches in his shoulder from his war injuries worse.

While Kitty was busy, Matt decided he would take his notebook and papers from the bureau and jot down what they had learned during the course of the day. It would be interesting to go over matters with Kitty over supper and hear her thoughts.

He had covered a couple of pages of jottings when there was a knock at the front door. Matt set aside his notes on the coffee table and with Bertie at his heels went to see who could be calling at the house at this time of day.

'Alice, Dolly and Betty, what a pleasant surprise. Come in, ladies.' Matt stood aside to allow the girls into the small hallway while Bertie greeted them happily.

Once the girls had hung up their coats, Matt showed them into the lounge and went to the kitchen to alert Kitty and to offer to make tea. He judged that something was afoot to bring both Miller sisters and their cousin to Churston on a Sunday evening.

'Alice, what a lovely surprise to see you all. Matt is just making tea.' He heard Kitty greet her friends as he filled the kettle and placed it on the hob to boil.

Alice was a frequent visitor to the house when she was not at work and Dolly often came too. Betty, however, hadn't called before and he could only surmise that this visit must be connected with the pageant and Peggy's murder.

He heard the hum of chatter as he added more china cups and saucers to the tray that was kept ready for visitors on the kitchen side. Once the water had boiled, he added the last of the jam tarts onto a plate and loaded everything onto the tray.

The visitors were seated on the sofa as he re-entered the lounge. Kitty had closed his notebook and put it aside so that he could place the tray on the coffee table. He took a seat on the armchair opposite Kitty and waited for their visitors to help themselves to refreshments.

'I take it you have come about Peggy's murder?' Kitty asked once the women each had a cup of tea.

Alice and Dolly both looked meaningfully at their cousin.

'We heard it said in the town this morning as Peggy's room had been burgled yesterday while her brother was working in the pharmacy.' A spot of high colour had bloomed on Betty's cheeks.

'Yes, that's right. We don't know if anything was taken as nothing valuable seemed to be missing but it was clear that whoever did it was looking for something. The constable said the room was in some disarray and her jewellery and money hadn't been touched,' Kitty said.

Dolly nudged her cousin's arm causing a bit of Betty's tea to slosh over the edge of the cup and land in the saucer.

'Oi, be a bit careful,' Betty admonished the younger girl.

'Do any of you have any idea what the burglar may have been looking for?' Kitty asked.

Alice and Dolly both looked at Betty.

'Well, it's like this, Miss Kitty. 'Tis only a tale though, but Peggy well, you know she weren't too popular in some quarters?' The colour on Betty's cheeks deepened.

'So I've gathered,' Kitty said. 'Why was that exactly?'

'She were always nosy, Peggy. She heard and saw a lot being in the chemist's and she liked nice things.' Betty looked at Alice and Dolly as if needing their encouragement to continue.

The Miller sisters nodded in agreement.

'Like the expensive bottle of perfume that Dorothy thought an admirer had given to her?' Kitty said.

Betty nodded. 'I don't know if'n anyone did buy her that perfume. They might have or she could have bought it for herself. She always had plenty money and it weren't from what she earned working in the shop. Her brother didn't pay her that well.'

Kitty frowned. 'Where did Peggy's money come from?'

Matt suspected he knew what Betty was about to say and if it were true it would open up the motive for the girl's murder.

'She blackmailed people?' Kitty put his thought into words. She had obviously drawn the same conclusions that he had made.

Betty nodded again. 'She liked knowing things, and she would wait until she had a spot when it could be useful to her. Dorothy doesn't like her because Dorothy Dodo Martin likes to steal stuff. Her father for all he's a councillor is mean with her allowance and Dodo likes pretty bits and pieces, so she pinches things. All the local tradespeople knows it but won't say anything because of her father. Everyone knows how he is. I know as Peggy caught her once in the shop a week or so ago.'

This confirmed Matt's ideas about why several people might have a reason to kill Peggy. 'I see.'

'It was said as she had a little book as she kept notes in about things she'd found out. People was a bit afeared of her and tried to watch their tongues when she was about,' Betty said.

'Betty, do you know of anyone other than Dorothy who Peggy may have known a secret about?' Kitty had wriggled forward to the edge of her seat.

'I don't know for certain, but I think as the Hardcastle girls, both of them were very wary of her and Peggy, well, she seemed to lord it over them a bit when she thought as no one were taking notice. Felicia thought so too,' Betty said. 'When I was still working at the house, I heard Miss Araminta warning Miss Victoria about her. That's why it struck me as a little bit queer when we were at the pageant as they behaved like they hardly knew her. I thought perhaps as they was being snooty as she were a shop girl.'

'You didn't catch what the warning was about?' Matt asked.

Betty took a sip of her rapidly cooling tea before answering. 'I don't rightly know as they stopped when they realised I was in the room, but I think it was to do with that Dominic Peplow. He's why they fell out.'

'I thought there was something. Araminta always sounds a little envious of Victoria when she talks about Mr Peplow,' Kitty said.

Betty's immaculately pencilled brows rose. 'I think Miss Araminta introduced him to Miss Victoria and had her nose put out of joint when he showed more interest in her sister.'

'Sir Vivian dislikes Mr Peplow and doesn't approve of his friendship with Victoria.' Matt moved the plate with the last of the jam tarts out of Bertie's reach.

'I'm not surprised by that. He's in a fast crowd if you catch my meaning and Miss Victoria, well she seems to have dived in headfirst.' Betty gave him a meaningful look.

'Drugs?' Kitty asked.

'I would say so. I don't know for certain, but I think as Miss Victoria may have taken something in the interval of the pageant.' Betty looked uncomfortable.

Dolly's eyes widened at this revelation and Alice's lips set in a disapproving line.

'Hmm, that's something that Peggy may have noted,' Matt

mused. Araminta had said she had seen Peggy near Victoria and Mr Peplow at the bar in the intermission.

'Did anyone know for certain that Peggy kept a notebook where she wrote these kinds of things down?' Kitty asked. 'It would certainly provide a motive for someone to search her room, but did such a thing ever exist?'

The Miller sisters looked at their cousin.

'Felicia told me as she saw her writing in something once. It were about a month ago. She had it in the pocket of her shop overall. Felicia saw her hiding up a corner and writing something just after that Naomi had been in the shop. Felicia asked her if she were writing a love letter. Teasing her like. Peggy said as she was balancing her books.' Betty finished the last of her tea and set her cup and saucer back onto the tray. 'Felicia thought it was an odd thing to say but afterwards she thought as Miss Naomi had seemed uncomfortable while she was in the shop. Felicia didn't take much notice as she was choosing a new lipstick but now, well, with what's happened...'

'I see. Thank you, Betty. It looks as if we shall need to speak to Felicia, Naomi and Victoria,' Matt said.

'Dorothy Martin may be able to confirm if Peggy asked her for money,' Kitty said.

'And our need to speak to the evasive Mr Peplow also grows more pressing.' Matt looked at Kitty.

Alice looked at the chrome clock on Kitty's mantelpiece and gave a small squeak of alarm. 'Robert will be here at any minute to collect us. Thank you so much for the tea, Miss Kitty.' There was a flurry of activity as the girls collected up their belongings before heading to the hall for their coats.

'I'm very grateful to you, Betty, for coming to see us,' Matt said as the ladies prepared to depart.

'She came and told us as she was worried when we heard about Peggy's room being robbed,' Dolly said as she adjusted the position of her hat in the hall mirror.

'Well, you did the right thing,' Kitty assured them.

'Will I have to tell that new policeman all this?' Betty suddenly looked apprehensive.

'Don't worry about it for now. We'll contact Inspector Lewis and if he feels it may help his case then I'm sure he'll be in touch with you,' Matt said.

'Yes, please don't worry about it.' Kitty gave the girl's arm a comforting pat.

Matt heard the sound of Robert Potter's taxi pulling up in front of the house. A moment later after a quick round of goodbyes, the girls were gone.

'That was enlightening.' Matt removed his arm from Kitty's shoulders after they had waved their guests off from the front step.

'It certainly was,' Kitty agreed as she came back inside and closed the front door once more.

'Blackmail. That may be where all the money came from in Peggy's room.' Matt helped Kitty to clear away the tea things ready to wash up.

'Do you think Peggy really did keep a notebook of all the secrets she knew?' Kitty asked as she carried the tray into the kitchen and started to put the crockery into the large white sink.

Matt frowned. 'I don't know if she would have written down what she knew necessarily but if Felicia is correct, she probably kept a note of who paid her.'

Kitty paused from where she was adding hot water to the washing up. 'That would be as incriminating as anything else though, wouldn't it? It certainly provides a motive for her murder.'

Matt pulled a tea towel from the rail on the front of the range ready to assist with drying up. 'Yes, it definitely does. It looks as if we will be kept very busy tomorrow following all of this up.'

Kitty dipped her hands in the water and scrubbed the cups. 'And we shall have to tell Inspector Lewis what we've learned.' She pulled a face at the thought.

Matt grinned at his wife. 'Well, that's something for us both to look forward to.'

CHAPTER FOURTEEN

Kitty's immediate plans to assist Matt the next morning with the investigation were somewhat stymied by the realisation that there was a Jubilee committee meeting scheduled at Mrs Ponsonby-Bell's home.

'I wish I could get out of going to this wretched meeting,' Kitty grumbled as she finished her breakfast.

'It will only take an hour or so,' Matt said soothingly as he tried to divert the kitten from pouncing on his slippers under the table. Bertie had accepted a sausage to make up for his injured feelings and was watching the cat from a safe distance.

'Even so, it's very annoying.' Kitty patted the corners of her mouth carefully with her linen napkin. 'Especially when we have so much to do.'

'While you are with the ladies, I'll call into Paignton and try to see Felicia. She should be at the picture house changing out the foyer advertising today before the matinee later.' Matt peered under the table to where his wife was busily extricating her new pet from the hem of his trousers.

'What shall we name her?' Kitty asked as she emerged clutching the tiny kitten to her bosom.

'You are definitely keeping her then?' Matt grinned.

Kitty gave him a look. He knew full well that she had intended keeping the kitten from the moment she had rescued it from the alley. 'I shall give her name some thought.'

Matt kissed her on the cheek as she placed the kitten safely back in its basket. 'I shall too. I'll meet you back here when you've finished with Mrs C and company. Hopefully Felicia may be able to tell us more about Peggy and her book.'

* * *

Kitty was rather pleased when she arrived at Mrs Ponsonby-Bell's large detached red-brick villa on the outskirts of Dartmouth to discover that Naomi was also present.

It seemed that, rather like Kitty herself, Naomi was there under duress as a favour to her godmother. The girl was seated, rather sulkily, beside the tea trolley and had obviously been tasked with offering refreshments.

Mrs Craven was seated opposite Mrs Ponsonby-Bell and Kitty's grandmother had arrived earlier with another two ladies who Kitty recognised from other meetings.

'Kitty, my dear, I heard from Dolly that you seem to be making strides in the investigation into Peggy's death,' her grandmother greeted her with a kiss on her cheek.

Naomi's attention was clearly caught by the conversation as she almost over filled one of the lady's cups. This caused a minor outbreak of clucking and the brandishing of napkins.

'Yes, we have some new things to consider.' Kitty kept her voice low, hoping Mrs Craven hadn't heard her.

'What was that, Kitty? Has that new inspector caught Peggy's killer yet? I heard there had been a robbery too at the Blaines' home. Shocking, quite shocking. I expect they were after drugs you know, being above the chemist's,' Mrs Craven proclaimed.

'Oh yes, my dear, drugs are everywhere today, aren't they? Or so it seems. I saw in the servants' newspaper only yesterday the most garish story.' Joan Ponsonby-Bell gave a discreet shudder.

'The state of the world today. I wonder if the man who wrote those ghastly letters has been apprehended yet? I'm certain he must be responsible for Peggy's death. Probably out of his mind on something or other,' Mrs Craven mused as she prepared to open her notes ready to start the meeting.

'That's if it was a man. It might have been a woman,' Naomi suggested.

'Oh no, it was definitely a man.' Kitty wished she could take back her words as several pairs of beady eyes were now fixed upon her.

'Has the inspector arrested him? Tell us what you know, Kitty,' her grandmother urged.

'I believe that the inspector has traced the letter writer, but whether he is the murderer remains to be seen, I suppose.' Kitty tried to give away as little information as possible.

'I take back my assessment of Inspector Lewis if he has found the right man so speedily. I must admit he struck me as a bit of a fool when I spoke to him. Quite lackadaisical. But perhaps he has hidden depths after all,' Mrs Craven said.

'We shall see, my dear. He was most rude to me if you recall when I first approached him on the matter of the letters. If only he had listened to me then poor Peggy might still be alive,' Joan Ponsonby-Bell declared with a sniff.

'But you do not think he was the killer, or you and your husband would not still be investigating,' Naomi pointed out, casting a sharp look at Kitty.

'We do have other cases which may have a connection with Peggy's death. Those matters have to be explored.' Kitty tried to give a non-committal reply.

She could see that Naomi was not satisfied and probably

would have pressed her further, but Mrs Craven was keen to return the meeting to its proper purpose. The matter was left, and the ladies turned their attention to the upcoming jubilee party for the children of Dartmouth.

Kitty was compelled to keep her mind on the notes she was taking for the meeting as Mrs Craven allocated tasks and briefed everyone on the monies raised from the pageant.

'Felicia as Miss Dartmouth Jubilee, will preside over the party, of course. I have ascertained that she has a suitable white gown and will wear the winner's tiara and sash. She will give out the souvenir gifts which Joan has ordered. Cups with a picture of their majesties, tastefully done of course.' Mrs Craven peered at Kitty. 'You have all of this down, Kitty?'

'Certainly, Mrs Craven.' Kitty dutifully read back what had just been said and resisted the urge to stab Mrs C with a teaspoon.

The meeting continued and Kitty made individual notes for the various members so they could take away their own lists of jobs at the close of the meeting. Naomi rather grumpily agreed to be Felicia's understudy, should Felicia be indisposed for any reason on the day of the party.

It was after eleven when the meeting finally ended. Kitty's grandmother was staying to lunch with the other ladies and declined Kitty's offer of a lift back to the Dolphin.

'I don't suppose you could drop me off near the boat float, could you?' Naomi asked as Kitty was gathering her things ready to leave.

'Of course. I have to go back through the town to take the ferry, it's no trouble,' Kitty assured her.

She said goodbye to her grandmother and the others while Naomi fetched her hat and coat.

'Oh, thank heavens. I am so glad to be out of there,' Naomi declared as soon as the front door had closed behind them, and they were on their way to Kitty's car.

Kitty understood the girl's feelings. 'I must admit I rather regret having allowed my grandmother to persuade me into assisting in this venture.'

Naomi settled herself in the passenger seat and produced a small, brightly enamelled pocket mirror from her handbag to check her lipstick. 'Aunt Joan is terribly generous, but I shall be glad to return to London. Mummy has promised a trip to Paris soon which should be rather fun.'

Kitty started the car. She wondered if she and Matt would ever get to go on a belated honeymoon, or even a holiday. So far the brochures they had sent for were still sitting unread in a drawer in the bureau.

'Did you know Peggy well?' Kitty asked in a casual tone as she drove along the tree lined street towards the main road leading down the hill towards the river.

'No, not really, I've only been here for a few months while Mummy and Daddy have been travelling. Daddy works for the government. I'd seen her in the shop, of course, when I went for Aunt Joan's medicines.' Naomi's reply came quickly leaving Kitty to think the girl had been expecting the question.

'Why did you think the letter writer might have been a woman?' Kitty applied the brakes as they drove down hill past the naval college.

Naomi tucked her mirror back into her black patent handbag. 'I don't know. It just seemed to me to be something perhaps a jealous woman might do. You know, if they thought their husband might be led astray by us in our evening gowns.'

Kitty could see Naomi's reasoning. 'Did Peggy ever ask you for any money?' She turned and drove the last few yards towards the boat float.

She had decided to be bold with her question in the hope of prising something useful from the girl. There was a shocked gasp from her companion. Kitty glanced across to see that Naomi's face had paled beneath her make-up.

'What makes you ask that?' she asked as Kitty drew to a halt.

'Peggy was rumoured to have a notebook of secrets that she wrote down about various people. It seems she often extracted money in return for her silence. I wondered if you might have been in her book.' Kitty turned in her seat to fully face Naomi.

Naomi licked her lips, smudging her recently applied lipstick. 'Has anyone found the book?'

'I don't know. Whoever broke into Peggy's room was probably looking for it,' Kitty said. 'Naomi, if your name may have been in it, then tell me now. Inspector Lewis will be wanting to question everyone who has any connection at all with Peggy and it will be better if you come forward first.'

The girl threw her gloved hands up to cover her face as if needing a moment to recover herself.

'I don't wish to upset you,' Kitty continued gently, 'but Peggy is dead, and no one deserves that, even if it seems that she was not a very nice person.'

Naomi slowly removed her hands from her face and Kitty could see that the girl was close to tears. 'I paid Peggy a couple of times. I very foolishly became involved with someone I shouldn't have back in London. A married man. That's why I came here to stay with Aunt Joan. Mummy found out and thought staying with my godmother would get me out of London for a time. Except, what no one knew... not even me until... well, until, I lost the baby.' Naomi blinked hard and fumbled in her bag for a handkerchief.

'Oh, Naomi, I'm sorry. And Peggy found out?' Kitty asked gently.

Naomi nodded miserably. 'The doctor was very discreet, but I think she guessed from the prescription that her brother dispensed. I bled rather a lot.' She sniffed and dabbed the end of her pert nose with the lace edged handkerchief.

'I'm so very sorry. That must have been quite awful.' Kitty

could see how distressing it must have been for the girl. To be
banished in disgrace and then to suffer physically as well as
mentally must have been terrible.

'I thought that once I was back in London then she would
be forced to stop. I could just ignore her.' Naomi took out her
mirror once more and checked her make-up for signs of damage.
'But if there is a book, and she wrote everything down... Oh,
Mrs Bryant, whatever shall I do?'

'Don't panic. The police are working on the case and
there is no real proof that there was a book, let alone that
there was much in it. It could just be a list of sums of money.'
Kitty tried to reassure the girl while her brain was busy
thinking through the implications of the information Naomi
had given her.

'If you discover anything, please, tell me, and if you can
keep what I've said private I will be very grateful. Aunt Joan
doesn't know about, well, about the baby. She just thought I was
unwell and anaemic. She's been very kind to me.' Naomi looked
despairingly at Kitty.

'I shall be as discreet as possible, I assure you.' Kitty pulled
over as they arrived at the dock and reached across to give the
girl's hand a comforting squeeze.

'Thank you.' Naomi dropped her belongings back inside her
bag and opened the passenger door to climb out.

Kitty remained parked for a moment after the girl had left
the car. It seemed that the case was becoming more complicated
by the minute. It would be interesting to compare notes with
Matt and to hear if he had learned anything from Felicia.

* * *

Matt had taken his Sunbeam motorcycle down into Paignton.
The picture house where Felicia was employed was at the top
of the high street near the railway station. He parked up at the

side of the road and looked up at the red-brick building with its impressive cream stone portico.

The cinema was not due to open to the public until the afternoon, but he knew that the staff were often there earlier, especially on Mondays when the displays inside the foyer were changed to reflect the week's films. He ran lightly up the couple of steps to the large glass doors and knocked.

Inside the foyer he could see a cleaner, clad in a wrap-around floral pinafore, her hair bound up in a headscarf pushing a broom across the floor. At the sound of his knock, the woman stopped her work and came over to the door.

'We'em shut. Come back this afternoon,' she shouted through the locked door.

'I'm here to see Miss Felicia Felling. Is she there?' Matt tried not to bellow as the street was busy with people passing by and he had no wish to draw attention to his mission.

'That depends, who wants her.' The cleaner eyed him suspiciously.

'Captain Bryant. She knows my wife, Kitty. I need to speak to her for a few moments,' Matt replied.

At first, he thought the woman was about to leave him waiting on the steps. Instead, she turned and walked out of his sight only to return accompanied by Felicia. Felicia was dressed for her day's work in a smart navy skirt and jacket and crisp white blouse.

She produced a large bunch of keys from her pocket and unlocked the door to allow him in.

'Captain Bryant, this is a surprise. Is everything all right?' Felicia asked.

The cleaning lady made no move to leave the foyer and Matt realised she hoped to hear their conversation.

'I'm sorry to bother you at work, Miss Felling, but I need to talk to you for a moment.' He looked at the cleaning lady who resumed her sweeping. 'In private.'

'The manager's office is free. He doesn't come in until after lunch on Mondays.' Felicia led the way to a closed door near the ticket booth. She produced another key and unlocked it before ushering him in.

'Now, how may I help you?' she asked once the door was closed behind them.

'Kitty and I are looking into Peggy Blaine's murder, and I hoped I might be able to ask you a few questions about her,' Matt said.

Felicia leaned back against the manager's desk. 'I thought this might be about Peggy. Did Betty send you?'

'She did. Betty thought you might be able to shed some light on a possible motive for Peggy's murder,' Matt said.

'Peggy wasn't a very nice person. I'm sure several people will have told you that already. She always used to creep about poking her nose into other people's business and then she would lord it over them or try and use what she'd found out to her advantage,' Felicia said with a sigh.

'Betty said that you thought she had information about Naomi, that you'd seen something that might be relevant.' Matt looked at the girl.

Felicia nodded slowly. 'I was in the shop getting a new lipstick. I'd lost mine, a lovely carmine colour. Naomi was at the counter, and I heard Peggy say something to her. I wasn't really paying attention but then I saw Naomi slide something quick like across the counter. It was odd, as if she didn't want to be seen. Not like she was paying for something from the shop, if you know what I mean. Naomi left and Peggy tucked herself up a corner all furtive like where Alastair couldn't see her. She was scribbling something in a tiny little book. I teased her a bit, you know about it being a love letter. She got a bit snotty and said something funny about balancing her accounts.'

'And you thought this was to do with Naomi?' Matt asked.

'Yes. I'm sure of it. When we were in the dressing room

getting ready for the pageant there was a funny atmosphere. Naomi seemed to be really wary around Peggy like she didn't want to have anything to do with her. Dorothy Martin hated Peggy. She was jealous of her for a start as Peggy had nice things and Peggy had turfed Dorothy out of the shop a week or so ago,' Felicia said.

'Shoplifting?' Matt asked.

Felicia gave him a quick look. 'I think so. Anyway, she didn't want her father to hear about it. Or her grandmother for that matter.'

'That's understandable I suppose. Betty said too that there was something between Victoria and Araminta and Peggy?'

Felicia fiddled nervously with the edge of the blotter on the desk. 'There was something, but I can't quite say what it was. Victoria was, well, she seemed out of it a lot of the time. Like as if she wasn't quite the full shilling. Araminta was quite snippy with her. I think she has a bit of a thing for Victoria's boyfriend. Good-looking fellow he is, but cocky. I don't know, Peggy had this sort of smug, gloating air over both of them. Like as if she knew something that they didn't.'

'I see. This is very helpful, thank you.' Matt appreciated the information. The picture he was forming of Peggy's character was not very flattering.

'My pleasure. I hope they catch whoever did it. I didn't like Peggy, but she shouldn't have been killed,' Felicia said as she showed him out of the cinema.

'I agree. Thank you for your help.' Matt made his way back to his motorcycle. A glance at his watch told him that it was likely to still be a while before Kitty finished her meeting.

He hopped onto the Sunbeam and pulled on his leather gauntlets. There was just enough time for a quick trip into Torquay before returning home.

CHAPTER FIFTEEN

Matt pulled to a stop at his destination and parked his motorcycle at the kerb. He could only hope that Dr Carter was at work in the morgue. He knocked on the green-painted door, hidden away at the side of the red-brick building.

After a moment the doctor himself appeared to greet him with a cheerful smile. 'Captain Bryant, what the Dickens brings you here? Come on in.'

Matt followed the doctor along a whitewashed corridor into a small office which smelled faintly of disinfectant and other chemicals.

'Tea?' the doctor offered. 'I was just about to make some.' He indicated a small spirit stove and various accoutrements for tea making situated on a low wooden cupboard beside a hanging display of a human skeleton.

'I thought I would call in to see if there was any new information about Miss Blaine's death, and to take a closer look at the knife if I could,' Matt explained once he had divested himself of his leather greatcoat and motorcycling cap.

The kettle started to whistle, and Dr Carter removed it from the stove. 'You're out of luck with the knife, old boy. Inspector

Lewis has whisked it off to be tested for fingerprints.' The doctor poured the boiling water into a small, brown china teapot.

Matt took a seat on one of the plain deal chairs in front of the doctor's desk. 'Inspector Lewis is a stickler for procedures.'

The doctor handed him a blue and white striped thick china Cornish-style mug. 'So I understand. Help yourself to milk and sugar. There are some ginger biscuits in the tin.' He indicated a battered square metal tin bearing the legend *Proctor's medical instruments*.

Matt added milk and declined a biscuit. 'How are you finding working with the inspector?' he asked curiously as he stirred his tea with a slightly grubby-looking teaspoon.

Dr Carter's eyes twinkled. 'It's somewhat different shall we say. Inspector Lewis sets great store by protocol and modern policing methods.'

Matt grinned. 'He does indeed.'

'One interesting fact from Miss Blaine's death, not that you've heard this from me of course – Miss Blaine was pregnant, about twelve weeks along. She would have started to show within the next few weeks.' Dr Carter dunked a ginger biscuit into his mug.

Matt stared at the doctor. 'I see. This adds a whole new dimension to the case.' He was very surprised to hear of Peggy's pregnancy. Did Peggy's lover know about the baby? Was this the motive for her murder and for the burglary? Was he a married man who wished to be rid of the girl?

'The inspector seemed to feel the same way. By the by, I don't have the knife, but I did take several photographs for my files.' Dr Carter gave an impish grin.

Matt smiled at him. 'I noticed it was an unusual design,' he said as he looked inside the manila folder the doctor passed to him.

'Some kind of ornamental brass paper knife would be my

guess, see the stones and enamelling on the handle? But the blade has been sharpened.'

Matt passed the folder back to the doctor. 'A premeditated murder then? The blade readied, waiting for the right moment?'

The doctor helped himself to another biscuit. 'That would be my thoughts but of course as a physician I can only state the facts.' His gaze met with Matt's.

'I'm very grateful for your help.' Matt finished his tea. He needed to get back to Churston to share what he'd learned with Kitty.

'Any time, dear boy. A word of caution, Inspector Lewis doesn't view private investigators with a friendly eye,' the doctor warned.

Matt tugged on his coat and set his cap firmly on his head. 'Yes, we discovered that in Yorkshire. He also has somewhat traditional views on the role of women.'

The doctor laughed out loud, his shoulders jiggling with amusement. 'Oh dear, he's about to discover that Mrs Bryant is a force to be reckoned with.'

'He is indeed,' Matt replied with a wry smile. He would have thought the inspector would have realised that from the case in Yorkshire.

* * *

Kitty arrived home to discover that Matt had not yet returned from Paignton. Thankfully Bertie and the kitten still appeared to be behaving and her housekeeper had no objections to the new arrival. It had taken a while for the older woman to adjust to Bertie, who could still be quite naughty and destructive if left alone too long. The last thing Kitty had wanted was to cause an upset in the smooth running of the household by introducing the kitten.

A few minutes later, she heard the rumble of Matt's motorcycle outside and a flurry of woofs from Bertie announced her husband's return. They exchanged information over an informal lunch of corned beef sandwiches as Kitty didn't wish to get underfoot while her housekeeper was tackling the washing.

'Well, it seems we've both discovered some very interesting things.' Kitty slipped Bertie the last corner of her sandwich under the table. 'Who shall we tackle first this afternoon? Dorothy or Victoria?'

Matt leaned back in his seat; his forehead creased in thought. 'We also need to do more to talk to this Peplow chap. Especially as he and Victoria were at the bar in the intermission when Araminta saw Peggy.'

Kitty had almost forgotten Sir Vivian's commission in her excitement over the information Naomi had provided. Now though she could see that perhaps a visit to Victoria could potentially provide them with more information on the elusive Mr Peplow.

'Victoria first then, we can kill two birds with one stone there. We can find out what she knows about Peggy and more about Mr Peplow,' she suggested.

'I'll telephone first and see if she is at home this afternoon,' Matt said.

'Very well, then if we get the chance later, we can try Dorothy Martin too.' Kitty cleared the plates.

Luck was on their side when Matt telephoned the Hardcastle residence and Victoria agreed to meet them in an hour's time.

Kitty decided as she drove to Paignton that it might be better if Matt started the questions. She knew that sometimes her natural curiosity could make her a little blunt and she had a feeling that Victoria might prove to be difficult to interview.

Despite the fresh, sunny afternoon the house still appeared dark and gloomy as they turned into the drive.

'It's not the nicest house that Sir Vivian could have chosen to rent,' she observed as she halted near the front door. The grass on the small lawn at the side of the drive was overgrown and the shrubbery badly needed a gardener's attention.

'Perhaps it was cheap,' Matt suggested as he exited the car ready to ring the bell.

Victoria opened the door to them herself and Kitty wondered if she had perhaps been watching out for their arrival.

'Come through to the library, there is a fire there,' Victoria suggested. Kitty thought the girl looked thin and pale beneath her layers of woollen cardigans. 'If you wished to see Araminta she has gone for a hack with some friends at Preston,' the girl said as she opened the library door and stood aside to allow them in.

Once they had entered and taken their seats on the shabby armchairs, Victoria curled up on the sofa in much the same way Araminta had done the previous day. She smoothed her thick woollen skirt down over her legs and pulled a thin crocheted blanket across her stocking-clad feet.

'We called yesterday and spoke to your sister,' Matt said.

'Daddy said you had called. Minty isn't talking to me at the moment.' Victoria plucked mindlessly at the blanket covering her legs. 'Is this about Peggy? The girl from the chemist's?'

'We're trying to discover why someone may have wished to harm her. We know she was a difficult girl to get along with. She didn't have many friends,' Matt said.

Victoria looked slightly bored by the conversation. 'Well, she wasn't a friend of mine, or as far as I know of Minty's. I'm not sure why you think I can help you.' She fixed her wide blue eyes on Matt as if challenging him.

'Several people have said there was a strange atmosphere between you, your sister and Peggy. As if she had some kind of hold over you.' Kitty saw fear flash across Victoria's pallid features.

'Then they were mistaken.' The girl's tone grew sharp.

'I don't believe they were. We know that Peggy often knew secrets about people. Secrets she was thought to note down in a book and use to extract things from her victims,' Matt said.

Victoria froze, her anxious fidgeting at the blanket stilled and her eyes were wide and frightened. She reminded Kitty of Bertie when he had been caught in the middle of doing something he shouldn't and was trying to decide what to try in order to escape chastisement.

'Why would Peggy know something about me?' Victoria asked.

Kitty thought it interesting that she didn't include her stepsister in that question.

'Perhaps because of Dominic Peplow,' Matt said.

Kitty knew her husband was fishing now, hoping he would hit the right note to get the girl to talk. If Sir Vivian was correct about Victoria being enmeshed in cocaine addiction then it was no surprise that the girl was scared.

'Dominic is a friend, that's all. We see one another from time to time. He... He's enormous fun.' Victoria sounded a little breathy as if she were panicking.

'Victoria, we know about the kind of fun Dominic supplies.' Matt was gentle but firm.

The girl's lower lip started to tremble. 'I don't know what you mean.'

'I think you do. Dominic is your supplier, isn't he, and Peggy had put all the pieces together. Working in a chemist's, she knew the signs of addiction,' Kitty said.

Tears spilled down Victoria's thin cheeks and she fumbled at her cardigan pocket to retrieve her handkerchief. 'Father will be furious. I promised him that I wouldn't fall back into it again.

He hates Dominic, but he's just helping me. Otherwise, I don't feel well.' The girl broke into choking sobs.

'Did Peggy speak to you about Dominic?' Kitty asked.

Victoria hung her head. 'She kept hinting. Nasty, snide little hints. I told Dominic but he said not to worry. He would deal with her as he knew something about Peggy that would shut her up.' As soon as she had finished speaking, Victoria lifted an anguished tear-stained face. 'Oh no, I don't mean... He wouldn't have harmed her, not really. He would just have warned her off.'

'Dominic was at the pageant, wasn't he?' Matt asked.

'Yes, he came with a group of our friends. I popped out to see him to get some champagne and he, well, he slipped me a little pick me up to calm my nerves before the talent show.' Victoria looked agitated again now and her hands were busy once more, fidgeting and plucking at the blanket.

'Did you see him speak to Peggy at all? We know she collected a drink from the bar as she took it back to the dressing room and Felicia told her off,' Kitty said.

Victoria shook her head. 'No, I drank my cocktail and went off to the ladies'. There was a queue, so I didn't see anyone else until I got back to the dressing room and Peggy had gone missing.'

'Do you know why Araminta and Peggy were at odds?' Kitty asked.

'I'm not sure. I think something was said after one of Father's lectures at the museum. Peggy used to go to those, she told me, she said she was fascinated by the discoveries.' Victoria shuddered. 'Why someone would wish to hear about embalming and mummies, I have no idea. The jewels and gold are pretty but, ugh, the rest of it is quite repulsive really. Minty used to help Father out sometimes but I never did.'

'Thank you for being so frank with us,' Matt said as he took one of his cards from the silver card case he kept in his pocket.

'We need to speak to Mr Peplow as soon as possible. We are not the police so he would do better to speak with us, before he finds Inspector Lewis knocking on his door.'

Victoria took the card and turned it nervously between her fingers. Kitty could see that the girl's nails, despite being painted a dark crimson, were bitten to the quicks. 'I don't know.'

'It's important, Victoria. Otherwise, he could find the finger of suspicion for Peggy's death being pointed very firmly in his direction,' Matt insisted.

The girl tucked the card inside her cardigan pocket. 'You won't tell Father about Dominic?' she pleaded.

'It would be better if you sought some help, proper help to stop taking the stuff he's been giving you. How much money has it cost you?' Kitty asked. She doubted that Peplow was supplying Victoria out of charity, even if he was Victoria's lover. Yet the girl seemed to have relatively little money of her own.

'I don't know what you mean. Dominic is very kind to me.' Victoria's gaze flew towards the library door.

'How have you found the means to pay him?' Matt asked.

Victoria looked panic-stricken. She shrugged off the blanket and rose from the couch. 'Dom's my friend. I've told you more than enough. I think you should go now.'

They had little choice but to obey her.

CHAPTER SIXTEEN

'I think we hit a nerve,' Kitty said as they climbed back into her car.

'I think you're right. This whole commission from Sir Vivian is strange. Victoria is his stepdaughter, and he doesn't seem like a very family-orientated man. Why is he so concerned about Peplow? He could insist that Victoria goes away for treatment, Switzerland or somewhere, and yet he's employed us to look into the man.' Matt sounded thoughtful.

'You're right. Dominic is apparently who he wants us to focus on, so why not just tell you that upfront? And there is that business about money. Victoria has to be paying Dominic somehow if he is her supplier. She says he is not her boyfriend, but their relationship appears more than just that of friends. She clearly is paying him or she would have reacted differently.' Kitty started up her car ready to drive to the Martins' house in Kingswear.

'Let's go and see what Miss Dorothy Martin has to say for herself.' Matt settled back in his seat.

'Hopefully her father will be out, and Dorothy will be able to talk more freely,' Kitty said. Dorothy's father was known locally as being very controlling and she was pretty sure he would not like them talking to his daughter about Peggy's murder.

The Martins lived in a smart, detached villa on the hill at Kingswear. Dorothy's mother had died some years ago and Dorothy and her father lived with her paternal grandmother. Kitty found a spot to park on the precipitous road and they made their way together to the dark-crimson front door.

A slightly harassed-looking young maid answered the bell and showed them inside, informing them that Miss Dorothy was in the sitting room.

'Mrs Bryant, Captain Bryant, do come in. Father and Gran are out at the moment. Would you like some tea?' Dorothy had her hand on the bell pull as she greeted them.

'No, thank you. This is just a short visit,' Kitty assured her as they took their seats on the old-fashioned leather sofa. The room was crowded with knick-knacks and potted plants. A collection of family photographs in silver frames stood on a small rosewood side table and little lace doilies covered all the surfaces of the furniture. A fire crackled in the hearth and the room felt hot and oppressive.

Dorothy herself was perched on the edge of her armchair near the fire. 'How can I help you? I presume this is about Peggy?' the girl asked.

Matt looked at Kitty and she took the lead with the questions.

'Dorothy, we know that Peggy was unpopular for many reasons. She liked knowing things about people, and it was believed that she kept a record of these secrets in a book. Her room was ransacked, and the police think whoever killed her may have been searching for those notes. We know that you had an altercation with Peggy a few weeks ago in the shop.' Kitty halted to give Dorothy the opportunity to digest what she had said. The girl's complexion had paled and she looked frightened.

'Oh, yes. It was frightful, so embarrassing. She flew at me from behind the counter. It came from nowhere. She was making all kinds of baseless accusations,' Dorothy said.

'She said you had stolen something,' Matt commented and drew an indignant glare from Dorothy.

'Like I said, she made all kinds of accusations. One doesn't like to speak ill of the dead, but Peggy was not a nice girl.' Dorothy tilted her small, pointed chin upwards.

'Did you ever hear anything about Peggy keeping a record of secrets about people?' Kitty asked.

Dorothy's gaze dropped and she stared into the fire for a moment before answering. 'Yes, I know she did. She told me so herself.'

This was an unexpected piece of information. 'She told you?' Kitty asked.

Dorothy nodded. 'After we had our well, disagreement, she told me she had made a note in her book, and I shouldn't think that she would forget about it.'

Kitty looked at Matt.

'Did she ever ask you for money or favours in return for not making your theft public?' Matt asked.

Dorothy fidgeted uncomfortably. 'She knew I hadn't much money but she liked to know things so she would try to get me to tell her information.'

'Information?' Kitty was puzzled.

'She knew that Father attends a lot of meetings as a councillor. She liked to know what went on and things like that,' Dorothy explained. Spots of high colour had appeared on her cheeks.

Kitty was starting to see how Peggy had operated and it wasn't a pretty picture.

'Did you see Peggy speak to anyone during the intermission or before the start of the pageant?' Matt asked.

Kitty knew that they had asked the girls this previously but now they had all had time to reflect she hoped that they might remember something new. Or might reveal something they had previously been hiding. No matter how trivial a detail it might still prove helpful.

Dorothy shook her head once more. 'I'm sorry, Mrs Bryant. I saw her near the bar when she was getting a drink. Father and Gran were there with Sir Vivian, so I went the longer way around. I didn't want to get involved in Father's political stuff. Victoria was with her boyfriend and his friends. Araminta was in the ballroom, oh, and I passed Naomi on my way to the ladies'.' Dorothy's brow was furrowed in concentration. 'I suppose though as somebody must have spoken to Peggy as she had a cocktail in her hand. She wouldn't have bought it herself, too tight for one thing.'

'Felicia said she bought a cocktail back into the dressing room. You think someone would have bought it for her?' Kitty asked.

'Definitely, Peggy never paid for anything herself if she could help it and it wouldn't be *ladylike*, would it, for her to go to the bar,' Dorothy said.

Kitty thought the girl made a good point. She knew which staff members had been working that day. Hopefully they might recall one of the pageant contestants getting a drink.

'If the person who got her drink also suggested meeting her, then perhaps we might discover who killed her,' Kitty said. 'Thank you, Dorothy, that's very helpful.'

'Not at all, Mrs Bryant. I wouldn't be surprised though if her brother didn't know something.' Dorothy gave a sly smile.

'Alastair? What makes you say that?' Kitty asked.

The girl shrugged. 'There's a bit of talk about him and that Mrs Dobbs, you know the widowed lady. I had wondered if

Peggy had something on her brother. He didn't want her to be in the pageant and I asked Peggy how come he had changed his mind. She gave that smug little laugh she had and said, "How do you think? I can be very persuasive.'"

'Hmm, thank you, Dorothy.' Matt rose from his seat and Kitty joined him. She would be glad to escape the overcrowded, oppressive room with this talk of secrets and gossip.

The discussion and the atmosphere made her feel sullied somehow and dirty. She was glad when they had said their farewells and were back outside in the cool late afternoon air.

'Let's go home,' Kitty suggested. She knew the bar staff she needed to speak to would not be working again until tomorrow night. After all the revelations of the day she wanted to return to their home, and play with Bertie and her new kitten. It might help assuage the murky feelings that were pressing in on her after leaving Victoria and Dorothy.

'Good idea.' Matt gave her an understanding smile and patted her gloved hand.

* * *

They arrived home just as their housekeeper was leaving.

'I've left supper ready in the kitchen, Mrs Bryant. It just needs hotting up. That rascal of a kitten is in its basket out of yon pesky dog's reach.' The older woman tucked her cotton scarf around her neck.

'Thank you. I hope they haven't been too much of a nuisance?' Kitty instantly felt guilty. Mondays was always a busy day, and she hoped the new addition had not caused Mrs Smith extra work.

'' 'Tis all right, Mrs Bryant. I'll see you tomorrow.' The woman strode away in the direction of the common, her wicker shopping basket on her arm.

They had not been home long when there was a knock at

the front door. Matt went to answer as Kitty was busy in the kitchen.

'Inspector Lewis, this is a surprise, do come in.' Kitty dried her hands on a tea towel as soon as she heard Matt greet their visitor. She patted her curls into place and went through to find out the reason for the policeman's visit.

'Inspector, can I get you a drink?' Kitty asked as she entered the room. Inspector Lewis was seated on one of the fireside chairs with a black expression on his foxy face.

'No, thank you, Mrs Bryant. I have not called to socialise.'

Kitty's eyes widened at the inspector's somewhat rude reply.

'I see. Perhaps then, you would care to cut to the chase, Inspector.' Matt's response was polite but frosty in tone.

'Very well, Captain Bryant. I have released the man who admitted sending the anonymous letters to the ladies involved with the pageant. He has been warned and severely rebuked about his behaviour. However, without further evidence I cannot link him with Miss Blaine's murder.' Inspector Lewis glared at Matt and Kitty.

'Or with the search of Peggy's room,' Kitty murmured.

The inspector fixed his attention on her. 'Miss Blaine's death is a police matter. I thought I had made myself clear that I was in charge of this investigation.'

'But of course,' Kitty agreed mildly.

'So why then do I find you two constantly under foot? Talking to witnesses, muddying the waters, poking around asking questions. This wretched letter writer fellow. You should have come to me about approaching the newspaper offices.' Inspector Lewis was clearly quite cross.

'I'm sorry, Inspector, but we know that you haven't the resources to be chasing up all kinds of odd whims. We thought we were assisting you, freeing you to focus on *important* policing matters,' Kitty said.

'I have made my position clear, Mrs Bryant. I thought I had done so when I was in Yorkshire. Serious crimes such as murder are no place for well-meaning amateurs.' He almost spat the last comment out.

'We are hardly amateur, Inspector, as I'm sure your chief inspector has informed you. We are also commissioned by a client to investigate another matter which seems to be entangled with Miss Blaine's death. If we have information which we feel may assist you, how then do you wish us to proceed?' Matt asked.

The inspector stood and glowered at them. 'If you have concrete facts and evidence that I can use to charge and convict someone then by all means inform me. Any suppositions, guesses and half-baked notions keep those to yourself and do not impede my investigation.'

'I see. Very well, Inspector.' Matt's tone was suspiciously agreeable.

'Now, if you'll excuse me, I have a lot of work to do.' The inspector took his leave, closing their front door behind him with a bang.

'Oh dear, well, that told us.' Kitty sank down on one of the chairs beside the fire after the policeman had gone.

'Oh dear, indeed. It seems that we can longer enjoy the mutually beneficial relationship we had previously with our constabulary.' Matt took the chair opposite and rubbed the top of Bertie's head.

'I wonder if he is aware of Peggy's notebook and the reason for the search of her room?' Kitty asked.

'I doubt he will learn much from Victoria or Naomi. That's if he questions the girls again. He may be trying a different method to find the murderer.'

Kitty was puzzled. 'Such as?'

'Perhaps using his manpower to question people in the

town, potential witnesses? Looking for a pattern of similar killings?'

Kitty sighed. 'Well, he was quite clear about not wishing to hear from us. I can speak to the bar staff tomorrow evening to see if they recall serving Peggy.'

'Let's hope we can find an opportunity to talk to this Peplow character too, although I suspect that may be difficult. He seems to have done a good job of evading us so far and I'm certain that he knows that we wish to speak to him,' Matt said.

'What else can we try? It seems to me we are running out of options.' Kitty tried to think of any leads they had not yet followed.

Matt drummed his fingers on the leather arms of the chair. 'We need to speak to Peggy's brother but that may have to wait a few days. This business about Sir Vivian is niggling me. Perhaps if we try the museum tomorrow. The staff there may remember Peggy attending the lectures and I would be interested to discover more about the donations he has made to the exhibits there.'

'He certainly had lots of things in his study, didn't he? Victoria mentioned gold and jewels. I don't know an awful lot about his career, do you?' She looked at her husband.

'No, but I have some people in London who may know more.' He grinned at Kitty.

She knew from his previous line of work that a telephone call to his old employer in Whitehall might well yield the information they wanted.

CHAPTER SEVENTEEN

Matt made his telephone call early the following day. Brigadier Remington-Blythe, his former employer, cheerfully promised to dig around and pass on any information he could find on Sir Vivian and his expeditions to Egypt.

He went back into the sitting room to tell Kitty the news only to find her extricating her new kitten from the curtains.

'I think Mrs Smith was right, this kitten is a rascal.' She fished the cat out of the fabric and held it up to study it. 'Rascal, I think that might just be the perfect name for you.'

Matt chuckled. 'Rascal it is then. I suppose we should find a collar with a bell on it so that the birds are not harmed when it grows big enough to let it out into the garden.'

Kitty smiled back at him as she deposited Rascal back inside her basket. 'Is the brigadier able to assist us?'

'Yes, he seemed intrigued by the request. Hopefully he will get back to us quite quickly.'

'Let us head to the museum then, and this evening I shall call at the Dolphin to ask the bar staff if they remember serving Peggy at the pageant.' Kitty scrambled back to her feet from where she had been kneeling with the kitten.

* * *

The museum was a handsome building built of pale grey stone. A shallow flight of steps led to the front entrance and the black wrought-iron gates were ajar indicating that they were open.

Kitty parked her car higher along the street in front of the neighbouring church. 'I do feel as if this is perhaps clutching at straws,' she said as she closed her car door.

'Perhaps it is rather, but at least we will have been thorough, and you never know, there may just be something that proves to be useful.' Matt offered her his arm.

The tiled floored entrance hall was deserted although they could hear the sounds of voices coming from the galleries above their heads on the next floor.

'We need to find a member of staff,' Matt said as they looked around.

'Let's try the gift shop,' Kitty suggested.

A small area had been set aside to sell souvenir pencils, postcards and a few knick-knacks. An older man was busy stocking the shelves with a selection of books covering aspects of local history.

'We're sorry to disturb you but wondered if you might be able to assist us?' Matt reached inside the breast pocket of his jacket and produced one of his business cards.

The museum employee set aside the books and took the card, holding it to the light from the window to study it more closely.

'I'll do my best, sir. In what way can I help?' the man asked in a puzzled voice.

'A young lady was murdered on Saturday evening in Dartmouth, a Miss Peggy Blaine. She often came to the museum to attend lectures by Sir Vivian Hardcastle. I wondered if any of the staff might remember seeing her?' Matt asked. He had a press clipping in his pocket that had a somewhat blurry photograph of Peggy with the other contestants and he showed it to the man.

'Come to Sir Vivian's lectures, did she?' the man asked as he squinted at the picture.

'Yes, Peggy was a very pretty girl. We wondered if anyone might recall seeing her or if she ever came with anyone. We've been told she sometimes used to stay behind to ask Sir Vivian questions,' Kitty said.

'Stay behind, you say.' The man's brow cleared. 'Oh yes, that does ring a bell. Yes, I remember her now, always last to leave she was. Very interested in the lectures. I think as Sir Vivian walked her out a few times.'

Kitty gave Matt a significant look.

The man chuckled as he passed the newspaper cutting back to Matt. 'Got an eye for a pretty face, has Sir Vivian. I think as he may have given the young lady supper once or twice. Not as he liked his daughter, Miss Araminta, to know. She used to get proper shirty if'n she thought her father were paying too much attention to the ladies. Mind, seeing as how many times he's been wed, I don't suppose as you can blame her.'

'No, I suppose not,' Matt agreed. 'You say that Sir Vivian took Miss Blaine to supper?'

The man nodded. 'Oh yes, gave her a lift in his car and I heard him say as they would stop off at the Imperial for something to eat.'

'I see, thank you. The museum has an extensive collection of artefacts from Egypt so I've heard? I expect Sir Vivian has donated quite a few things?' Matt remarked as the man resumed his shelf-stacking activities.

'We have a big collection but not much from Sir Vivian for all his travels. Mostly pottery and such,' the man said.

'No jewellery or valuable items?' Matt asked.

The man chuckled. 'Oh no, sir, nothing like that. I expect anything like that would go to a bigger museum than us. I think as Sir Vivian is more an expert on hieroglyphs though so I doubt as he ever found much in the way of treasure.'

Kitty wandered off to look around at the small display of Egyptian-themed souvenirs available for purchase. Within a minute she was back and tugging at Matt's sleeve. 'Darling, come and look at the paperknives.'

Matt took a couple of steps and immediately saw the display that had caught Kitty's eye. The handles on the daggers were identical to the sharpened blade that had been used to murder Peggy.

'Fine collection of paperknives, those. Good quality brass and steel with enamelling on the handle. That young lady as you was asking about, God rest her soul, she was admiring those a few weeks ago,' the museum employee said affably.

Kitty's eyes were wide as she looked at Matt. He knew that they had no choice but to go and annoy Inspector Lewis further with this fresh information.

* * *

Kitty's mind was busy as she turned her car in the direction of Torquay police station. Could the knife that killed her have been Peggy's own? Could she have she bought one? The knives in the museum didn't have sharp blades and Matt had told her that Dr Carter said someone had deliberately tampered with the one used to kill Peggy.

She doubted if Inspector Lewis had found Peggy's knife amongst her things or surely he would have noted its similarity to the murder weapon. Or had he, and just not said anything? Really, the man was too vexing for words.

Then there was Sir Vivian. He had implied that he barely knew Peggy and yet the man at the museum had said that he had taken her to supper.

The foyer of the police station was busy when they entered

with the desk sergeant booking in a very drunken man who appeared to be clinging to the counter for support. Kitty waited quietly with Matt until a constable had taken the man through to the cells before they approached the counter.

'Good morning, Captain Bryant, Mrs Bryant, how can we help you today?'

'Is Inspector Lewis available at all?' Matt asked.

The sergeant coughed and looked a little embarrassed. 'I'm very sorry, sir, but I've had instructions as the inspector is not to be disturbed.'

'You mean he is not to be disturbed by us,' Kitty said with a wry smile. 'It's quite all right, Sergeant, we do understand. However, we think we have located the source of the murder weapon used to kill Peggy Blaine, and who the owner of the knife may have been.'

The sergeant's attention was clearly caught by her words. 'Oh yes, Mrs Bryant?'

'Tell Inspector Lewis to check the museum's gift shop and to talk to the museum attendant about Miss Blaine.' Kitty winked at the sergeant. 'You can say an anonymous informant came in if you'd rather not mention our names.'

The grizzled older man cracked a knowing smile. 'Very good, Mrs Bryant, and thank you. I'll see as the information gets through.'

They turned and left the police station.

'We could have asked if the chief inspector was in,' Kitty mused as they settled themselves back inside her motor car.

'That's true, but I think it may annoy Inspector Lewis still further and really we need to persuade him that we are his friends rather than his enemies,' Matt said.

Kitty could see his point. It would make their work so much harder if they continued to antagonise the inspector. Even though she would dearly like to set the man back in his place.

They decided to return home until later in the day when

Kitty planned to go into Dartmouth. She had a list of jobs to complete for Mrs Craven for the children's party on the 12th of May and then she intended to talk to the hotel bar staff.

* * *

It was mid-afternoon when Kitty took the ferry back across the river into Dartmouth. She decided to make her purchases first, before calling at the hotel.

She parked her car near the boat float marina and strolled towards the Butterwalk in the spring sunshine. The chill had finally gone from the air, and it seemed as if the weather was finally settling down. The shops were decked in red, white and blue for the jubilee and daffodils and tulips nodded their heads in the formal beds. Kitty greeted several people who she knew as she made her way to the shops.

It wasn't strictly on her route to go past the Blaines' chemist's shop, but she decided a small detour wouldn't go amiss. Not that she expected it to be open, at least not for a few days. Even so she took her time strolling past. A black-edged notice had been posted on the front door informing passers-by that the shop was closed for the foreseeable future due to an unexpected death in the family.

Kitty wondered if Alastair was in the flat above the shop. It must be very hard for him, losing his sister. He had been almost like a father to Peggy. He had never married and until this latest friendship with Celia Dobbs there had never even been a rumour of a romance in his life.

She knew Celia Dobbs vaguely from various social events and a couple of chance meetings. She was of a similar age to Alastair she supposed, plump and amiable with fair hair, rosy cheeks and a kindly disposition.

Mr Dobbs had been unwell for years. He had been several years older than Celia and she had nursed his mother before nursing her husband. Their marriage had never been blessed with children. Matt had known Mr Dobbs a little from his business meetings at the council.

The last time Kitty had seen Gabriel Dobbs he had been in a wheelchair, and she had helped Celia to push the chair up one of the steep slopes in the town onto the pavement. The man had been painfully thin, and despite being bundled up under layers of woollen blankets had complained to Celia of feeling cold.

His death a few months ago had surprised no one and most of the town had agreed that Celia deserved a rest after a lifetime of caring for others. She must have come to know Alastair Blaine on her many trips to the chemist's to collect her husband's medications. It was little wonder they had become friends.

Dorothy's words about Peggy having some kind of hold on her brother, however, forced Kitty to examine the relationship through a more critical lens. Gabriel Dobbs had clearly been suffering in his final days. Had Alastair and Celia contrived to hurry his end forward a little? Was that the hold that Peggy had hinted at to Dorothy? No one would have suspected anything, and many would have thought it a kindness. Or had Celia and Alastair been having an affair while her husband was still alive?

Both ideas made Kitty uncomfortable however and she was lost in thought, staring into the window of the closed shop for a few moments before she collected herself.

'Excuse me, Mrs Bryant?'

Kitty struggled to maintain her composure when the woman she had been thinking about suddenly appeared beside her.

'Oh, Mrs Dobbs, good afternoon.' Kitty felt her face growing warm and she hoped the other woman hadn't noticed her gazing into the closed chemist's shop.

Mrs Dobbs appeared a little flustered. 'I wondered, Mrs Bryant, if you might be able to spare me a moment? Mrs

Ponsonby-Bell said as you and your husband were looking into Peggy's death.'

'Yes, of course, shall we go and have some tea?' Kitty offered. The woman's request was unexpected, and Kitty was eager to hear what she might have to say. Especially after the ideas which had struck her while she had been staring into the closed shop window.

The nearest tearoom was quiet, and they selected a small table in the far corner where no one was likely to be able to overhear their conversation. Once the tea had been ordered, Kitty drew off her gloves and waited for Mrs Dobbs to reveal what was troubling her.

Celia seemed to be nervous, straightening the cutlery on the table while waiting for the waitress to deliver their order. Kitty waited patiently until the tea things were in front of them and the waitress had gone about her business.

'How may I help you?' Kitty asked as she set out the delicate floral teacups.

'You may have heard that well, Mr Blaine, Peggy's brother and I, have a friendship,' Celia said, fixing her gaze on Kitty's ministrations with the teapot.

'I understand that's so,' Kitty agreed as she poured tea from the pot through the metal strainer on the top of the cup. She wondered what the woman was about to confess.

'I'm worried about Alastair, Mrs Bryant. This terrible business with Peggy's death.' The woman stumbled to a halt as if still trying to marshal her thoughts into order.

'It must have hit him very hard. He raised Peggy from when she was very young.' Kitty removed the strainer and offered her companion the milk jug.

'Sometimes it felt as if she were more like his daughter than his sister,' Mrs Dobbs said as she added milk and two spoons of sugar to her cup. 'Peggy, well, she wasn't an easy person to take to.'

Kitty wasn't certain if that last part was a question or a statement. 'No, unfortunately she wasn't. A lot of people have said they found her challenging.' She wondered what Mrs Dobbs wished to tell her that was so difficult. Had she and Alastair been conducting an affair? Or was it the darker, more deadly thought that Kitty had considered?

'Alastair did his best for her, but Peggy was secretive, and he always gave in to her. She liked money and nice things, and she liked knowing other people's secrets. Like it gave her power over them.' Celia raised troubled blue eyes to gaze at Kitty. 'I feel disloyal talking about her like this. You shouldn't speak ill of the dead, should you?' She bit her lip.

'Please don't worry. Anything you tell me I shall keep to myself unless of course it is pertinent to the investigation. Then naturally I should have to pass it on to Inspector Lewis.' Kitty privately intended to tell the inspector as little as possible since he had made it clear that he didn't wish for their assistance in the case.

Celia stirred her tea which was cooling rapidly in the cup. 'Let me be frank. Peggy was blackmailing people. She kept a little black notebook where she wrote things down.' The words came out in a rush.

'I presume that must have been what the person who searched her room was looking for,' Kitty said.

Celia sighed and laid her spoon back on the saucer. 'I think so. I'm afraid as one of the people in her book might have killed her. It was part diary and part accounts.'

'You saw the book?' Excitement leapt in Kitty's stomach, and she tried to stay calm.

Celia lifted her large cream leather handbag onto her lap and opened it. 'I have it here.'

Kitty closed her open mouth with a snap as she accepted the small book from Celia across the table. 'How do you come to have it?' She tucked the book inside her own bag without looking at it. There would be time for that when she was back at home. One woman had already been killed for that book and she had no intention of being the second.

Celia blushed. 'When the police told Alastair that Peggy had been killed, he was in a terrible state. I went round to the flat as soon as I heard. You know what Dartmouth is like, Mrs Bryant, news travels fast. I made him a cup of tea and insisted as he went to bed. He was trembling all over with the shock of it all. I was tidying up when I suddenly thought what if somebody killed her for that book? So, I went to her room, and I saw at once as it was all in disarray.'

'No one else had been inside that evening? Alastair hadn't entered it? Or the police?' Kitty asked.

'No. I thought as I might have been too late, but I knew where Peggy kept it.' The colour in Celia Dobbs's cheeks deepened. 'I'd seen her the one day when I was at the flat and she hadn't realised as I was there. Her door was open, and I saw her lift a loose board by the side of her bed and hide something under it. I never let on. I mean it was none of my business and it would have looked as if I were spying or something.'

'So you checked her hiding place and you discovered it. You didn't call the police though?' Kitty asked. Why hadn't Celia told the inspector that she had the book or that she had found the room in disarray the night of Peggy's death? Instead, it had been the following day before the police had been alerted.

Celia dropped her gaze. 'I shouldn't have been in that room. I had no right. I was frightened of what might be in that book, Mrs Bryant. That she might have put something in that would hurt Alastair. He's a good man. I know as folks thinks he's a bit dour, but he has a heart of gold.'

'I see, and is there anything in the book about Mr Blaine?' Kitty asked. It seemed as if the thoughts that had struck her earlier were correct.

Celia closed her eyes for a moment as if gathering her

courage. 'The diary is in code when it comes to names but some of them you can work out who she's referring to. She wrote about my late husband's death.'

'Your husband was a very sick man,' Kitty said gently.

A tear leaked out and ran unchecked down Celia's plump cheek. 'He only had days left and he was in terrible pain. He was begging me to help him. You wouldn't let a dog suffer the way he was suffering. He was taking morphine...' Her voice trailed away.

'There was an anomaly in the register?' Kitty guessed. She knew that pharmacists kept such strong medicines under lock and key and every grain had to be accounted for in some way.

'Morphine takes away pain, but it depresses the lungs.' Celia raised anguished eyes to Kitty's face. 'Gabriel passed peacefully in my arms.'

'I'm so glad his death was peaceful,' Kitty said softly, seeing how upset Celia had become. 'Did Peggy ever speak of this to you or to her brother?' Kitty asked quietly.

Celia pulled out a delicately embroidered handkerchief and dabbed at her eyes. 'She hinted that she knew something to me and to Alastair, but Alastair was having none of it and told her to be careful about what she was doing and saying.'

'How did Peggy take that?' Kitty asked. Peggy, with her sharp eyes and tongue, had seldom seemed to be afraid of anything or anyone. From what Celia had already said, it seemed that Alastair had rarely refused his sister anything, or ever said no.

'She backed off. I think she could see that it would be worse for her if Alastair were to get in any trouble.' Celia frowned as she spoke. 'She seemed just lately as if she had found something else, or someone else. She was sort of gloating and smug. She dropped a few hints, saying things like, "when I'm the lady of a fine house". It was as if she had expectations of some kind.'

'What else did you find in the diary?' Kitty asked bluntly.

Celia blushed once more. 'I skimmed through it. I were really only interested in what she might have put about Alastair or my husband. I didn't know what to do with it. I thought as I might be in trouble with the police for taking it and well, if Peggy was killed for it then I might get murdered as well.'

'Does Mr Blaine know that you have Peggy's book?' Kitty's mind raced.

'No, he's enough on his plate and well, he didn't really know about everything as Peggy got up to. When the police found all that money in her room, he was shocked. He's proper cut up about Peggy. He keeps saying as he can't understand who could have done something so terrible,' Celia said.

'But you knew where it had most likely come from?' Kitty could see that Celia was a much more astute judge of Peggy's character than Alastair had been.

Mrs Dobbs sighed. 'I put two and two together. I knew what she was capable of more than Alastair did.'

'Did you know who Peggy's boyfriend was? Does she talk about him in her diary? I presume this was where her expectations had come from about a fine house?' Kitty asked.

Celia fidgeted with the strap on her handbag. 'She talks about someone in code but doesn't give a name. You'll see, Mrs Bryant, when you read it.'

'One more thing, Mrs Dobbs, do you know if Peggy possessed a paper knife? One she had acquired from the museum?'

Celia blinked. 'Yes, she did. A brass and steel one with a fancy handle. She said it was a gift from a friend.'

Kitty could see that Celia was anxious to be gone, having unburdened herself and given her the diary. 'I see. Thank you, Mrs Dobbs. I'll make sure this is safe and will pass it to the police if there is anything inside it that may help them.' So, Peggy had persuaded someone to buy her the knife she had admired at the museum.

Celia stood and gathered her things. 'They don't need to know how you come by it?' she asked anxiously.

Kitty shook her head. 'Don't worry. I'll think of something.' She wasn't sure if she should have said that, but Celia had entrusted her with so many secrets.

The older woman scampered away, leaving Kitty with the bill for tea and Peggy's diary burning a hole in her handbag.

CHAPTER EIGHTEEN

Kitty hurried about the town completing the tasks on Mrs Craven's list, her mind still busy mulling over everything she had just learned from Celia. It seemed her speculation that Gabriel Dobbs's demise had been brought forward by a few days was correct. She wondered what other secrets Peggy's diary might hold.

She stopped off at the ironmonger's and purchased a tiny pink collar with a bell for Rascal from the limited selection of pet supplies. Her errands completed, she walked swiftly to the Dolphin where she knew her evening staff would be reporting for work.

The bartenders who had been working on the day of the pageant usually waited tables in the dining room for evening meals before moving to the ballroom to look after the bar. At this time of day, they would be in the kitchen snatching a cup of tea and setting up the tables in the dining room.

She greeted Mary, the hotel receptionist, and popped her head into the office to say hello to Dolly and Mr Lutterworth before heading to the dining room. The spacious room at the

Dolphin was a handsome one with the best table in the bay window affording a view of the embankment.

She found both the men she was looking for placing cutlery and folding the starched linen napkins ready for the evening meal service.

'Afternoon, Miss Kitty.' They both greeted her affably, having been employed by her and her grandmother for a long time.

She responded to their greeting, and not wishing to delay them in their work, plunged straight into her questions.

'You were both bartending on the afternoon of the beauty pageant?' she asked, fully aware that this had been the case.

'Yes, Miss Kitty?' The older of the two paused in between polishing the wine glasses.

'Miss Blaine, the girl that was murdered, acquired a drink, a cocktail, during the intermission. Do either of you recall serving her or serving someone else who purchased the drink for her?' Kitty asked.

She knew the question was something of a long shot, but long shots seemed to be paying off for them just lately.

The older man shook his head. 'No Miss Kitty, I can't say as I served her.'

The younger member of her staff had also stopped in his tasks and his brow was deeply furrowed in concentration. 'It was right busy at the bar that afternoon, Miss Kitty. I'm a trying to think.'

Kitty waited patiently, knowing the man was doing his best to recollect the events of that afternoon.

'There was a young man who came with a crowd, they was buying plenty of champagne, and ordering cocktails,' the older man suggested.

'No, it weren't him as bought Miss Blaine a drink, although he did give some of his champagne to both of Sir Vivian's daughters. They was in the pageant too.' The younger man continued to puzzle over the question.

'I thought the one of 'em was agoing to chuck it over him,' the older man chuckled.

Kitty suspected that must have been Dominic Peplow's group and perhaps it had been Araminta who had looked as if she wished to hurl the champagne back.

'There was a group come up to the bar right after they had moved away. Councillor and Mrs Martin and Sir Vivian. That were it. I remember now as it struck me because everyone knows as the councillor has short arms and long pockets. He bought drinks for himself, his mother, Sir Vivian and Miss Blaine. I thought at the time perhaps she was to take it to Miss Dorothy.' The man snapped his fingers satisfied that he had remembered.

'Councillor Martin bought the drinks? Hmm.' Kitty was somewhat surprised by this piece of news. Had he intended Peggy to take the drink to Dorothy?

'Old Mrs Martin didn't seem too impressed by his generosity, mind. I reckon as she would rather have had some champagne instead of a ginger ale.' Both men seemed to find this quite amusing.

Kitty thanked them both for taking the time to talk to her and returned to the lobby.

'Your grandmother is out, Miss Kitty, if you were thinking of calling on her. Mrs Craven has invited her to an early supper,' Mary informed her as Kitty was about to head for the stairs.

'Oh, thank you, Mary. Please tell her I dropped in. I'll head back home then.' Kitty smiled warmly at the receptionist.

Feeling slightly guilty at her sense of relief that she could leave sooner, Kitty hurried back to her car. She was eager to get home so she and Matt could examine Peggy's diary.

When she arrived home, she was surprised to find her usual parking space occupied by the familiar black motor car that

Chief Inspector Greville usually drove. She pulled up beside it and hopped out. Surely Inspector Lewis hadn't taken his complaints higher up the chain of command?

She let herself into the hall and took off her hat and coat. The murmur of masculine voices reaching her from the sitting room. She guessed that there must be refreshments on offer as Bertie had not bumbled out to greet her in his usual lively fashion.

'Kitty, my dear,' Matt greeted her with a kiss on the cheek as both men stood when she entered the sitting room. The remains of one of Mrs Smith's ginger cakes was on a plate and empty teacups were on the coffee table.

'Good afternoon, Mrs Bryant. I thought I would drop by and see you both. A little bird told me that my new inspector may not have been keeping you fully in the loop, so to speak.' Chief Inspector Greville resumed his seat on the sofa and self-consciously brushed a few stray crumbs of ginger cake from his tie.

Bertie, who was lying at his feet, looked up hopefully in case any larger titbits might follow.

'I'm sure the inspector is a very busy man,' Kitty said as she sank down onto a vacant chair opposite her husband. The guilty secret about the contents of her handbag weighed heavily on her conscience.

She knew she should speak up and offer Peggy's diary to the chief inspector, but she desperately wanted to read the contents for herself first before handing it over.

'From what Captain Bryant has told me it seems you have both uncovered a lot of information which the inspector appears to have missed.' Chief Inspector Greville looked quite unhappy about this.

'I expect it's difficult when you're a stranger to learn who you need to speak to. Torquay is quite different from Yorkshire.'

Kitty saw Matt's brows rise slightly at her gentle defence of the inspector.

'Even so, Mrs Bryant, I appreciate Inspector Lewis has some very modern ideas on policing, but I shall be keeping a close eye on him. I'd appreciate you continuing to pass on any information that may be useful to myself and obviously to Inspector Lewis. I have suggested to him that he may wish to reconsider his stance on some aspects of police work.' Chief Inspector Greville prepared to take his leave.

'Of course, sir. Thank you, we appreciate that.' Matt rose too and went to see the policeman out while Kitty remained, once again feeling guilty.

Matt returned after a few minutes and Kitty heard the police car pulling off the drive.

'Well, Mrs Bryant, what is going on?' Matt asked as soon as he was back in the sitting room.

Kitty picked up her handbag and took out Peggy's diary. 'I ran into Celia Dobbs in Dartmouth, and she gave me Peggy's little black book. The one everyone has been searching for.'

* * *

Matt stared at his wife and released an oath under his breath. 'How did she get it? Have you looked at it yet?'

'Not yet, no.' She explained everything she had learned from Celia Dobbs and from the bartenders at the Dolphin.

Matt leaned back in his chair once she had finished. 'We shall have to give this to Inspector Lewis.' He looked at the small black leather-bound book.

'I know. Celia says that Peggy made most of her entries in code. The diary is at the front of the book and her accounts are at the back.' Matt could see that Kitty was itching to study the notebook's contents.

'And she couldn't work out who Peggy's boyfriend might have been?' Matt asked. Someone had got the girl pregnant.

Kitty shook her head and her blonde curls danced. 'No, shall we have a look through?' she suggested.

'We'll have to give it in first thing tomorrow,' Matt warned as he moved from his seat to the sofa, collecting his notes from the bureau on his way. He was as eager as Kitty to see what they could learn from Peggy's diary. However, the chief inspector had done them a great service by asking Inspector Lewis to work with them. This discovery of the diary could jeopardise that, if not handled correctly.

'Of course', Kitty agreed as she came to join him so they could study the contents of the book together.

'Start at the back first. You said that's where Celia said the accounts were kept? If we can work out who she has received money from then that might help to decode the diary portion of the book,' Matt suggested.

Kitty flipped the book open at the back to reveal neat columns of pounds, shillings and pence. Dates and initials were inscribed at the side.

'Goodness, how much money was in Peggy's room?' Kitty looked at the figures.

'And yet nothing of value was taken,' Matt said. It was a considerable sum. He found that quite curious. Had the person who had killed Peggy and searched her room had no need of the money? Or had they been worried that they might be traced in some way if they had taken it?

'Right, who are these people?' Kitty asked.

'NC, that must be Naomi, the date next to the initials lines up with what she told you.' Matt scribbled in his notes.

'DM must be Dorothy but no money, instead she's put an I in the column. Presumably as Dodo Martin's currency was information.' Kitty was clearly stunned by the planning Peggy had put into her blackmailing business.

'VC, Victoria Carstairs, Sir Vivian's stepdaughter. Hmm, quite a sum there too. Where is Victoria getting her money from? She was paying Peggy off, and she has to be giving Peplow money. I can't see him providing her with free drugs.' Matt frowned as he made a note.

'Sexual favours?' Kitty blushed as she made the suggestion.

Matt grinned. 'Perhaps. There are a few entries here I don't recognise. JM?'

Kitty leaned back for a moment. 'This may be a stretch, but Dorothy's father is James. What if the drink he bought at the pageant *was* for Peggy and not Dodo? He could be another of her victims.'

Matt nodded slowly. 'Yes, that's a distinct possibility. We know it was an unusual gesture from him and he bought his own mother a ginger ale rather than a cocktail.' If they were correct, then it might give Councillor Martin a motive for murdering Peggy. The information Dorothy had given Peggy could have been used against the councillor in some way.

Kitty waited for Matt to make a note of all the initials and dates in the accounts section of the book.

'Right, let's start from the beginning and see what we can work out,' Matt said as he scribbled the last note.

'I feel rather odd about reading Peggy's private diary even though she was clearly a rather wicked and dangerous girl,' Kitty said as she turned back the pages to the start of the notebook.

Matt knew what she meant. It left a feeling of being somehow sullied and tarnished with something of Peggy's nature on every page that was turned.

'It seems to be something of a journal, rather than a daily diary. She has just dated a page and made an entry when it seems something she felt was significant occurred,' Kitty said as she flipped through the first couple of pages before starting to read.

'Let's see, then.' Matt waited for Kitty to turn back to the first page.

'The first entry is dated a year ago.' Kitty watched as Matt made a note 'There aren't as many entries as I'd expected.'

The first entry consisted of the dead girl vowing to change her life, speaking of how unhappy and trapped she felt working in her brother's shop.

'Well, that seems to be the motivation for the blackmail,' Kitty said. 'It's dated from her eighteenth birthday.'

'She was just nineteen when she was killed. A life cut short.' Matt was sombre as he read the short entry.

'The next entry mentions one of the sets of initials we can't identify. It says she heard something to her advantage in the shop. "*A casual remark to EW and I'm several shillings better off.*"' Kitty's eyes widened. 'That was clearly the beginning of her blackmail career.'

There were several more entries along similar lines as the year moved forward.

'Here is the one that must be about Celia Dobbs and her brother easing Gabriel Dobbs's death.' Kitty read it aloud. 'A is infatuated with CD and GD continues an impediment. A dispensed a new script today and I think this may be the one. He made a fuss of a spill in the dispensary and afterwards I happened to glance at the register to see the counts had been altered. I shall remember this should he try to stand in my way.'

'That gives Celia and Alastair strong motives for Peggy's death,' Matt remarked as he made his own notes. 'Yet, her brother was in the dispensary all day when Peggy was killed. The assistant stood alongside him all afternoon. I suppose Celia could have done it?' He looked at Kitty.

'We don't know if she had an alibi but then why would she approach me with this book? Surely if she or Alastair were implicated, she would have burned this, and no one would have been any the wiser.' Kitty turned the page.

Matt thought his wife made a good point. The next entry noted the death of Celia's husband two days later. The following entries mentioned various initials with cryptic remarks about misdemeanours.

'Those tally up with various payments that she listed in the back of the book, usually within a week of the entry,' Matt said.

'No clue yet to her love life.' Kitty frowned. 'Perhaps this was just used for her blackmail victims, as a record.'

Matt smiled gently. Kitty sounded disappointed and he guessed that she'd hoped the book would provide more clues to who the father of Peggy's child might have been.

'Oh, wait!' Kitty said, as she turned over the page.

CHAPTER NINETEEN

Kitty's frown deepened as she read aloud. "*Today I met the key to my escape. He seems taken with me so I shall use this to my advantage. I shall engineer meetings to find out more and use my spies.*" What do you suppose that means? She has marked the entry with a star and it's clearly very important. Is this the gentleman friend do you suppose, or does she think this is a wealthy victim for her blackmail scheme?'

Matt studied the entry. 'I see what you mean, it could be taken either way. You said that Celia told you she had read these entries and couldn't work out who Peggy's beau may have been?'

'That's what she said, and I think she was telling me the truth. She was very frank about everything else,' Kitty said. 'There are only a few more entries.'

'There is the one about Naomi and the one about Dorothy.' Matt pointed to the page and tapped it with his finger. 'Back there she hints at information from Dorothy that has been lucrative.'

"*One of my admirers has gifted me the perfume I wished for, at my suggestion of course. I have told him of my expectation of a little stranger. I think our wedding will surprise more than a few people.'"* Kitty looked up at Matt. 'She knew she was pregnant and told the father. She thought he would marry her.'

'Or decided she would make sure he did. It's the last but one entry.' Matt reached and turned the page.

"'I have entered the pageant. A little jealousy may bring the desired results sooner rather than later as my patience is being tried. Not that he has a choice if he wishes to retain his standing." What does she mean by that do you think? Was her boyfriend not keen on marrying her?' Kitty flicked on for a few more pages to see if there was anything else in the book but it seemed that the entries had ended.

'A little jealousy. Hmm, that suggests that she might be playing one man against another, perhaps? She wrote *one of my admirers,*' Kitty said.

'Yes, it's a distinct possibility. There is a lot in that diary. More than a few people had a motive to kill Peggy,' Matt said as he leaned back on the sofa and looked at the notes he'd made.

Kitty closed the book and drummed her fingers on the cover. 'I can see why a killer might want to get hold of it. Even with the cryptic initials and the cagey references, this thing is dynamite.'

'First thing tomorrow, we'll take this to the police station.' Matt picked up the book. 'I'll lock it away for now in the bureau. At least it will be safe there overnight.' After locking it away, Matt tucked the key to the drawer in the pocket of his jacket.

Kitty petted the top of Bertie's head as he nudged against her knee, reminding her of his presence. She hoped the inspector would be more amenable to working with them when they gave him the book. It would be awful if the good work Chief Inspector Greville had done on their behalf with Inspector Lewis were to be damaged in any way.

* * *

The air still held a chilly note when they set off for Torquay the next day after an early breakfast. Kitty shivered as they exited the car to walk up the steps into the police station. Matt had retrieved the book from the bureau and had it safely inside his coat pocket.

'Captain Bryant, Mrs Bryant, good morning, how can I help you today?' The desk sergeant greeted them affably as they entered the lobby.

'I'm afraid we do need to trouble Inspector Lewis about the Blaine murder, and it is very important,' Matt said when they reached the desk.

The sergeant's bushy eyebrows rose slightly but he picked up the receiver of the black Bakelite telephone on his counter and dialled.

'Yes sir, I know sir, but I have visitors in the reception with very important information regarding the Blaine murder.'

Kitty's own curiosity was piqued by the sergeant's subterfuge at not giving their name to the inspector. She could only assume that Inspector Lewis was still resisting Chief Inspector Greville's instructions that he work with them.

'Very good, sir.' The sergeant replaced the receiver. 'The inspector says he can spare you a few minutes.'

They followed the policeman through the door behind the counter and into the familiar corridor with its faint scent of disinfectant and day-old cabbage. The sergeant knocked on the door of the inspector's office, and at the summons to enter, left them to go inside.

Inspector Lewis was seated behind his desk as they entered the room. It struck Kitty anew at how tidy the room seemed compared to the chaos that had prevailed when Chief Inspector Greville had occupied it.

The inspector looked up and rose briefly from his chair on

seeing Kitty next to Matt. His expression indicated resignation at their appearance in front of his desk. 'Good morning, please take a seat.' He waved an indifferent hand at the two deal chairs which were clearly reserved for visitors.

'Good morning, Inspector, we hope we are not disturbing you.' Kitty was determined to be polite no matter how irritating or unmannerly the inspector might prove to be.

'My sergeant informs me that you have *important* information about Miss Blaine's murder.'

Matt reached inside his coat pocket and drew out Peggy's notebook and passed it across to Inspector Lewis. 'Peggy's diary came into our possession late yesterday and we felt after seeing the contents that you should have it. It may assist in the hunt for her murderer.'

Kitty marvelled at the bland tone of her husband's voice.

The inspector stared at the small, black book lying before him on his blotter. 'Peggy Blaine's diary?'

'It contains her accounts and coded sources of who had paid her. Peggy seemed to have established a successful blackmail business. It seems likely it was what the killer was searching for when her room at the flat was ransacked,' Kitty said.

The inspector gaped at them for a moment. 'Where did you get this?'

Matt glanced at Kitty. 'That's not really important. The person who had it hadn't realised the significance of the book. Once they did, they gave it to us to pass to you.'

The inspector's lips compressed into a tight line and his cheeks inflated into two crimson balloons. Kitty thought the man might be about to have a stroke.

'I had heard rumours obviously about Miss Blaine. I have had officers all over Dartmouth asking questions and combing the town to establish if this book exists, and you, you... turn up with it.' The inspector paused to glare at them. 'Now, who gave you this book and how did they obtain it?' His voice rose to a dull roar, and he thumped the desk for emphasis making the small brass pen holder vibrate on the wooden surface.

'The book had been hidden by Peggy in her room. The person who found it knew of Peggy's hiding places. Once they knew her room had been searched, they checked and found it was still where Peggy had hidden it. As Matt said, they didn't realise fully the significance of their discovery until yesterday evening.' Kitty stretched the truth slightly. She had no desire to get Celia into trouble. After all, the woman could have kept quiet and destroyed the book. No one would have been any the wiser.

'They knew where Peggy hid things in her room!' the inspector exploded. 'And didn't come to the police?'

'Sometimes people worry about being involved in police matters, especially matters as serious as a murder,' Matt said.

'I take it our information about the knife was of use?' Kitty asked as the inspector picked up the diary, trying to change the subject.

'That was you, was it, Mrs Bryant? I might have guessed when my sergeant was so coy about telling me he'd received a tip-off.' Inspector Lewis looked as if he had sucked on a lemon.

'The knife was a gift to Peggy from an admirer,' Kitty explained and saw the inspector's expression grow even more sour.

At that moment the telephone on the inspector's desk gave two short rings and Kitty guessed this must signal the transfer of an internal call from the front desk.

Inspector Lewis excused himself and picked up the receiver. Kitty could hear the rumble of the desk sergeant's voice but couldn't make out the nature of the call.

'Get one of the constables to bring the car around and telephone Dr Carter. I'll be right there.' The inspector replaced the receiver in its cradle before standing. 'I'm afraid the matter of this diary and how you came by it will have to wait. I'm needed at Sir Vivian's house.'

Kitty picked up her bag and rose to join Matt. 'Oh dear, I presume something bad has happened if you have requested Dr Carter to attend?' What could have happened at the Hardcastle house? Was it one of the girls? Or Sir Vivian himself?

The inspector collected his hat and coat from a hook on the wall in the corner of his office.

'You might say that Mrs Bryant, Miss Victoria Carstairs has just been found dead in her room.' He ushered them out of the office, locking the door behind him.

A moment later they were outside the front of the police station and the inspector was being driven off towards Paignton.

'Good heavens, poor Victoria. An accident, do you think, or murder?' Kitty asked as she rested her gloved hand on Matt's arm for support. The unexpected news had left her feeling more than a little shaken. They had been with Victoria only yesterday.

'I don't know. I expect we may learn more in the next few hours. If it is connected in some way to Peggy's death, then no doubt Chief Inspector Greville will find a way of informing us,' Matt said as he covered her hand with his, sensing her distress.

'It may be suicide,' Kitty mused. 'Victoria seemed to be quite an unhappy girl. I just wish we had not parted from her the other day in such unhappy circumstances.'

'I know darling, it's most distressing. We also cannot rule out an overdose.' Matt's expression was sombre as they walked the short distance to her car.

'Let's go home for now,' Kitty suggested. There seemed little else they could do until they knew more about what had happened to Victoria.

* * *

They had scarcely been back at the house for half an hour when the telephone rang. Kitty waited in the sitting room where she had been playing with her kitten while Matt took the call in the hall.

'We have a visitor on his way over,' he said as he re-entered the room.

'The chief inspector?' Kitty asked as she rolled up the piece of yarn she had been dangling for the kitten. She would need to check with their housekeeper to make sure they had cakes or biscuits to hand.

Matt shook his head. 'No, it appears Mr Peplow has decided to call and see us.'

'Dominic Peplow?' Kitty scrambled to her feet and brushed down her skirt. This was an unexpected twist in an extraordinary day.'

'The very same. He sounded perturbed. He said Victoria had given him our card and after hearing of her death he wanted advice.'

Kitty sank down on the sofa. 'I see.'

Victoria's death must have greatly distressed the man if he had finally decided he wished to speak to them. He had been avoiding them for long enough. Kitty let Mrs Smith know that a guest was expected, and they waited for Mr Peplow to arrive.

The rumble of a powerful motor engine outside the house a few minutes later alerted them to his arrival. Bertie bounced to the door, tail wagging in joyful expectation to greet their guest when the bell rang.

'Kitty darling, this is Mr Peplow, Mr Peplow, my wife and business partner, Kitty Bryant.' Matt made the introductions as he showed the man into the sitting room before alerting Mrs Smith to bring tea.

'Do take a seat, Mr Peplow. I'm very sorry for your loss. We only learned of Miss Carstairs death a short time ago.' Kitty waited for the man to take a seat on one of the fireside armchairs.

Close up in daylight she could see that he was somewhat younger than she had first thought. Perhaps in his late twenties, the dashing air of cocky confidence which always seemed to surround him had dissolved. One thing was certain. Dominic Peplow was a frightened man.

CHAPTER TWENTY

Mrs Smith carried in the tray of tea, deposited it on the coffee table and made a discreet exit. Matt took a seat on the sofa.

Kitty busied herself with pouring tea for their unexpected guest, herself and Matt. Bertie stationed himself at Matt's feet, his eyes fixed on the plate of shortbread biscuits which Mrs Smith had placed on the tray.

'Now, how may we help you, Mr Peplow?' Kitty asked once tea had been dispensed and the niceties dealt with.

She saw the Adam's apple bob in his throat before he spoke. 'Victoria telephoned me yesterday and said that you wished to speak to me. I had heard that you had been making enquiries in Torquay.' Mr Peplow's gaze flitted to Matt.

'And yet you didn't come forward?' Kitty said.

'Sir Vivian Hardcastle, Victoria's stepfather disapproves of me. I suspected it was he that was really looking for me in order to poke his nose in my affairs.' The man's voice took on a harder tone.

'Why would that be a concern? Victoria was of age, and he was her stepfather. He and her mother had divorced, and I understand Victoria's mother is currently on honeymoon with her new husband.' Kitty kept her tone mild. There was a lot she didn't understand about Dominic Peplow's relationship with the Hardcastle family, and she was determined to get to the bottom of it all.

'Sir Vivian is an influential man. He's hoping to be adopted as an electoral candidate. He's not a man you would wish to cross.' Dominic's gaze shifted again.

'How did you and Victoria meet?' Matt asked.

Dominic swallowed again. 'Through Araminta. Minty and I are old chums, we know a lot of the same crowd. She introduced me to Victoria when they returned to Torquay from Egypt.'

'Araminta doesn't seem to be especially friendly towards you at the moment, was this because of Victoria?' Kitty asked. She had wondered if Araminta had been Dominic's love interest to start with and had been supplanted by her stepsister. It would account for the rivalry that had seemed to exist between the two girls.

Again, Dominic's gaze seemed to skitter around, and he shifted in his seat. 'I don't know, I think Minty may have been jealous of Victoria.'

Kitty looked at Matt. She was unconvinced by Dominic's replies and decided she might as well just be blunt with her questions. 'Was she? Or was she concerned because she knew you were supplying Victoria with cocaine?'

Dominic jolted, spilling some of his tea into the saucer. 'I... um...'

'That's why you are here, isn't it? Victoria's death is linked to an overdose of a drug that you supplied and now you are concerned for your own neck?' Kitty wasn't going to pussyfoot around. He'd been avoiding them for days and if he wanted their help, then he had to tell them the truth. It was a bit of a punt to guess how Victoria may have died but there had to be a connection. Why else would Dominic look so afraid or have come to seek them out?

'It was all meant to be a bit of fun.' Dominic set his cup and saucer back down on the tray and buried his face in his hands.

'Supplying someone with cocaine so they became addicted and were dependent upon you for their supply? How is that a bit of fun?' Matt asked, picking up the questioning.

'Victoria was already an addict. She had developed a problem when they were in Egypt, but she had convinced her mother and Sir Vivian that she had stopped. She discovered that I sometimes provided a few grams for my friends. No one was meant to get hurt. But Victoria wanted more and more.' Kitty could see tiny beads of sweat forming on Dominic's temples.

'How did she find the money to pay you? I don't suppose this generous provision was a gift?' Matt's tone was stern.

Kitty waited for Dominic Peplow's answer. This was the question that had been troubling them since they had learned about his relationship with Victoria.

'I... um, she took things from the house. Once she'd used up the allowance her mother had given her. She was only staying with Sir Vivian as she had nowhere else to go and no real money of her own. Her allowance was small as her mother didn't want her to get sucked back into addiction.' Peplow shifted uncomfortably once more in his seat.

'And yet you were happy to facilitate her need for cocaine. What kind of things did she steal?' Kitty asked.

Dominic seemed to shrink in his seat. 'Sir Vivian didn't declare a lot of the things he had found on his digs in Egypt. A lot of smaller finds, precious things set with gold and jewels, he stuck to them and brought them back to England. He would sell them on the black market when he was strapped for cash. Victoria knew about them and, well, she took a few for herself. Sir Vivian found out, of course. That was why he hated me; he wanted to find out what I knew and how I had obtained the pieces. I suspect one of the dealers I used tipped him off.'

Kitty blew out a breath. This certainly answered the question why Sir Vivian wished to know more about Dominic Peplow. It wasn't concern for Victoria but more about the missing antiquities. 'I see,' she said.

'Victoria knew that Sir Vivian couldn't go to the police. There would be a lot of awkward questions to answer about where the things had come from,' Dominic said miserably. 'With his political ambitions, it wouldn't be good.'

'How did you learn of Victoria's death?' Kitty asked.

'Minty telephoned me. She said that Victoria was dead, and it was all my fault. She'd taken too much stuff and choked in her sleep.' Dominic leaned back in the armchair, his shoulders slumped. 'She said the police would want to question me.'

'And you thought that you would make contact with us to see what your options might be?' Matt fixed the man with a stern look.

'I suppose something like that. Minty suggested that I had something to do with the murder of that other girl. The one from the chemist's shop,' Dominic said.

'And did you?' Kitty asked.

'No, why would I?' Dominic seemed to recover some of his strength in order to deny any involvement in Peggy's death.

'Because she recognised that Victoria was in the grip of drug addiction and she had you pinned as her supplier. She was blackmailing Victoria. Someone else leaching off her.' Kitty had little sympathy for the man in the chair opposite her.

'I didn't know that.' Dominic seemed genuinely startled by this revelation. 'I mean she had said this Peggy kept passing comments, but I'd told her not to worry. But not actual blackmail. I thought it was just well, girlish spite.'

'Victoria had not confided in you?' Kitty frowned as she posed the question.

Dominic shook his head. 'I knew she was troubled about something. She'd passed on more items for me to sell. Victoria was a complicated girl. She was deeply unhappy about her mother swanning off and abandoning her. Sir Vivian is not a nice man but at least he gave her a roof over her head, and I think in his way, he was kind to her. She was upset too that she and Minty had fallen out. She wanted to count on her as a true sister.'

'Did you know Miss Blaine? The girl that was murdered?' Matt asked.

Dominic gave a slight shrug. 'Only from Victoria and Minty's connection to her. I think they knew her vaguely. She was at a couple of parties that I threw but I'm not sure who had invited her. I'd heard that she was nasty piece of work. I saw her at the pageant obviously but she was talking to that councillor and Sir Vivian so I steered well clear.'

If Dominic was telling them the truth, then it was unlikely that he was responsible for Peggy's death. He appeared genuinely ignorant of the extent of Peggy's blackmailing activities.

'The police will want to talk to you,' Kitty said.

'I suppose they will have to know about the cocaine?' Dominic licked his lips, a hopeful note in his question.

'That will be unavoidable. If what Minty said was correct and Victoria died of an overdose, then questions will be asked by the coroner at the inquest. I would strongly advise you to make a full and frank confession to Inspector Lewis of your activities on that front.' Matt's tone was stern. 'Do not be foolish enough to think you can evade the police or you may well find a murder charge for Peggy Blaine's death hanging over you.'

'But I just told you, I didn't know anything about that girl blackmailing Victoria. Even if I had known I would just have warned her off. I had no reason to kill a woman I barely knew,' Dominic protested.

'All the more reason to put yourself forward to the police

now, and you may find they deal with you more kindly than they would otherwise,' Matt advised.

Dominic bowed his head and Kitty could see he was thinking through what they had just told him. He appeared to resign himself to the inevitable. 'Very well, I can see I have no other options. I suppose this may lead to a jail sentence?'

'For supplying? Very possibly, but who knows. A good barrister and a lenient judge may make all the difference. Go and see a solicitor and then go to Inspector Lewis at Torquay police station. It will be in your best interests, I assure you,' Matt said.

'Thank you, you have been kinder to me than I deserve.' Mr Peplow rose, ready to depart. 'For what it's worth, I did really like Victoria, she was nice girl and I'm very sorry for her death.'

Matt saw their guest out of the house while Kitty leaned back in her seat with a sigh.

Bertie promptly took advantage of her laxity to snaffle the last biscuit from the plate on the table.

The door had barely closed behind Dominic Peplow when the telephone rang.

'Hello, Brigadier Remmington-Blyth, how lovely to hear from you, sir. I'll just get Matt.' Kitty handed the receiver to Matt as he entered the room. 'The brigadier, for you.'

'Hello, sir,' Matt greeted his former employer and listened intently to the information the brigadier had discovered on Sir Vivian and his expeditions.

Since the brigadier always conducted his telephone conversations by shouting, Kitty overheard a few snatches as she tidied away the tea things. She smiled to herself as Matt gingerly held the receiver a little away from his ear.

'I see, thank you, sir, that's most helpful.'

'Well?' Kitty asked once Matt had replaced the handset. 'I heard him mention Egypt and diplomatic incident.'

'Yes, the brigadier's information seems to back up what Mr

Peplow told us.' Matt sat back down on the sofa.

'Oh?' Kitty resumed her own seat and waited for him to tell her the rest of the story.

'Sir Vivian has made several expeditions into Egypt, and other parts of the region. He has had some quite good finds which were naturally shared with the British Museum and the museum in Cairo. However, there was trouble on the last two archaeological digs that he ran. His backers were disappointed with the finds produced. While they added to the sum of knowledge, there was a distinct lack of valuable pieces. Those in the know began to suspect that not everything that was uncovered was being logged correctly.'

'So Sir Vivian was definitely taking finds for his own purposes?' Kitty said.

Matt nodded. 'That was the rumour. It confirms what we've discovered so far from the museum staff in Torquay and from Mr Peplow. It seems that the museum in Cairo sent out one of their own men to observe Sir Vivian's latest dig but there was an accident.'

'What kind of accident?' Kitty asked. She was beginning to regret the biscuit she had eaten with her tea. This whole morning had taken a horrid turn.

'The car the official was in came off the road and crashed. He, and the driver, were killed. Sir Vivian closed the dig and returned to Torquay. He has been unable to find new backers to resume his work and Egypt has quietly let it be known they will not issue him a permit.' Matt sounded thoughtful.

'Quite the whiff of scandal, and now he wishes to stand for Parliament. No wonder he wanted us to look into Mr Peplow. If some of those black-market items had found their way to the sales rooms it could lead to some awkward questions about where they had come from originally. Surely Sir Vivian must have known we would uncover something like this?' Kitty said. 'But where does that leave us with Peggy's murder? Did she discover any of this? Was she blackmailing Sir Vivian? Or was it just Victoria? She must have been attending those lectures for a reason.'

'We still don't know who Peggy's lover was. It could have been Peplow for all his denials. He was the right age for Peggy, and wealthy,' Matt said.

Kitty considered the idea. It was certainly possible and would provide Peplow with a very strong motive for murdering both Peggy and Victoria. Especially if Victoria had begun to discover more about a relationship with Peggy. She tried to think who else they knew of who might be in the frame.

'Or perhaps Sir Vivian?' Kitty suggested. 'We know he has an eye for the ladies.'

The furrows deepened on Matt's brow as he considered her suggestion. 'Perhaps, or was she at his lectures to discover more information about the stolen artefacts that Victoria had been selling? She could have had him in her sights as a possible blackmail target.'

'There is always the possibility of Dodo Martin's father being Peggy's beau? He bought her a cocktail at the pageant. That was such an uncharacteristic thing for him to do. If she had been flirting with both Councillor Martin and Sir Vivian, then they could have been the men she spoke of in her book. The ones she wished to make jealous. Although I suppose that could also apply to Mr Peplow,' Kitty mused.

'Celia couldn't offer a suggestion to his identity. Do you think perhaps her brother might have a clue?' Matt asked.

'I suppose it's worth a try, although Celia thought he was unaware of who it could be, and she seemed to have a better understanding of Peggy. The shop is still closed as far as I know so we shall have to call at the flat.' Kitty rose. 'Our other option is to try and speak to Councillor Martin.'

'Indeed, surely one of them must help us get closer to the truth,' Matt replied.

CHAPTER TWENTY-ONE

After letting their housekeeper know that they had to go out again, they set off for Dartmouth.

'Is everything in hand for the children's party?' Matt asked as she drove them down the hill towards Kingswear. 'The jubilee is almost upon us, and Mrs Craven will be after you.'

Kitty sighed as they passed the station and saw the River Dart sparkling in the sunshine. 'I have completed my portion of the errands she set me, but I daresay she will try to persuade me into more committee work.'

The idea of being inveigled onto more charity committees filled her with dread. This whole experience of being involved with the activities to celebrate the King and Queen's silver jubilee had been more than enough. She had hoped that after stepping back from managing the Dolphin and becoming a partner in Matt's business, her days would be full. Awful though Peggy's murder was, it had given her own life more purpose.

'Perhaps when this is over, we should study those holiday brochures we have in the bureau and book our honeymoon trip.'

Matt smiled sympathetically at her as they waited for the ferry to dock.

'A holiday would be rather nice.' The South of France did sound quite appealing. Her cousin Lucy had honeymooned there with her husband Rupert the previous year. Time away from Dartmouth and indeed crime, not to mention Inspector Lewis, might be rather pleasant.

Once across the river, she drove towards the boat float so they could park at the side of the marina before walking the short distance to the chemist's shop.

'Where is the party to be held?' Matt asked as she stopped the car.

'In the park if it is fine. If the weather is wet or too cold, then Grams has offered the use of the hotel ballroom once again. I rather fear that may be a tight squeeze and I'm not looking forward to having hordes of children in the hotel.' Kitty locked her car door.

'Let us hope for sunshine.' Matt's smile widened as Kitty took his arm and they set off along the narrow street towards the building that housed the chemist's premises.

The closure notice was still in the window as they passed by. Kitty led the way along the street to where two doors stood inconspicuously side by side. One was for the flat above the chemist's and the other door was for the flat above the tobacconist's shop next door. Kitty sniffed the air curiously, certain she could smell roses or vanilla.

Matt rapped on the door of the Blaines' flat, and they waited for a response. At first Kitty thought no one was going to answer but then the sound of feet descending a wooden stair sounded from behind the closed door.

The dark blue door cracked open, and Celia's round, pale face peeked out at them.

'Oh, Captain Bryant, Mrs Bryant, we weren't expecting you. Do come on up.' The woman opened the door wider, and they ascended the narrow staircase once Celia had shut the door behind them.

Celia bustled up the staircase to join them on the narrow landing, which was lit by a single light bulb dangling from the ceiling on a length of twisted black cable.

'Go on through to the sitting room,' Celia urged as she indicated a cream-painted door in the dimly lit corridor.

Kitty followed Matt into the room and Celia scurried in behind them. The room was surprisingly dark given the bright sunshine beyond the leaded bay window. Heavy red velvet drapes, yellow and sun-faded at the edges, framed the glass which was largely obscured by a vast aspidistra plant in a painted ceramic pot.

The furniture in the room was dark oak and there was a lot of it. The wallpaper on the walls had a heavy red brocade pattern and like the curtains showed signs of fading and age. Pictures of landscapes and sentimental style art hung from ribbons. The effect was depressing and gloomy added to by Alastair Blaine himself who was seated in front of the meagre fire.

'Good afternoon, Mr Blaine, we are sorry to intrude at such a sad time. I'm sure Celia has told you that we are trying to discover who may have killed your sister, and I wonder if we could speak with you?' Kitty said as she approached the grey-faced man seated in the high-backed chair.

She knew Alastair vaguely from seeing him at the shop and around the town. He had always appeared to her a somewhat dour and stern individual. Clearly older than Peggy, her death seemed to have aged him even further. Celia stood near the door wringing her plump hands together.

'Please take a seat, Mrs Bryant, Captain Bryant,' Alastair said at last.

Matt sat on the dark red brocade covered sofa and Kitty took her place beside him.

'Yes, Celia told me that you were assisting the police with their investigation.' Alastair seemed to be finding it a huge effort to speak. His voice sounded weary as if talking cost him all his energy. His eyes seemed sunken and the lines at the corners deeper.

'We wondered if you might be able to tell us anything that might help us. Sometimes we find that given a few days after a terrible event such as Peggy's death, people sometimes recollect things they had forgotten,' Kitty said carefully.

She thought perhaps it had been a mistake to call. Alastair had clearly been greatly affected by his sister's death. She had no wish to cause him further distress.

Alastair lifted his hand from where it rested on the arm of the chair in a tired gesture. 'Ask me anything you wish, Mrs Bryant. Nothing can restore my sister's life, but I dearly want her murderer to be caught and justice to be served.'

'Thank you, sir, we appreciate how difficult this must be.' Matt looked as uncomfortable as Kitty felt.

Alastair's mouth twisted in a grim line. 'You would think that Peggy's death would have been the worst thing I would have to face. Instead, the revelations that have come to light about her and her life since her murder have been far, far worse.'

Matt exchanged a glance with Kitty, and she saw the distress on Celia's face at Alastair's words.

'I have told Alastair about Peggy's notebook and the contents. The police inspector hasn't yet been to ask us about it.' Celia twisted her hands together trapping some of the dark grey material of her dress between her fingers.

'We passed the book on to the police first thing this morning. We didn't reveal how exactly we had acquired the book. Inspector Lewis has been called away to another urgent crime so it may take him a little while before he comes to see you.' Kitty picked her words carefully. Since they were unsure of what exactly had happened to Victoria, she felt that they couldn't reveal that there had been another death.

'What was your reaction to the contents of the book, Mr Blaine?' Matt asked.

The corners of Alastair's mouth tilted upwards but there was no mirth in his smile. 'I was profoundly shocked. We discovered a large sum of money in Peggy's room. I knew that my sister was frugal, and I have always paid her well for assisting me in the shop.' He broke off with a sigh and shook his head before continuing. 'However, this was far beyond anything that she might reasonably have saved. It was clear from the book that she had been using people's secrets against them for her advantage. Sometimes it seemed it was for monetary gain, at other times it was for some other unknown reason.'

'Did she try to do this to you, sir?' Matt asked.

Kitty held her breath as she waited to see how Alastair would respond.

Celia gave a small, choked sob and pressed her handkerchief to her lips.

Alastair moved his head in a brief affirmative nod. 'I know that you are already aware of some of the details. Celia's husband was terminally ill. At best he had about a week or so left, and he was in great pain. The cancer had virtually destroyed him. As a pharmacist, I knew he needed a stronger dose of morphine, but his doctor was unwilling since the effects of the relief would hasten his demise.'

'You would not have left an animal to suffer as my husband was suffering. No decent person would have wanted that, not even for their worst enemy,' Celia broke in, her voice cracking with raw emotion.

Kitty released her breath and waited for the rest of the story to unfold.

'I dispensed a stronger solution, but without a prescription, it would have caused a shortfall in the register if the stock were checked. We have to be very careful with opioids. To balance the books, I had to pretend to make a spill in order to account for the missing amount. Celia's husband passed peacefully later that night. I – we – regret nothing.' Alastair's face was blank.

The room fell silent for a moment broken only by the ticking of the large oak clock on the mantelpiece and the crackle of a log in the hearth.

'Peggy knew what you had done,' Matt said.

'My sister was a very clever girl. She saw the entries in the drug register and my entry recording the wastage and put the events together. She never challenged me directly. After all, I had raised her since she was a young girl and she regarded me as more of a parental figure than as a sibling. Even so, she hinted that she knew and would keep her knowledge to herself in return for my turning a blind eye to some of her affairs.' Alastair sighed deeply.

A shiver ran along Kitty's spine at the bleak expression in Alastair's dark eyes. She could only guess at how much he regretted that decision.

'Were you aware, sir, of Peggy's condition at the time of her death?' Kitty asked.

Celia sobbed quietly into her handkerchief.

'No, Mrs Bryant, not until Dr Carter kindly paid me a visit. He wished to tell me himself as he was uncertain if the information would be made public at the inquest. Naturally, it would cause a great deal of scandal and gossip if this were the case. He wanted to prepare me for such an event, as a personal kindness.' Alastair's lips compressed as if he were struggling with his emotions.

'I'm so sorry to have to continue with this line of questioning, Mr Blaine. I can see this is very painful for you, but it may have a bearing on who could have killed your sister,' Matt said. 'Did you know of a steady boyfriend? Was there anyone that

Peggy may have mentioned who could have been the father of the child?'

Celia sniffed and dabbed fiercely at her eyes before speaking. 'This is the most shameful thing. We only learned of it earlier today.' Her lower lip trembled.

Alastair sighed once more. 'I'm afraid to say that my sister may well have been intimate with more than one man.' He looked at Celia as if to gain strength for what else he was about to reveal.

'Tell them, Alastair,' Celia urged, her voice tremulous behind her handkerchief.

'This morning, quite early, there was a hammering on the door. Celia had only just arrived, but she went down to answer it.' Alastair paused once more as if to gather himself before continuing. 'It was Councillor Martin. It was clear from his demeanour that he was angry about something.'

Kitty was puzzled. What could have happened to trigger such a strong reaction from the councillor? She knew he had a reputation for being mean and brutish, but to intrude on Alastair's grief seemed shocking.

'He smelt of stale alcohol, his eyes were red-rimmed and he had worked himself into a fine temper. He shouted that Alastair should come down the stairs and speak to him about his harlot of a sister.' Tears spilled down Celia's cheeks.

'I went down and told Celia to go back upstairs. The man had clearly lost his mind. I asked him what the matter was. He said that he had learned from his daughter that Peggy had been trying to blacken his name, just because he had been kind to her and bought her a few small gifts, perfume and a gold necklace.' Alastair was trembling as he spoke.

Celia picked up the story. 'I could hear him shouting and raving like a man possessed. In a minute half the town would hear him. I ran into Peggy's room and picked up the perfume. I knew which one he meant; it was the one she took to the pageant. I came back downstairs and threw it at him telling him to take it and be gone. Alastair slammed the door and threw the bolt.' Celia looked at Alastair.

Kitty guessed this would account for the scent she had detected downstairs by the front door. It sounded as If Dorothy had argued with her father and let slip a few home truths sparking the councillor's rage.

'He carried on shouting and banging on the door for a minute or two longer, then he staggered off. We watched him go from the window in here.' Alastair appeared to crumple into his chair with the effort of telling this story.

'Do you think he may have been the father of Peggy's child?' Matt asked in a gentle tone.

Kitty closed her mouth, suddenly aware that she was gaping. The entry in Peggy's journal had strongly suggested that he might be.

'I think it may be a possibility. However, she was also seeing other men. I don't know their names, but she would let slip that she had dined at the Imperial or the Grand or had been taken to Totnes or Newton Abbott,' Alastair confirmed. 'After what she'd discovered about Gabriel's death, I had no choice but to let her do as she wished.'

'Her journal seemed to indicate that she had informed someone of her pregnancy, someone who she believed was the father? Do you think it really may have been Councillor Martin?' Kitty asked, anxious to know if her supposition was correct. Or could it have been someone else?

Alastair gave a faint snort of derision. 'I have no doubt that she would select someone who was in a position to provide for her and convince them of that even if it were not true. Councillor Martin is a wealthy man, if rather mean.'

'But he might not be the only candidate?' Matt asked.

'I gave up arguing with my sister about her moral choices some time ago. I hoped that as she grew older, she might settle down. She always took good care to keep her liaisons secret. Most of her life outside of the shop was a mystery to me. I knew some of the men she was seeing were much older than her. Although there was a young man with a fancy motor car who dropped her off one night outside the shop a couple of weeks ago.' Alastair pressed his fingertips to his temples. 'How I wish now that I had done things differently when she was younger.'

Celia left her seat to kneel at the side of his chair, her hands on his arm. 'Alastair, my love, there was nothing you could have done.'

Kitty privately agreed with Celia. It seemed that Peggy's affairs had been far murkier and more complex than any of them had realised.

'I'm so very sorry, Mr Blaine,' Kitty said.

Alastair lifted a grief-ravaged face to meet her gaze. 'I loved my sister, Mrs Bryant, despite everything. She was all I had. I had watched her grow from a little girl into a beautiful young woman. I sacrificed everything for her when I was young. I passed up my chance to marry, to move away, to advance my career, everything, in order to provide her with a safe and secure home and livelihood. Promise me that you will do your utmost to catch whoever did this?'

Kitty's heart ached at the undeniable grief and confusion in his voice. 'We promise.' She gathered up her bag and gloves ready to depart.

Celia struggled back to her feet. 'I'll see you both out.'

They made their farewells to Alastair Blaine and followed Celia out of the room and back onto the gloomy landing.

'He's in a terrible state,' Celia confided in a hushed tone as she led the way back down to the street door. 'That man turning up this morning, shouting and blustering. It broke him, Captain Bryant.' Celia turned at the bottom of the stairs to reveal a tear-ravaged countenance. 'I threw that bottle of perfume at him and told him to clear off. Heaven only knows what the people in the street must have thought. I had to go out later to get the bits of glass up and wash the perfume away.'

'I'm so sorry, Mrs Dobbs,' Matt said. 'This must be dreadful for both of you.'

'Alastair is a good man. He doesn't deserve any of this. Please, just do your best to solve Peggy's murder. It would be a small comfort to both of us,' Celia said as she unlatched the door to let them out.

'We shall do whatever we can.' Matt patted the woman's arm before stepping out into the street.

'Indeed, we shall,' Kitty affirmed as she followed her husband.

'Thank you.' Celia closed the door.

Kitty slipped her hand into the crook of Matt's arm, grateful for his solid strength as they walked silently together back towards her car. The revelations about Peggy and Councillor Martin had taken them both by surprise. Kitty wasn't certain now how the case would proceed.

She had been convinced that if they could discover who the father of Peggy's baby might be, then that person would be a strong suspect for her murder. Now however it seemed that this was not necessarily the case.

They were also none the wiser about who Peggy had selected as the most likely candidate to marry her and to be the child's father. Councillor Martin was now a firm possibility. His reaction to whatever he had wormed out of Dorothy was certainly quite extreme.

Or was it Dominic Peplow, despite his denials? She doubted that he was the most truthful or reliable of witnesses. Had he lied to them about the extent of his involvement with Peggy though? He could have been the young man with the expensive motor car.

Then there was Sir Vivian Hardcastle, a known womaniser with a liking for young girls. Had he been involved with Peggy?

They knew he had lied about only knowing her from her attendance at his lectures. The museum staff had been convinced
there was more to it than that. There was also the question of
his own dodgy dealings. It was all so complicated.

They reached the boat float and Kitty released Matt's arm
in order to unlock her car. 'I suppose we should return home. If
the councillor was in his cups just a few hours ago we are
unlikely to be able to talk to him.'

'I think so, there seems to be little more we can do for now,'
Matt agreed.

Kitty slipped behind the wheel. 'It's so frustrating. I wish
we could have gone to the Hardcastles' house to discover
exactly what happened to poor Victoria.'

'Yes, it would be good to ask Sir Vivian a few more questions. Especially about those artefacts.' Matt looked across at
Kitty as she started the engine.

'And to talk to Araminta. From what Dominic said today,
there is a lot that she must know that she deliberately hasn't
shared about Peplow and Victoria. I'd love to know if she is
aware of her father's dealings and of how Victoria was affording
her cocaine habit,' Kitty said as she pulled away from the kerb to
drive to the ferry.

'I know, but those questions will have to wait. Inspector
Lewis was very clear that we are to stay away,' Matt said.

'Then we shall have to think of another approach.' Kitty
smiled as she pulled onto the boat to cross the river.

CHAPTER TWENTY-TWO

Matt was surprised not to be greeted by Bertie when he entered the house. Usually, the spaniel would come bouncing towards them, tail wagging with joy at their return. Mrs Smith, the housekeeper, had departed for the day and there was no sign of either Bertie or Rascal in the kitchen or scullery.

'Where is Bertie?' Kitty asked as she paused at the hall stand to remove her hat and coat.

Matt pushed open the door to the sitting room and, stifling his laughter, called Kitty to witness the sight before them. Bertie was curled up in front of the fire with Rascal nestled into him, fast asleep.

'It seems we need not worry about the two of them getting along,' Matt said.

Kitty chuckled. 'Indeed. Although they only seem to do this whenever we are both out.'

After realising they had missed lunch, Kitty disappeared into the kitchen to prepare something to eat. Mrs Smith had left a casserole in the oven which would be ready later for their supper.

While Kitty was busy, Matt took the opportunity to take out the notes he had made so far on Peggy's murder. He wanted to capture all of the new information they had gathered during the course of the day. Writing it all down would help him to order his thoughts.

It seemed to him too that they would have to make a report to Sir Vivian at some point. He was after all, still their client. Quite how matters would stand now in the light of Victoria's death, he wasn't sure. The man might not wish them to report their findings on Dominic Peplow. Or he might wish to use anything they had discovered to get the man arrested, despite the risk to his own reputation.

Ordinarily, Matt would have assumed that Sir Vivian would have been seeking to have Dominic incarcerated and charged, but the alleged theft of antiquities complicated matters. There was no way that he could see Sir Vivian wishing that allegation to be aired in a public arena, even with Victoria's death.

Bertie lifted his head hopefully when Kitty entered the room bearing a tray laden with sandwiches and slices of fruitcake.

'I thought this would keep us going until suppertime,' she said as she set down the tray.

'Thank you, darling. I decided I'd update the notes I made on Peggy's murder.' Matt set the papers to one side and helped himself to cheese and pickle sandwiches and a slice of pork pie.

'Have you any new thoughts on the matter?' Kitty asked as she poured them both a steaming cup of coffee from the elegant chrome-plated pot that had been a wedding gift from her cousin.

Matt leaned back in his chair and munched on his food while he considered the notes he'd just made. 'I have to confess that nothing obvious is leaping out at me. To my mind, unless there is someone else in the picture that we are unaware of, the obvious suspects must be Councillor Martin, Sir Vivian and

Dominic Peplow. All have a motive, all had opportunity and none of them have told the truth or behaved very well,' he said after he'd swallowed his sandwich.

Kitty loaded her own plate and frowned thoughtfully. 'What about the other girls? If we set aside the pregnancy, then it seems to me that Naomi and Dorothy could have had motives for killing Peggy. Indeed, so could Victoria. We don't yet know if her death was an accident, murder or even suicide.'

Matt could see her point. Peggy's murder could have been committed by any of the people Kitty had mentioned. The other girls could have asked Peggy to meet them quickly away from the pageant with the promise of money or a juicy secret. It would have been the work of an instant to kill the girl and return to the hotel ballroom.

If Peggy had been in the habit of carrying her paperknife with her in her bag, then they could have extracted it and sharpened it at the rehearsal. That implied a degree of premeditation that made his blood run cold.

Equally, the same access to the knife could have been gained by any of the male suspects, depending on when Peggy had last met with them.

He picked up his coffee and took a sip. 'Who is the most likely suspect in your view?' He was curious to hear her thoughts. Kitty often had a way of working things out from the tiniest of clues.

She brushed a few crumbs from the front of her cherry-red serge frock and considered his question. 'I don't know. It's all such a jumble in my head at the moment. I think Dominic Peplow has to be near the top of the list, however. We must find a way to get to the Hardcastles' house and investigate what has happened there. Is it linked to Peggy's murder or is Victoria's death just a ghastly coincidence? I think knowing more might help us get to the bottom of all this.'

Rascal seemed to stir at her words, opening a tiny mouth in a huge yawn before rolling away from a relieved-looking Bertie.

'Poor Bertie.' Kitty called the dog to her side to pet him and reward his patience with the kitten by slipping him a sliver of cheese.

'I think I'll try the police station later and see if I can speak to Chief Inspector Greville. He may be able to tell us a little of what has gone on. Perhaps later we can try and speak to Councillor Martin,' Matt said.

'Inspector Lewis may even have arrested Mr Peplow already if he has followed our advice to obtain a solicitor and go to the police voluntarily.' Kitty stacked the used crockery back on the tray ready to return it to the kitchen.

'Very true,' Matt agreed.

Kitty carried the tray away and returned to the sitting room a few minutes later carrying Bertie's leash. 'I think I'll take Bertie out onto the common for a walk. It might help to clear my head. Do you want to come?' she asked as the dog bounced happily to her side at the mention of a walk.

Matt shook his head. 'Would you mind if I stayed here? I would like to go over these notes again. I keep thinking that we've missed something.'

Kitty laughed and assured him that she didn't mind before attaching Bertie's leash to his collar.

A few moments later, the front door closed, and he heard the sound of Kitty's shoes crunching on the gravel driveway as she set off on her walk. The kitten came to mew at his feet, and he spent some minutes playing with the tiny creature before picking up his notes once more.

He started to read through the papers once more, wishing he could work out what was niggling him about the case. The ring of the black Bakelite telephone cut into his thoughts and he dislodged the kitten from his lap to answer the call.

'Chief Inspector, I had intended to telephone you later.' Matt greeted the policeman warmly on hearing his familiar voice.

'Inspector Lewis has informed me that you and Mrs Bryant delivered Miss Blaine's journal to the police station this morning.'

'Yes, sir, we obtained it after your own visit to our house.' Matt decided it was best to blur the truth of when Kitty had acquired the notebook. He knew the chief inspector would have been very annoyed had he known they were in possession of the book already when he had called.

'I also hear that you were with the inspector when the news came in of Miss Victoria Carstairs' untimely demise,' the chief inspector said.

'That's correct, sir, we were about to leave when the inspector took the telephone call.' Matt wondered where this conversation might be leading.

'I presume too, that Mr Peplow's visit to the station this lunchtime with his solicitor was also after he had spoken to you and Mrs Bryant?'

Matt confirmed this had been the case. 'We had been trying to speak to him for a few days as Sir Vivian had engaged us to investigate, as he was wary of Mr Peplow's motives for his friendship with Miss Carstairs,' Matt said.

A gusty sigh reached him through the telephone receiver. 'Inspector Lewis is most unhappy about your involvement with the case. As you know he had already spoken to me about it. He is insistent that you take no further actions in the investigation.'

'I see, sir. Of course, we have no wish to antagonise the inspector, or indeed to hamper him in any way. Quite the reverse, I rather think we have been most helpful.' Matt decided that he was not about to take this lying down. Without his and Kitty's help the inspector would not have obtained Peggy's journal and Dominic Peplow would most likely have disappeared.

Chief Inspector Greville sighed again. 'Personally, I feel that you and Mrs Bryant have indeed given the inspector quite a lot of assistance in the case. Certainly, you have provided him with evidence and witnesses that he would not have found himself. However, he seems to think now that a case may be built where Mr Peplow may have been responsible for Miss Blaine's murder and has requested that he has the time and space to put this supposition together.'

'I see. What of Miss Carstairs' death, sir? May I ask if it was accidental or suicide or murder? Mr Peplow indicated that Miss Carstairs had choked to death in her sleep.'

'Dr Carter has indicated that Miss Carstairs was a regular opioid user. A supply was discovered in a small silver box in the locker beside her bed. She was discovered in her bed by her sister, Miss Araminta Hardcastle, after the maid could not rouse her. Dr Carter has suggested that she choked in her sleep due to the influence of cocaine. He will confirm this, no doubt, when he finishes the autopsy. As you know, Mr Peplow has admitted supplying her with the drug, although he states that he only uses it himself for recreational purposes and shared it with Miss Carstairs since they were romantically linked.' Matt thought it sounded as if the chief inspector was reading from his case notes.

He was certain that Dominic Peplow's solicitor would have suggested that Peplow only had enough for his personal use so that he could not be charged for supplying and dealing in the drug on a larger scale. It was clearly the forerunner to painting Peplow as a victim of the drug himself rather than the root cause of misery and addiction for others. His dislike of the man kicked up a notch at the thought.

'So, no suicide note, or evidence of murder?' Matt asked. He had wondered if perhaps Victoria might have killed Peggy and overcome by remorse might have taken her own life. It was an unlikely theory, but he wished to rule it out.

'No note, and if there had been one, I think it unlikely that Miss Hardcastle or another family member would have destroyed it and not removed the cocaine,' the chief inspector said.

'An accident then? Or is murder still possible?' Matt's brain raced. When he had been in the far east, he had known people to die when their regular supply of drugs had been tampered with. The introduction of a much stronger version had killed them when taken unwittingly.

'We shall have to wait for Dr Carter's report and his tests on the contents of Miss Carstairs' silver box.' The inspector seemed to be confirming his ideas.

'Right, thank you, sir. Obviously, events have overtaken us, but we will have to make contact with Sir Vivian at some point, since he is still our client.' Matt was not sure quite what he could report. It seemed to him that he would have to be very careful when it came to the allegations of Sir Vivian's theft of artefacts.

'Sir Vivian is obviously very distressed by Miss Carstairs' death, and I believe he has been trying to reach the girl's mother who is on her honeymoon. Perhaps once Mr Peplow has been formally charged might be the most appropriate time?' the chief inspector suggested.

Matt suppressed a smile. Chief Inspector Greville was clearly attempting to walk a diplomatic tightrope of his own making between appeasing his newest inspector and allowing Matt and Kitty to complete their own work.

'Of course, sir, it's to be expected. He seemed to think a lot of Miss Carstairs,' Matt agreed.

'Very good. I'm glad we understand each other. Please give my regards to Mrs Bryant.' The chief inspector ended the call and Matt replaced the handset with a thoughtful air.

'Well, Rascal, my little chum, what do we make of that?' Inspector Lewis thinks Dominic Peplow is Peggy's killer and he certainly supplied Victoria with the cocaine that killed her.' He tickled the kitten's tiny, rounded belly as Rascal attempted to bat at his fingers with his paws.

He picked up his notes once more and added in the contents of the chief inspector's phone call. There was quite a lot to tell Kitty, it seemed, when she and Bertie returned from their walk. The chief inspector had sounded confident that Peplow was their man.

He added another piece of wood to the fire in the grate and prepared to head into the kitchen to finish tidying up the tea things when the telephone rang once more.

'Hello?' At first, he thought there was a problem with the line as all he could hear were faint scuffling sounds and crackles. 'Hello, is someone there?'

'Captain Bryant?' A young woman's voice, faint, breathy and scared.

'Speaking.'

'It's Araminta Hardcastle, can you come to the house? Please come, it's urgent. I'm so frightened.'

'Miss Hardcastle, what is frightening? Is someone in the house?'

'Yes, he's here, and...' The line went dead before Matt could find out more.

He sat for a moment deliberating what to do. There was no sign yet of Kitty returning. He went to the front window to see if she was coming back yet across the common. With no sight of her he tore a sheet of paper from the pad and wrote her a note. He placed it on top of the other papers on the coffee table so that she would see what had happened in her absence.

The girl had sounded terrified and desperate. Had Peplow been released from the police station and gone to see Araminta? Was it the councillor, still intoxicated, hurling threats at Sir

Vivian? Surely if her father was home then she would not be so scared. He popped the kitten back in its basket and hurried into the hall to collect his leather greatcoat and motorcycle cap. There was no time to waste. He locked the house and jumped onto his Sunbeam motorcycle to set off for Paignton and the Hardcastle house.

CHAPTER TWENTY-THREE

Kitty was enjoying her walk across the common and down into Galmpton village. After the events of the morning, it was good to get away for a little while. She decided to call in at the village store for more boiled sweets, since she had used her last bag to pay her young informants when they had been searching for Preacher Bob.

She dawdled on her way back up the hill, admiring the view, then turned to walk across the common, making the most of the last of the late afternoon sunshine. At last, it seemed as if spring was finally arriving, with wildflowers springing into bloom in the hedgerows. Bertie trotted happily at her side, nose to the ground sniffing for rabbits. His tail an erect plume of happiness at the pleasure of a long walk.

Kitty was approaching the turn towards her home when she saw the dark green omnibus pull into the stop and a familiar female figure alighted.

'Alice!' Kitty waved at her friend.

'I was just in Torquay running some errands for mother and thought as I'd stop off on my way home,' Alice explained as she hefted the large wicker shopping basket she was carrying further along her arm.

'Well, I am delighted to see you. Can you stay for supper, do you think? I'm sure Mrs Smith will have left enough for three,' Kitty said as she linked arms with her friend.

Bertie gave a happy woof of agreement, and the girls started the short distance to Kitty's home.

'Oh, Matt's motorcycle is missing.' Kitty stopped as she saw the Sunbeam's usual parking place was empty. 'That's odd. Perhaps he's had a message from someone and had to go out.' It was not out of the ordinary for Matt to ride out and fetch them a small treat like cream buns or a jug of cider. Or sometimes a prospective new client needed an urgent meeting if they discovered a theft or damage to their property.

She opened the front door and while Alice was removing her hat and coat, Kitty went straight through to the kitchen to put the kettle on and prepare a tea tray.

'I'll do that, Miss Kitty, you go and take your outdoor things off.' Alice bustled in behind her and laughingly shooed her out of the way. Bertie sat himself at the side of the range and looked up hopefully at the biscuit tin.

'You are my guest, Alice.' Kitty laughed back at her friend and rewarded Bertie with half a biscuit before going to the hall to hang up her own things.

She checked on the table beside the telephone in the hall in case Matt had left a message for her there. He often did so on his way out of the house when called away unexpectedly. The last message she found however was a note from their house-keeper from the other day, nothing from Matt.

Kitty shrugged and went to assist Alice in the kitchen with the tea tray. Matt was sure to be back before too long. She could find out where he had been then on his return. Once the tray was ready, and the boiling water added to the teapot, Kitty picked it up to carry it into the sitting room.

'Oh, Alice, can you move Matt's notes onto the bureau please so that I can put the tray down,' Kitty requested when she saw the coffee table was still covered with papers from where he had been working.

Alice duly obliged, bundling the papers together quickly and setting them aside on the bureau. 'Oh, what a darling kitten!' Her friend spotted Rascal who was snoozing peacefully in his basket.

Kitty took a seat and poured their tea while she told Alice the story of where she had found the cat. She knew Alice adored cats and cared for the hotel's resident mouser. Rascal awoke while they talked, and Alice took him out of his basket to play with her.

'I can't believe it. What a palaver, 'tis terrible.' Alice was shocked when Kitty updated her with everything they had discovered so far about Peggy's murder.

She was confident that Alice would keep the information to herself as she had been involved with several of their previous cases. 'Indeed. Poor Mr Blaine is terribly distressed.'

'No wonder at it. And that other poor girl, Miss Carstairs. She was such a fragile, pretty little thing when I saw her at the pageant. I hope as that man who supplied her with that stuff gets sent to prison for a long time. Disgraceful, it is.' Alice was indignant when she heard of Dominic Peplow's role in Victoria's death.

'I sincerely hope so.' Kitty finished her tea. 'I must admit though, I'm still not certain that he was responsible for Peggy's murder. I know that he could have done it but then again so could several other people.'

Alice nodded. 'It certainly sounds like it could have been any one of them. None of them are very nice. I mean, we know as Councillor Martin is a horrid man. That Sir Vivian sounds ghastly as well although from what you say he was very fond of

Miss Victoria. I mean he did give her a home after her mother divorced him. It's a terrible thing knowing now as Peggy was pregnant when she was killed. I know from what Mr Blaine told you as Peggy wasn't a very nice person but even so, it's horrid. It makes you wonder why she had to be killed then, too? I mean she was in the beauty pageant so she could have been killed any time, couldn't she?'

Kitty knew what Alice meant. It was something neither she nor Matt had considered. Alice was right, there was no reason why Peggy couldn't have been killed before the event or later that evening. The sharpening of the paperknife suggested premeditated murder but what had triggered the girl's death that it had happened when it did? Was it to do with the letters? Why kill her during the pageant?

'You have a good point, Alice. Perhaps there's something we missed. Let me look at Matt's papers.' Kitty set down her cup and saucer and picked up the documents from the bureau. After lifting up the first sheet of paper, she realised there was a note.

'Oh, Matt left me a message, how odd. I wonder why he didn't put it by the hall telephone.'

'Where has he gone?' Alice asked.

'He says, "*Just had a call from Chief Inspector Greville, will tell you later. Just got an urgent call to go to Hardcastles' house. Araminta is in trouble.*"' Kitty looked at her friend, stricken with guilt. 'I need to go into Paignton.'

Alice was already on her feet. 'I'm coming with you.'

They hurried into the hall and tugged on their hats and coats.

'Alice, you should get back home. I'll be all right.' Kitty attempted to dissuade her friend from accompanying her. She had no wish to bring her into any danger, and who knows what they might find at the Hardcastles' house.

'I'm coming with you and that's that,' Alice said as she jammed her pale green felt hat firmly on top of her auburn curls.

Kitty jumped into her car and started the engine as Alice seated herself in the passenger side.

'Won't your mother wonder where you are? You have her shopping,' Kitty said as she pulled off the drive and out to the main road.

'Hang the shopping.' Alice glanced across at her. 'This is more important than a few links of sausage and Mother's knitting pattern.'

Kitty drove as fast as she dared along the coastal road towards Paignton. Matt had been gone for well over two hours at least now and he hadn't telephoned the house which was concerning. Especially as he had said in his note that Araminta was in trouble.

Alice emitted a squeak and placed a hand on her hat as Kitty took the turn towards the Hardcastles' rented home a little quickly.

'Mercy me, miss, slow down a touch. We want to get there in one piece,' Alice reproved her.

'Sorry, Alice, I can't shake off the feeling that something is terribly wrong. I just need to know that Matt is safe.' Kitty could see the entrance to the Hardcastle's drive up ahead of her.

She steered her car to a halt near the front door. Matt's Sunbeam motorcycle was parked on the one side. Sir Vivian's Rolls Royce was next to it with a large trunk strapped to the back. There was no sign of any of the police vehicles so she assumed they must have left.

'It looks as if Sir Vivian is here as well as Matt. That's his car over there.' Kitty jumped out of the car with Alice at her side and they headed for the front door.

The bell sounded deep inside the house when Kitty pushed the worn and dirty brass button.

'I reckon we might be waiting a bit afore anyone answers the door, miss. Our Betty says as Sir Vivian has dismissed most all the staff lately. No money for wages so she heard,' Alice remarked tartly.

'Well Matt must be here, his motorcycle is parked up there.' Kitty frowned as she spoke. It seemed as if her friend was right, no one was coming to the door. She pushed the bell once more.

'Hang on here, miss. I'll nip around the back and see if I can see anyone inside the house or if the servants' door is open,' Alice suggested.

Before Kitty could stop her, Alice hurried away across the weedy gravel. Kitty gave the doorbell another impatient push. As the final peals of the bell died away, she stepped back from the step to look up at the house searching for any signs of life.

The blank, dark windows stared back at her, the ancient leaded glass reflecting the dying light of the sun where evening was starting to set in. She wrinkled her nose as a disturbing scent reached her. An unpleasant burning smell. One that smelled of old papers and wood.

Kitty walked further back and shaded her eyes with her hand to try and determine the source of the smell. It reminded her of when the gulls had made a nest in one of the chimneys at the Dolphin and had almost caused a fire.

With that thought in mind, she peered upwards looking at the ornate brick chimney stacks at either end of the building. No sign of nests or curls of smoke were visible on the red terracotta chimney pots.

A faint movement in one of the small dormer attic windows caught her attention. Kitty squinted, trying to make out what or who she could see. After a moment she realised that there was a woman in a pale blue dress banging on the glass of the dormer window as if trying to attract attention.

'Araminta?' Kitty wondered if the girl was trapped or locked in. Why else would she be behaving so oddly? And where was Matt?

The singed smell was growing stronger. Kitty suddenly realised that faint wisps of smoke were beginning to curl over the dark grey slate roof. Where was Sir Vivian? Was he in the house with Matt? Had Araminta started a fire and become trapped? Was she the one behind Peggy's murder and her step-sister's death? Was there evidence that she was attempting to destroy?

Kitty felt as if her feet were glued to the gravel of the driveway for a moment. Alice, she had to find Alice. They had to get help. She turned and ran towards the overgrown shrubbery at the side of the house to follow the path Alice had taken when she said she was going to try the back door.

'Miss Kitty, the door is locked, and I can't make nobody hear.' Alice cannoned into her on the narrow path almost knocking her off her feet. The smell of burning was growing stronger the closer they had gone to the rear of the house.

'I think Araminta is in the attic. I can see someone up there and there is a fire. I can smell it.' Kitty grasped her friend's arm. 'We have to get help.'

'I couldn't see no flames, but I can smell burning,' Alice confirmed, her thin face pale with fear. 'Do you think as Captain Bryant is inside?'

'I don't know, but clearly Araminta is in there. Can you go and try the neighbours' houses and see if any of them has a telephone. Call for the police and for the fire brigade,' Kitty instructed.

Alice went to sprint off but paused. 'What are you planning to do, miss?'

'I'm going to try and break in to see where my husband is, and Sir Vivian. Araminta may have locked them in or harmed them and set fire to the house, she may be behind the murders or she could be about to be the next victim,' Kitty spoke quickly, her thoughts all over the place at the unfolding drama.

'Don't go getting yourself killed. I'll be back as fast as I can.' Alice hitched up her skirt and ran away down the drive towards the street.

Kitty thought her best chance to get into the house would be at the back. The front door was secure and the front bay windows were quite high and she would struggle to climb in, even if she were to manage to break any of the glass.

She hurried to the back of the house. When she and Matt had visited before she recalled seeing leaded French windows in the library just beyond the grand piano. If she could smash one of those, she might be able to put her arm through to open the door to gain access.

Above her head now, she could hear crackling and guessed that the fire was beginning to take hold. She found the French windows and looked around the overgrown and unkempt garden for something she could use to force an entry into the house.

Spying a large, moss-covered stone, she prised it loose from the rockery, ignoring a shower of dispossessed beetles and woodlice. Her crimson kid driving gloves, at least, would afford her some protection from the glass shards, she thought as she took hold of the boulder in both hands and smashed it into the French windows.

The sound of breaking glass seemed impossibly loud, startling the crows nesting in the tall trees at the end of the garden. She skipped backwards as a large piece of glass fell out and shattered at her feet. The birds flew off in a chorus of disapproving caws as Kitty used the rock to try to clear as many of the jagged pieces of glass away from the door as possible.

Once she was satisfied it was safe and the hole was large enough, Kitty slipped her arm through the gap to turn the handle from the inside.

'Yes,' she breathed triumphantly as the latch clicked and the door swung open. Thank heaven it wasn't locked. More shards of glass crunched under the soles of her shoes as she entered the room.

No one was in sight as she exited the library to search the rest of the ground floor. The kitchen and scullery were as empty and deserted as the library.

'Sir Vivian! Matt!' she called out as she searched.

The sitting room too was empty, the ashes in the fireplace were cold indicating the room hadn't been occupied that day.

Kitty hurried towards Sir Vivian's study. Where was Matt? He had to be in the house if his motorcycle was outside, and Sir Vivian's car was there too. She flung open the door to the study.

'Sir Vivian!'

Sir Vivian was engaged in tossing as many of the artefacts that adorned the shelves of his office into a box as he possibly could. He whirled around at the sound of her voice.

'Mrs Bryant.'

'I'm looking for my husband. His motorcycle is outside, and your house seems to be on fire.' Kitty could see that a great deal of the contents of the study had already been removed. Her mind whirled as she tried to make sense of what she could see.

'Nothing to worry about, my dear. I'm just ensuring these precious items are safe. I'm sure the fire brigade will be here shortly.' Sir Vivian continued to place items swiftly inside the straw-filled box.

'Your daughter? Araminta is in the attic near the blaze. We need to go and get her out. And where is my husband?' Kitty demanded, placing herself directly in his way as he went to retrieve another empty box from the other side of the room.

'My dear, Mrs Bryant, I must get these things to safety.' Sir Vivian attempted to dodge past her.

'Your daughter could die. She seems to be trapped near the seat of the fire and my husband is here somewhere.' Kitty stared at him. Surely, he could not be so focused on saving his precious artefacts that he was unconcerned about his own daughter's safety?

Sir Vivian's teeth bared in a snarl. 'I rather think that is the general idea, Mrs Bryant.'

CHAPTER TWENTY-FOUR

The blood in Kitty's veins turned to ice as the implications of Sir Vivian's words hit her. She had made a mistake, a dangerous assumption that could be about to cost her dearly.

'I must find Matt.' She edged back towards the study door ready to make a run for the stairs.

'I really can't allow you to do that, Mrs Bryant.' Sir Vivian's tone was conversational and light but the gun he had suddenly produced from the drawer of the desk was much more serious.

'The police and fire brigade are on their way. My friend has gone to summon help.' Kitty tried to keep her own voice calm.

'Then they will discover three bodies rather than two.' Sir Vivian waved the barrel of the gun at Kitty. 'Since you are so eager to find your husband and my daughter, please allow me to take you to them.' He advanced towards Kitty, forcing her out of the study and into the hall.

The smell of smoke and burning timber was stronger now and Kitty's heart hammered in her chest. Sir Vivian motioned towards the staircase with the gun. 'Come along, Mrs Bryant, we haven't much time, as you so rightly pointed out.'

When Kitty's feet refused to obey her swiftly enough, Sir

Vivian pressed the gun into her side. The hard metal dug in through her coat to push against her ribs.

'Move.' His breath was hot on her cheek as he snarled the word into her ear galvanising her into motion.

Kitty's brain raced as he forced her up the stairs to the first-floor landing. The sounds of the fire were louder now. She could hear the crackling and roar of the flames as the conflagration took a stronger hold above their heads. The surrounding air felt hot and fetid.

'The fire brigade will be here at any time, so will the police. You should just leave me here and make good your escape. If I die trying to rescue Araminta and Matt, then so be it,' Kitty said as he continued to force her forward towards the far end of the landing.

'Oh, but that would leave too much to chance, Mrs Bryant. This must look like an unfortunate accident. My daughter and your husband having an affair and you discovered them in the act. The fire clearly a crime of passion and revenge.' Sir Vivian gave a wolfish smile.

'No one who knows Matt or I would believe any of that nonsense.' Kitty swallowed hard. The man was delusional if he thought he would escape from a burning house unscathed with his precious artefacts, leaving three people dead inside.

'Why not, Mrs Bryant? People will believe anything, especially when laced with gossip and slander,' Sir Vivian said.

A loud crack came from above their heads and wisps of smoke began to curl into the landing.

'Miss Kitty!' A shout from behind them made Sir Vivian turn around. Kitty's heart leapt.

Alice had returned and must have followed behind them up the stairs.

Kitty took advantage of the momentary distraction to hit Sir Vivian's gun arm hard. Taken by surprise he dropped the weapon, and it skittered forward from the edge of the

Turkish carpet runner onto the polished wooden floor towards Alice.

Sir Vivian went to retrieve it at the same moment that Alice dived for it. Terrified for her friend's safety, Kitty launched herself onto Sir Vivian's back, gouging and kicking as she did so. The older man gave a muffled roar of rage as he attempted to shake her loose.

Alice scrambled for the gun, snatching it from Sir Vivian's outstretched hand as Kitty tumbled him onto the landing floor.

'You, get up.' Alice held the gun between both hands. The determined expression on her face contrasted with her tumbled auburn locks and lopsided hat. She pointed the gun at Sir Vivian who was on his hands and knees before her.

Kitty released her grasp and stood up, dusting off her hands as she did so. 'Alice, I have to find Matt and Araminta. The fire is growing worse.' Kitty turned to glance fearfully at the narrow flight of stairs at the end of the landing. Smoke was already forming a hazy cloud now at the entrance. If Matt and Sir Vivian's daughter were trapped up there, then there was little time left to save them.

'Go ahead, miss, and be careful. The police and fire brigade will be here any second. I can manage him.' Alice skipped back nimbly as Sir Vivian attempted to grab at her legs as she spoke.

'If he moves again, Alice, shoot him.'

Kitty pulled up her coat collar to try and protect her nose and mouth from the smoke and headed for the staircase. The wooden handrail was warm to her touch as she raced up the short flight of stairs to the top floor which she assumed would normally have housed the servants.

The smoke on this floor was thicker and choking and the darkness made it hard to see. Ahead of her the fire roared like a ravenous beast. Kitty tried to remember which window she had seen Araminta standing in.

'Matt! Araminta!' She dropped her coat collar for a fraction of a second to shout.

'Here.' The voice was faint and followed by coughs.

It came from behind the first door. Kitty rattled at the handle knowing the door must be locked or the girl would have made good her escape already. The door was too sturdy for her to be able to physically break it down.

The air all around her now was oppressively hot and the smoke made it hard to breathe. Thinking quickly, Kitty pulled a pin from her hat and bent down to the lock, praying her skills would be enough to turn the tumblers. Dolly had shown both her and Alice how to pick a lock, but it had not been one of Kitty's strengths.

Tears streamed down her face as she probed and twisted with the pin before finally hearing the faint click that told her she had managed it. She opened the door to see Araminta kneeling next to Matt's prone body in a bare, smoke-filled room.

Kitty's heart leapt into her throat as coughing, she rushed to her husband's side. 'Matt, oh God no. What happened?'

'He's out cold, I can't wake him,' Araminta sobbed.

'You'll have to help me to carry him. Hurry, we have to get out of here.' Kitty hoped the girl was right and Matt had merely been knocked out.

She dropped to the floor, coughing and wheezing from the effects of the smoke, and draped one of Matt's arms around her shoulders. Araminta did the same with his other arm. Between them the girls staggered forward carrying the dead weight of Matt's body.

Another loud crash sounded close by and Araminta screamed as a blazing piece of timber fell through the ceiling onto the floor of the room they had just vacated.

'Quickly, the roof is collapsing,' Kitty panted as between them they coughed and spluttered their way through the wall of smoke to the stairs.

'It's too narrow, we can't get down like this.' Araminta turned a scared face towards Kitty.

'Take his top half and I'll take his feet.' Kitty could barely breathe now and talking was difficult.

Kitty pulled and Araminta did her best to protect Matt's head and shoulders as they made their way down the staircase to where Kitty had left Sir Vivian and Alice.

The landing was completely full of smoke and there was no sign of either her friend or Araminta's father. Kitty had no time to wonder where they might have gone, or if Alice was safe. More loud crashes were coming now from above their heads. Flames appeared, starting to lick at the cornicing at the tops of the walls.

'Hurry,' Kitty wheezed as they pulled and dragged Matt along the landing to the final flight of stairs.

Kitty could scarcely see her way in front of her now. The acrid scent of burning filled her nose, throat and lungs.

'We're at the stairs.' Araminta coughed. Kitty could hardly see her although she was standing almost next to her.

They started down the stairs together, both supporting the top half of Matt's body, feeling for each step as they went, unable to see the treads.

Suddenly Matt's body sagged forward catching Kitty off guard, and she staggered against the balustrade. She realised that Araminta had either collapsed or fallen, throwing all of Matt's weight onto Kitty.

Everything was blurry and Kitty could scarcely stand upright as she desperately tried to get Matt further down the stairs. She managed one more step before losing her footing and falling.

* * *

'Miss Kitty, Miss Kitty.'

Kitty coughed and retched as she opened her eyes at the insistent sound of someone calling her name. Alice's pale, anxious face was above her. 'Matt? Araminta?' she choked the words out, barely able to speak.

'Both safe, miss.' Tears ran down Alice's soot-stained cheeks. 'The doctor is with Captain Bryant now. The police have Sir Vivian.'

Kitty closed her eyes and tried to suck in more clean air. Her chest felt as if it were burning on the inside and she could taste ash on her tongue. She could hear male voices shouting out orders and the sound of running water which she realised must be from hoses.

'Now then, Mrs Bryant, let's have a look at you.' The familiar face of Dr Carter loomed over her as she reopened her eyes, and the doctor began to check her pulse and vital signs. 'Dearie me, you and that husband of yours get yourselves into some scrapes. This one was a bit of a narrow squeak. Good thing the firemen got you all out in the nick of time, thanks to young Alice here.'

Kitty's eyelids fluttered shut and tears started to leak from under her lashes. Thank heavens Alice had been with her and had managed to get help. The doctor was right, a few more minutes and they would all three have been killed.

'Matt?' she whispered.

'Fortunately, your husband has a hard head. Like you, he's taken in quite a lot of smoke, but he'll be as right as ninepence by tomorrow,' Dr Carter reassured her cheerily.

'That Sir Vivian bashed him over the head with one of them Egyptian stone carvings,' Alice explained as she gave Kitty's hand a comforting squeeze.

Kitty opened her eyes again and realised that Dr Carter had moved on, presumably to check on Araminta.

'Oh, Alice, however did you get out?' Kitty asked as she tried to sit herself up. Alice placed her arm around her shoul-

ders to assist her. Kitty realised that she was lying on the grass
lawn at the side of the driveway. All around them was darkness
illuminated only by a dull orange glow which she guessed must
mean the fire was not yet out.

'I kept that gun on him and backed him towards the stairs.
My heart was in my mouth, it was, and I thought *Alice, you'd*
better not mess this up or he'll kill you as soon as look at you. I
was about to get him outside when I heard engines out the front
of the house and shouting. I knew then as either the police or
the firemen must be here.'

'You were so brave.' Kitty broke off into a coughing fit as she
tried to speak.

'I shouted out for help and the firemen took an axe to the
front door. They was pretty surprised to find me holding a gun
on Sir Vivian. He tried to say as how I was robbing the house
and to let him loose. I told them as you'd gone up into the fire as
people was trapped upstairs.' Alice's small face was indignant.

'What happened then?' Despite her physical distress, Kitty
was desperate to know what had gone on while she had been
trying to rescue Matt and Araminta.

'Well, Sir Vivian tried to get past me. He claimed he had to
save his antiquities. I said as he was going nowhere till the
police came and just then that new inspector arrived. He took
the gun off me and handcuffed Sir Vivian. The firemen started
to get the hoses going and I told them as you'd gone up towards
the attics.' Alice gave her a comforting hug as she spoke.

Kitty dashed the tears away from her cheeks and tried to
struggle to her feet only to collapse back down. 'I must go to
Matt.'

'In a minute, miss, you'm not fit to go anywhere just for a
bit. He's all right. The doctor has seen to him and there's an
ambulance coming to take all three of you to the cottage hospital.' Alice's face was creased with anxiety. 'Bide here for a
minute or two.'

Kitty realised she was too weak to do anything other than comply with her friend's wishes. Alice kept her arm about her shoulders as all around them they could hear the sounds of the men fighting the fire.

After a few minutes, two uniformed ambulance men appeared out of the hazy night.

'Come along, Mrs Bryant, let's get you off to the hospital.'

Alice gave her a final hug and Kitty allowed herself to be borne away from the fire.

CHAPTER TWENTY-FIVE

Matt was unsure which part of him hurt the most: his head, where Sir Vivian had hit him with a heavy stone ornament; his lungs and throat from breathing in the soot-laden smoke where Sir Vivian had attempted to burn down the house; or his arms and legs which were covered in bruises from where Kitty and Araminta had dragged and pulled him to safety.

Safely back at home, after a night spent in the cottage hospital, he was grateful to be seated in his favourite armchair beside the fireplace. Bertie lay snoring contentedly at his feet and Kitty was seated in the chair opposite him with her kitten on her lap. Thankfully, despite their ordeal, she looked pale but unharmed.

Alice had arranged for Robert Potter and his father to retrieve Matt's motorcycle and Kitty's car from the Hardcastle home and bring them back safely to Churston and she had fed both animals and walked Bertie. Araminta had been detained at the hospital as she had not recovered as swiftly as he and Kitty had from inhaling smoke. She had likely been trapped up there with the growing fire before Matt had even arrived.

Mrs Smith, their housekeeper, had been horrified when she had learned of their adventure and had been constantly plying them with pots of tea and food ever since they had been allowed to return home.

Alice had accompanied Mr Potter in the taxi to collect them. She had insisted on staying and had spent her morning fending off telephone calls from Kitty's grandmother, Matt's parents and Mrs Craven.

She was in the hall at the moment, and he could hear her answering yet another telephone enquiry.

'That were Chief Inspector Greville, he said as he'll be 'ere shortly with that new inspector as he needs to take statements. I've asked Mrs Smith to have some cake and biscuits ready. I expect as the chief inspector will be hungry as usual,' Alice said as she entered the sitting room.

'Thank you, Alice.' He wished his voice was less raspy and that it took less effort to speak.

However, compared to what his fate could have been had Kitty and Alice not rescued him, losing his voice was a small price to pay. Kitty looked quite exhausted after yesterday's adventure and he knew that her voice too was somewhat hoarse with the after effects of the smoke.

Some twenty minutes later there was a knock at the front door and Alice went to admit the policemen. Chief Inspector Greville came into the room first and presented Kitty with a small bunch of daffodils wrapped in newspaper.

'A little something for you from my garden, Mrs Bryant.'

'Thank you, Chief Inspector, that's very kind.' Kitty smiled at their old friend as he took a seat on the sofa, while Alice bore the flowers away to the kitchen.

Inspector Lewis stepped inside the room after allowing Alice out. He greeted them both, then took his place beside Chief Inspector Greville.

'I hope you are both feeling well enough to be interviewed this morning?' Chief Inspector Greville asked, glancing from

Kitty to Matt. 'We took Miss Miller's statement yesterday evening after you had both gone to the hospital.'

'I think so, sir, although we are both a little hoarse,' Kitty confirmed.

'Now, Miss Hardcastle has been detained at the cottage hospital as her breathing is not quite as good as they would like just yet. They are hoping after some more oxygen as she can be discharged later today. Her older sister, Lady Artemis Fowler, is coming from London to take her back to them I believe. She is quite naturally very distressed.' Chief Inspector Greville settled back on the sofa while Inspector Lewis produced his notebook ready to take down their statements. 'We've had Miss Hardcastle's story of what happened and Miss Millers. Perhaps, Captain Bryant, you could tell us your version of events?'

Matt was aware that even Kitty had not yet heard exactly what had happened after he had taken the desperate telephone call from Araminta and had ridden off to the Hardcastle residence. They had been in separate wards at the hospital and he had been unable to speak for a few hours thanks to the smoke he had inhaled.

'I received a telephone call from Araminta yesterday afternoon while Kitty was out with Bertie. Miss Hardcastle sounded distressed, frightened. She urged me to come straight to the house. She said she was terrified, and the line then cut off.' Matt was forced to pause for a moment in order to clear his throat.

'Alice and I found the note Matt left much later when I returned from my walk, and we were taking tea. We didn't see it at first as it was with the case notes for Miss Blaine's murder and Sir Vivian's commission,' Kitty said.

Matt sensed that Kitty blamed herself for the delay in coming to his aid as she and Alice had missed his message.

'We usually leave messages in the hall near the telephone there which is why Kitty wouldn't have seen it.' Matt looked at his wife hoping that she would understand that missing his note had been a simple mix-up and he was really to blame for not placing it in a more obvious place. In his haste to aid Araminta, he hadn't given it a second thought.

'What time was this, sir?' Inspector Lewis asked.

'It was almost four o'clock I believe, when we found the message,' Kitty said.

'I think Araminta telephoned at about three-fifteen. She called shortly after I spoke to you, sir,' Matt added.

Alice returned to the room pushing a small gilt and onyx trolley laden with coffee things and plates of biscuits and slices of fruitcake. Matt saw Chief Inspector Greville's expression brighten when his gaze alighted on the cake.

'What happened then, sir?' Inspector Lewis asked as Alice dispensed china cups of coffee and refreshments.

'I took my motorcycle and rode over to the Hardcastles' house. I parked up near Sir Vivian's Rolls Royce. I noticed that he seemed to have various boxes on the rear seat of the car. There was a trunk strapped to the luggage rack.' Matt took a small sip of coffee, grateful for the moisture on his dry throat.

'I rang the doorbell. Sir Vivian answered the door himself. I was a little surprised as there seemed to be no sign of his staff or of Araminta. He apologised, saying that everyone was very upset after Victoria's death and that the police had not long gone. I expressed my condolences and asked for Miss Hardcastle. At this point I wondered if the shock of her stepsister's death had caused her to feel afraid for some reason.' Matt swallowed and took another sip of his drink while Inspector Lewis scribbled furiously in his notebook.

'Where was Miss Hardcastle?' Inspector Lewis asked.

'Sir Vivian seemed not to know, saying she was in the house, and he had last seen her going upstairs towards the attic. He suggested I go up there and offered to show me the way.' Looking back, Matt wondered that he had agreed, but he had been anxious to assure himself of Araminta's safety and there had been no reason to suspect that Sir Vivian might wish him any personal harm.

'So, you complied with his request?' Chief Inspector Greville brushed a stray cake crumb from his moustache which was instantly collected by a delighted Bertie.

'I had no reason to think he would harm me. He was our client and he seemed to be quite calm and rational, making small talk about his antique collection. I had thought that perhaps Miss Hardcastle wished to discuss Mr Peplow, who had called to see me earlier in the day. I thought he was the source of her concerns,' Matt explained.

'Mr Peplow had called here shortly after breakfast. Araminta had telephoned him and told him of Victoria's death. He knew that we had wished to speak to him as part of the investigation that Sir Vivian had commissioned,' Kitty said.

'I gathered from Mr Peplow that he had spoken to you. Sir Vivian's commission was for what exactly?' Chief Inspector Greville asked.

'He told us that he suspected Victoria was taking cocaine and that he wished to find her supplier. At least that was what he told us initially when we agreed to take his case,' Kitty said.

'And that changed?' Chief Inspector Greville leaned forward to look at Kitty, a shrewd expression in his sharp eyes.

'We learned very recently that Mr Peplow was indeed her supplier and Victoria had been stealing various small artefacts and trinkets from Sir Vivian to pay for her drug habit.' Kitty stroked the kitten that lay purring softly in her lap.

'If this was the case, why did he not come to us?' Inspector Lewis asked in a belligerent tone.

'The goods Victoria was disposing of were ones that Sir Vivian himself had stolen from his expeditions in Egypt. If it came to light that he was the source of these artefacts, then both his career as an archaeologist and any hope of a parliamentary career would be at an end. He wanted to discover who had the goods and where they had been sold, so thought we would unwittingly confirm his suspicions in that area. I suppose that he had thought we wouldn't discover that the items had been stolen by him in the first place, and that he owned them legitimately.' Kitty broke into a coughing spell and needed a drink of her coffee in order to recover.

'I can only assume that Sir Vivian used the items he had stolen whenever he needed money,' Matt explained.

'I see. What happened then when Sir Vivian led you to the attics?' Inspector Lewis asked.

'I heard banging noises, as if someone was trapped. I turned to ask Sir Vivian what the sound was, and everything went black. I don't recall anything else until I found myself lying outside the house on the wet grass with Dr Carter tending to me,' Matt said apologetically.

'What does Araminta have to say about what happened?' Kitty looked at Chief Inspector Greville.

The chief inspector stroked his moustache thoughtfully and gave a slightly regretful glance at the now empty china cake stand. 'Miss Hardcastle said that after the upset of the morning of finding her stepsister dead in bed she telephoned Mr Peplow. She said that she was very angry. She blamed herself for having introduced him to Miss Carstairs in the first place. She knew of his cocaine dealing but hadn't realised that Miss Carstairs was in quite as deep as she was.'

'Poor Araminta, she and Victoria didn't always get on, but it must have been horrible for her finding her like that,' Kitty murmured.

'Quite so, Mrs Bryant. Sir Vivian had dismissed all the servants, bar one, a day or so earlier saying he had to cut costs. The last remaining girl, a young maid called Enid, he let go that morning right after Miss Carstairs' death. That left Miss Hardcastle alone in the house with her father, once we had departed.'

The chief inspector drained his coffee cup and set it down on the table.

'Why did she telephone Matt?' Kitty asked.

'She saw her father had started to pack up the things in his study. He started as soon as our men had left the house. She knew that some of the things her father had done weren't quite on the level. She had been with him out in Egypt, where I understand some official from the Cairo Museum of antiquities was killed in a motoring accident on his way back from a site visit. They had left Egypt in a hurry not long after that.

'She had noticed her stepsister behaving oddly the night before she died. Acting as if she were afraid of Sir Vivian. At first, she had thought it was paranoia induced by the cocaine. Then Araminta says she overheard a snippet of conversation earlier that day which she didn't think much of until after Victoria died.' Chief Inspector Greville looked at Kitty.

'What did she hear?' Kitty asked.

'She says she heard her father tell Miss Carstairs that he knew she had the things and she had to get them back.' Inspector Lewis leafed back through his notes to quote Araminta directly in order to answer Kitty's question.

Chief Inspector Greville took up the tale once more. 'Araminta says she started to piece everything together. Her father leaving Egypt so quickly when the museum had wished to inspect his records from the dig. The accident in the desert. Now, her stepsister was dead, and he had dismissed the servants and seemed to be packing up the house without telling her. She knew too that there had been more to his connection with Peggy Blaine than he had led anyone to believe.'

'The museum staff said that he had taken Peggy to supper a few times after his lectures, and he is well known for having an eye for the ladies,' Matt said.

Chief Inspector Greville's brows rose slightly at this information. 'We think that Miss Blaine and Sir Vivian were lovers.

Miss Blaine was a somewhat mercenary young lady and when she became pregnant, we think she had expectations of Sir Vivian.'

'That would make perfect sense; she was playing Sir Vivian off against Councillor Martin. From Peggy's perspective she would have thought Sir Vivian could offer her more,' Kitty agreed.

'The last thing Sir Vivian wanted was another marriage, especially to a young woman with little to offer financially. He needed to find someone willing to back his new parliamentary venture. An impecunious marriage to a chemist's assistant would not provide him with money or social kudos.' The chief inspector's tone was sober.

'Awful, that's what it is, just awful. So he killed Peggy? To shut her up?' Alice's face was pink with indignation.

'That would seem to be the case, yes, Miss Miller,' Chief Inspector Greville confirmed.

'And Victoria? Was her death an accident?' Kitty asked.

'We are waiting on the results of the tests Dr Carter has ordered on the remnants of the cocaine found in her possession, but we think it's possible that a much purer form of the drug was placed in her box,' Inspector Lewis said.

Matt saw Kitty shiver. He knew that she had mentioned before that Sir Vivian was a likely suspect for Peggy's death. Even so, to have it confirmed in this way was quite awful. And that the man had killed his own stepdaughter and attempted to murder his daughter.

'Miss Hardcastle was frightened but she didn't want to believe her suspicions. She thought perhaps she was mistaken so she decided to telephone you, Captain Bryant, and ask for help. She had found your card with her sister's possessions.' Chief Inspector Greville's moustache twitched.

'I presume her father overheard her making the call?' Matt asked.

Inspector Lewis nodded. 'It would seem so. Shortly afterwards he lured her to the attic telling her that they were to go and stay in London with one of her sisters and could she help with one of the trunks.'

'That must have been when he locked her in. Then he waited for Matt to arrive and when Matt went to find Araminta he knocked him out and locked him in with her.' Kitty shuddered at the recollection.

'Now we come to you, Mrs Bryant, and Miss Miller. You found Captain Bryant's note and set off for the house together?' Inspector Lewis asked.

Kitty nodded. 'Yes. Like Matt, I initially thought perhaps Mr Peplow was responsible for Peggy's murder and obviously was implicated in some way in Victoria's death. Since Araminta had telephoned him, I thought he may have gone to the house, and she was afraid.'

'That's right, like I said in my account we talked about it on our way to Paignton. When we got there, we saw Sir Vivian's car next to the captain's motorcycle,' Alice agreed.

Kitty smiled at her friend and continued the story. 'No one answered the front door when we rang so Alice went to try at the back of the house in case any of the servants were in the kitchen.'

'Although I had heard the day before from my cousin Betty as the servants had been dismissed, so I weren't thinking as there was much hopes.' Alice smiled brightly at Inspector Lewis who was writing his notes with a slightly bemused expression on his face at the latter part of Alice's explanation.

'Alice couldn't see anyone, so she came back to meet me. As she did so we realised we could smell smoke and there were flames coming from the roof. I saw Araminta in the attic window, and I wasn't sure if she was trapped or if she was in fact the arsonist at that point,' Kitty explained.

'I run off to raise the alarm and Miss Kitty went to see if she could get inside the house as we knew Captain Bryant had to be in there.' Alice's cheek grew pinker as she retold her part of the story.

'This was when you, Mrs Bryant, broke in via the French windows,' Inspector Lewis said somewhat dourly.

'I was so concerned about Matt's whereabouts and safety, it took Sir Vivian pulling the gun on me to realise that he had in fact been responsible for everything.' Kitty talked the policemen through everything that had transpired afterwards.

'And Miss Miller here was heroically preventing Sir Vivian from making good his escape when we arrived. His car was loaded with his clothes and a veritable treasure trove of stolen artefacts. A man from the British Museum is on his way to collect them as we speak,' Chief Inspector Greville said.

A wave of relief mixed with exhaustion washed over Kitty. She felt this hadn't been a case that covered any of those involved in glory. She and Matt had almost been killed and her darling Alice had been put in danger too.

'I presume Sir Vivian has been charged with Miss Blaine's murder?' Matt asked, his voice still raspy from the fire.

'Indeed, and I think the Egyptian authorities may also look again at the death of their museum official.' Inspector Lewis closed his notebook and returned it to the inside top pocket of his jacket.

'Hanging's too good for such as him,' Alice remarked fiercely as she gathered up the used crockery to return it to the trolley. 'It's poor Miss Araminta, and Miss Blaine's brother as I feel sorry for. 'Tis terrible.'

Kitty was inclined to agree with her friend. Who would have thought a simple event like a beauty pageant to celebrate the king and queen's silver jubilee would end in such dark events?

Alice took the two policemen into the hall to see them out after they had made their farewells.

The small, discarded pile of colourful holiday brochures on the bureau caught Kitty's eye. 'After the children's party next week, what do you say to a little holiday? I think I've had all the adventure I can cope with for a while?' she suggested, smiling at her husband.

'If Mrs C can spare you, then I'm all for it.' Matt chuckled impishly at her expression.

'Hopefully somewhere murder free,' Kitty replied.

A LETTER FROM HELENA

Dear reader,

I want to say a huge thank you for choosing to read *Murder at the Beauty Pageant*. If you did enjoy it, and would like to keep up-to-date with all my latest releases, just sign up at the following link. Your email address will never be shared, and you can unsubscribe at any time. You also get a free short story!

www.bookouture.com/helena-dixon

This book is the first in the series after Kitty and Matt's wedding and I hope that you've enjoyed this new adventure. There are lots more stories to come with new characters to meet.

I do hope you loved *Murder at the Beauty Pageant* and if you did, I would be very grateful if you could write a review. I'd love to hear what you think, and it makes such a difference helping new readers to discover one of my books for the first time.

I love hearing from my readers – you can get in touch on my Facebook page, through Twitter, Goodreads or my website.

Thanks,

Helena

KEEP IN TOUCH WITH HELENA

www.nelldixon.com

 facebook.com/nelldixonauthor
twitter.com/NellDixon

ACKNOWLEDGEMENTS

My thanks as always to everyone in Torbay who has given me information, support, and sight of documents and pictures. Your help with my research is invaluable and I'm so grateful.

Special thanks to the members of Paignton Historical Society for their information, support and interest in the stories. Also special thanks to Basil and all the team at Torquay Museum who gave me such a good insight into the history of the museum. I loved the story about the Mummy.

Thank you to all my readers who gave me such a fabulous selection of names to choose from for Kitty's new pet. Special thanks and congratulations to Harriet Notley who came up with Rascal. A perfect fit!

Much love to the Tuesday zoomers and the Coffee Crew.

My thanks too as always to my fabulous agent, Kate Nash, and all the team and everyone at Bookouture who do such an incredible job to make my stories the best that they can be. It's much appreciated.

Printed in Great Britain
by Amazon

36631773R00148